LEERY ABOUT

Miss Margaret Caldecourt had learned well that love was not to be trusted.

The parents she loved had tragically died—as had her noble brother and the dashing young officer who had been her fiancé.

Now the only love she trusted was her love for her orphaned younger brother, Timothy . . . for her eccentric Aunt Celeste . . . and for the family estate of Caldecourt Manor, which was their only haven in a cold, cruel world.

But now Caldecourt Manor was about to be lost forever—unless Margaret threw herself at a man who made her trust herself even less than she trusted him. . . .

Lord Abberley's Nemesis

For a list of other Signet Regency Romances by Amanda Scott, please turn page . . .

Lord Abberley's Nemesis

by

Amanda Scott

A SIGNET BOOK

NEW AMERICAN LIBRARY

PUBLISHED BY
THE NEW AMERICAN LIBRARY
OF CANADA LIMITED

NAL BOOKS ARE AVAILABLE AT QUANTITY DISCOUNTS
WHEN USED TO PROMOTE PRODUCTS OR SERVICES.
FOR INFORMATION PLEASE WRITE TO PREMIUM MARKETING DIVISION.
NEW AMERICAN LIBRARY. 1633 BROADWAY.
NEW YORK. NEW YORK 10019.

First Printing, August, 1986

2 3 4 5 6 7 8 9

SIGNET TRADEMARK REG U S PAT OFF AND FOREIGN COUNTRIES
REGISTERED TRADEMARK — MARCA REGISTRADA
HECHO EN WINNIPEG, CANADA

SIGNET, SIGNET CLASSIC, MENTOR, ONYX, PLUME, MERIDIAN
AND NAL BOOKS are published in Canada by The New American
Library of Canada, Limited, 81 Mack Avenue, Scarborough,
Ontario, Canada M1L 1M8
PRINTED IN CANADA
COVER PRINTED IN U.S.A.

For Kevin
Best of Sisters

1

In 1818 and for many years thereafter, northbound travelers along the Great North Road met with an irritating check at the bottom of the wide marketplace in Baldock High Street, where they were forced to turn right into White Horse Street and then, after a few hundred yards, left again in order to resume their northward course. So popular was the Great North Road that nearly every traveling coach to pass through the marketplace executed that right-left jog. Thus it was that when two dusty, heavily laden coaches entered the town one chilly evening in late March and failed to take the left-hand turn, more than one person with late business in White Horse Street turned to give them a second, more searching look. When the lead coachman likewise failed to check his team where the Roman road from Bishop's Stortford crosses White Horse Street, one old gentleman squinted his eyes and peered first at the liveried footman perched up behind and then at the small crest, barely discernible through the dust on the door panel, and gave it as his opinion that 'twas her ladyship and young Miss Caldecourt returning at last from Foreign Parts.

Lady Celeste Fortescue, being merely the daughter of the third earl, had little right to display the Abberley crest, but she had never in the fifty odd years since her girlhood allowed that fact to deter her from displaying it. Therefore, since the present earl rarely bothered with the trappings of his position and since White Horse Street is no more than a diversion of the ancient Icknield Way, the most efficient route to both Abberley Hall and Caldecourt Manor, the only two great houses in the immediate vicinity of Baldock or Royston, the old gentleman made his observation in tones of certainty and he was—as, indeed, he was accustomed to be—quite correct in his surmise.

Inside the coach, twenty-two-year-old Margaret Caldecourt gently prodded the elderly, well-dressed lady snoring erratically beside her. "Aunt Celeste, we are passing through Baldock. Shall I tell Milsom to draw up at the Crown for some refreshment?"

Lady Celeste straightened first her spine and then the frothy confection perched precariously atop her complex arrangement of silver curls, after which she peered suspiciously out the coach window as if doubting that they could actually have traveled so far as Baldock. Then she turned back to her grandniece.

"No need to stop," she said briskly. "Only ten more miles to Royston, after all, and with the end in sight after a long journey, delay is nothing more than time wasted. If you tell Milsom anything, dear child, tell him to stir his stumps."

Margaret chuckled, and her smile lit up her oval face. She was a slim, elegant young woman with dark hair twisted into an intricate knot at the nape of her neck under a dashing slate-blue silk bonnet trimmed with ruchings of rather dismal charcoal ribbon. Her eyes were large and gray with black rims to their pupils and black lashes so thick they seemed to weight her eyelids. Set wide apart on either side of her straight little nose, under dark arched brows, those eyes had drawn more than their share of compliments over the years, but once Margaret's smile faded, the sparkle dimmed, leaving dark-gray pools of sadness.

The coach rattled off cobbles and onto the rutted roadbed between tall, straggly hedges, and as she stared out at the familiar bare downs sweeping away to the Midland plain, she saw a wood pigeon slope out of the twilight sky, dropping lower, with fewer and fewer wing strokes and longer and longer glidings upon half-closed wings as it drew near its home tree. It disappeared. Another, no doubt its mate, flew into sight and slanted downward with the same folding-in motion. Then there was only the rattle of their coach, echoed by the slightly lower-pitched rattle her keen ears detected from the baggage coach behind, and the empty road ahead. Involuntarily, Margaret's slender black-gloved hands gripped each other in her lap.

"Margaret?" Lady Celeste spoke gently, without her usual briskness.

"Ma'am?" Margaret turned to face her, noting in the distance beyond her ladyship's sharp profile a sprinkling of lights from the village of Ashwell. Dusk was rapidly turning to darkness.

" 'Tis no use trying to hide what cannot be hidden, my dear, but you must endeavor to appear cheerful once we reach the manor—for the boy's sake, you know."

"I know, Aunt Celeste, but I cannot help thinking we ought both to be wearing blacks when we arrive. Whatever will they think?"

"Fustian," replied her ladyship. "The servants have no right to be thinking anything whatever about our mode of dress, for mourning is in the heart, not in the garment. Our grief over your brother's death is clear enough without draping ourselves in black bombazine." She sniffed. "Hideous stuff. I thank God we had no time to arrange for more than black ribbons and gloves before we left Vienna."

"Well, if you had not long ago chucked everything I had with me from London, I'd have had plenty of proper mourning dresses."

Lady Celeste winced. "Three years out of date? Surely not, dear heart. What a figure you should have cut. No, no," she added when Margaret drew breath to protest, " 'twould be far worse to look a dowdy. And when I think what a chore it was to get you out of your blacks after young Culross was killed . . . well, I can only be thankful you haven't had time to acquire a new set."

"Nonetheless, I shall do so at once, now we are home again," Margaret said quietly. "We must set an example for little Timothy, after all, and I'll not have anyone saying I didn't show proper respect for Michael's memory.''

"To my mind, 'tis better for young Timothy to get on with life and not be surrounded by constant reminders of his father's death,'' said Lady Celeste more tartly. "The boy's only seven and already he's lost both mother and father. Moreover, by the time you reach my age, m'dear, you'll come to realize that life is too short to waste huge bits of it in repining.''

"I've already had more than my share of those bits,'' Margaret said, her tone laced with bitterness.

"That you have, but we must all learn to be content with our lot. None of those deaths was of your contriving, after all.''

Margaret turned away again, her eyes looking sadder than ever. Maybe she had not contrived, but surely it was no good thing for another person to be cursed by her love. More and more as years passed by it seemed that she had only to care deeply for another person to see that person cut down by Fate's cruel hand. Had she not thus far in her short life lost three out of four grandparents, both her own parents, her only uncle, her favorite aunt, and Frederick Culross, the only man to whom she had ever considered giving her heart? And now Michael, dear, dear Michael, cut down just before his thirtieth birthday in the very prime of his life by a fierce pain in his side that had grown worse and worse and then had ceased altogether, giving those around him cause to rejoice for his recovery. But their rejoicing had proved premature, for the end had come swiftly, two days later.

It had taken nearly two months for word to reach Margaret in the form of a typically formal note from Mr. Maitland, the vicar of their church, informing her that her brother, Sir Michael Caldecourt, had passed from this life to the next a week before Christmas. The details had come from the rector's daughter, Pamela, in a more emotional and much-crossed second sheet enclosed within her father's missive. Immediately upon receipt of the news Margaret and her ladyship had made preparations for the long journey back to England. Thus it was that Death, having sent Margaret to Vienna, now called her home again.

Her thoughts were interrupted just then as Milsom drew in to the side of the road long enough to allow Quinlan, the liveried footman riding up behind, to light the carriage lamps, before giving his team the office to continue their journey. Details of the landscape thus faded into darkness, and Margaret could see little now beyond the lantern's glow. She knew England's oldest road—for the Icknield Way dated from the Bronze Age or before—well enough to imagine what the passing countryside looked like, and she soon found herself playing a mental game she had played since childhood when she had first learned bits of the ancient road's history.

In her mind's eye she saw Neolithic warriors carrying spears as they trod a vaguely defined track above the thick, wild-animal-haunted forests that once covered Hertfordshire's undrained lowlands, having followed the crest of the Chilterns from Buckinghamshire, through Dunstable in Bedfordshire, before passing through what was now Baldock and traveling on to Royston. Many of the settlements in the area dated from the Iron Age, and Margaret's father had once taken her and Michael to Ashwell to view an Iron Age fort that was said to be two thousand years old. Closer to home, on Royston Heath, a long barrow and several round barrows—evidence of the county's ancient inhabitants—had been unearthed several years earlier.

The thick, impenetrable forests were mostly gone now, though some portions of the countryside were still heavily wooded with beech, lime, sycamore, and hornbeam trees, and Margaret knew she could look forward to some pleasant rides as winter turned to spring. Already there seemed to be little snow left on the ground, although their coachmen had slowed the teams as soon as the sun had disappeared behind the low ridge to the west, knowing they could expect to encounter icy patches along the road.

Nearly two hours passed before the coaches rolled into the village of Royston, and by then Margaret was only too glad to wrap herself in the fur rugs that were part of the coach's furnishings. She peered from the coach windows as they passed through the town, becoming more excited by the moment, despite her sadness, the nearer they came to home.

Whether Royston or its twelfth-century Augustinian priory had come first was a moot point, but there were documents showing the grant of a market and fair in 1189. Two more fairs came into existence during the next fifty years, and all of these were originally held in a cigar-shaped open space at the road crossing now largely taken up by High Street, King Street, and Lower King Street. As the two coaches passed from King Street into Lower King Street, Margaret could scarcely make out in the dim glow cast by erratically spaced streetlamps the block of millstone grit popularly known as Rohesia's Cross, which was said to be the socket of an old market cross. Only a tiny open space north of the cross still survived to remind people of the old marketplace, however, for the present marketplace, east of Ermine Street, had come into use during the previous century.

Margaret had once found a book, dated 1745, in the library at Abberley Hall, which commented enthusiastically upon the multitude of corn merchants, maltsters, and other dealers in grain who constantly resorted to the Royston Market, and what a vast number of horses laden with grain did fill all the roads on market day. Indeed, her own memory provided her with knowledge of the bustling, noisy crowds that filled the town on such days.

The coach turned south now onto Ermine Street, once the main route from London north into Hertfordshire and beyond until it was made nearly unusable by the constant traffic of heavily laden barley wagons and packhorses carrying their freight from all over the eastern counties to the great malting town of Ware. The two coaches lumbered along the badly rutted road for some fifteen minutes before turning west onto a gravel drive. They soon passed between two fat stone pillars, then wound their way through a wooded area to a tall, torchlit house. They were home, and they were clearly expected, for the tall, narrow windows of the first two floors glowed a welcome.

Margaret was grateful to Lady Celeste for having had the forethought to send a courier ahead from London to warn Mrs. Moffatt, her brother's motherly housekeeper, of their intended arrival. Quinlan had leapt to the ground as the coaches drew to a halt and approached the door, rubbing his gloved hands to restore circulation after having held on so long in the chilled air. A moment later he pulled open the door and let down the steps. Lady Celeste accepted his hand, allowing him to help her from the coach, but once her feet were solidly upon the ground, she stepped away from him, tacitly rejecting further assistance. In her mid-sixties, her ladyship was as spry and agile as a woman half her age, and she disdained to accept help she did not need, saying that she would need it soon enough and that there was no sense in anticipating one's decrepitude.

When the footman had helped Margaret to alight, her ladyship, who had been speaking to the two tirewomen who had descended from the baggage coach, turned back to him again, a slight frown of disapproval creasing her brow. "Quinlan," she said, "do you run up to the door and give that knocker a good clanging. I cannot think what is keeping Moffatt. We've made enough din out here to wake the dead. Mayhap he grows deaf in his old age."

Since Moffatt was, as clearly as Margaret could recall, easily ten or fifteen years younger than her ladyship, it was obvious that Lady Celeste was annoyed. That she had expected the door to be flung wide immediately upon her arrival and to find herself enveloped in a warm welcome by all and sundry was clear to the meanest intellect.

Margaret hid a smile. "Perhaps the servants are all in the kitchen having their supper, ma'am. 'Tis nearly nine o'clock, after all, and Timothy must be tucked up in the nursery by now."

"Poor child," said Lady Celeste, ascending the stone steps at her side. "Two months an orphan with only servants to look after him. How lonely he must be."

"For all we know, ma'am," Margaret replied, "Timothy is not even here but has been carried off to Abberley Hall instead. You know that his lordship had a great fondness for Michael. I should not be at all surprised to learn that he has taken Michael's only child under his wing.''

"Well,'' replied her ladyship tartly, straightening her hat, "for my part, I should be astonished to learn anything of the kind. Abberley taking notice of a six-year-old? I wish I may see it. From all I have heard from my friends who deign to include news of him in their letters, he has become little more than an irresponsible rake these past years, and is much more likely to be off gracing some duchess's house party or shooting in Leicestershire. Timothy would be much better off in the Moffatt's care than . . . Ah, Moffatt,'' she said without skipping a beat when the door opened at last to reveal a tall, plump man in a black suit and snow-white linen, "we had begun to fear the place had been deserted.''

"No, my lady,'' he replied in a quiet, well-modulated voice, affecting a slight bow. "Welcome home, my lady. And, miss, I'm sure 'tis good to have you back with us again. Young master . . . thãt is, Sir Timothy will be very pleased to see you both, I'm sure.'' Moffatt stepped aside as he spoke, ushering them into a spacious, well-lit hall, the highly polished floor of which was dotted with colorful Oriental carpets, acquired by an early-eighteenth-century Caldecourt who had extended his grand tour to the Far East.

A small but cheerful fire crackled in the large marble fireplace opposite the front door and candles glowed from an overhead chandelier and numerous wall sconces. Margaret, remembering her brother's habits of thrift, hoped the show was merely in honor of their arrival and not a habitual display. Lady Celeste, accepting the brilliance as her due, saw nothing amiss and paid no heed at all to the brightly lit room. She had matters of greater importance on her mind.

"Our people can dispose of our baggage, Moffatt,'' she said, "but we are famished, so I trust Mrs. Moffatt can manage to prepare something nourishing for us. We are accustomed, you know, to large midnight suppers.''

"Yes, my lady,'' replied the butler, his expression nearly concealing his opinion of habits in Foreign Parts. "In point of fact," he added with a slight twist of his lips, "I was on the point of serving tea in the drawing room when you arrived, and as it has been thought unnecessary to engage more than one footman at present, and him not being one of us and off to the village besides, supposedly to attend to important business, though how he can have business of any sort in a village far from his own—"

"Serving tea to whom?" demanded her ladyship. "Surely, young Timothy has been in his bed these two hours past."

"Indeed, yes, my lady, although not because he was wishful to go. Growing right stubborn is that lad," he added in an undertone as they moved to the graceful stairway at the rear of the hall and began making their way to the first-floor gallery.

Margaret, hearing, grinned at him, but her curiosity was quite as avid as Lady Celeste's. "Who is in the drawing room, Moffatt?"

The butler's features arranged themselves into nonexpression, and he avoided the eyes of both women. "Her ladyship and Mr. Caldecourt, miss," he said as he moved purposefully toward the drawing-room door.

"Her ladysh— Not Annis!" Lady Celeste quickly lowered her voice on the last word, for Moffatt—in self-defense, Margaret decided, hiding her own annoyance—had flung the doors to the elegant blue-and-white drawing room wide and was announcing their arrival to those within.

The scene upon which they intruded was a cozy one. The two persons now facing the door had obviously been indulging themselves in a generous tea. A silver tray reposed upon a low table near the plump, black-clad Lady Annis Caldecourt, and the platter beside the teapot, though a large one, bore but one lone sandwich and a dusting of crumbs. Jordan Caldecourt, a sleek, sandy-haired young gentleman sitting opposite his mother in a straight-backed blue-velvet chair near a fire larger than the one below in the hall, had been caught taking a generous bite of a heavily buttered muffin. He choked a little but rose to his feet with studied grace to greet Miss Caldecourt and Lady Celeste. His mother, unperturbed, set down the blue-and-white Sevres china cup and saucer she had been holding and nodded regally without making any effort to rise from her comfortable brocaded wing chair.

"So you are here at last, Celeste," she said. "Now Moffatt can put out all the lights downstairs except for the porter's lamp in the hall. Such a waste to have so many candles burning all at once." Her tone was placid but marked by an incipient whine that grated on Margaret's ears. She saw Lady Celeste's slim shoulders tense, though whether at the younger woman's words, tone, or use of her Christian name she was at a loss to say.

"We made excellent time," Margaret said. "At least, from London we made excellent time. Six weeks' journey from Vienna, even in winter, is scarcely noteworthy."

"No, indeed," put in Mr. Caldecourt, approaching her with both hands held out. "Why, one of my chums—Brevely, I believe it was—actually made the trip in half that time. Of course, it was summer then, and he hadn't to worry about a coachload of baggage and servants."

Margaret, fearing that he meant to embrace her, quickly held out one hand to fend him off, withdrawing it immediately when he showed a desire to retain it in his own. "How do you do, Jordan? I trust we see you well."

"Indeed, coz, and anxiously awaiting your arrival, unexpected though it was." He smiled at her.

"Unexpected? How could we be unexpected? Surely you must have known we would return as soon as we received word of Michael's death."

Jordan shrugged with a slanted, somewhat accusing glance at his mother, and Margaret found herself thinking he had not improved much in the three years she had been away. Two years her senior, he had been an irritating young fop who, whenever they met in London, had seemed to enjoy attaching himself to her in order to bask in the reflection of her popularity. Although Michael and Abberley had merely teased her about her conquest of the young man, she was certain that Frederick Culross would have soon sent him to the rightabout, once Michael had allowed an announcement of their betrothal to be posted in the *Gazette*. But it would not do to think of Frederick now. Resolutely, she pushed the memory into the nether reaches of her mind and regarded Mr. Caldecourt straightly, waiting for his response.

But it was not he who spoke. "You do not ask how I fare," said Lady Annis plaintively. "Of course, you do not realize that Doctor Fennaday has positively insisted that I be in my bed at nine o'clock. My health is tenuous, you know. But I must not complain of my sufferings. There could be no question, once your courier had brought us news of your intended arrival, of my going to bed without knowing you were safely at home. It is my nature to worry," she added with a sigh.

"But why on earth are you here?" demanded Lady Celeste, unbuttoning her gloves. She glanced pointedly at the interested Moffatt, who quickly effaced himself, before she looked back at Lady Annis. "I am sorry you worried, for there was no need. But surely you ought to be tucked up in your own bed in Little Hampstead."

Lady Annis drew herself up, her impressive bosom swelling with righteous indignation. "And leave my poor dead husband's little grandnephew to the mercies of mere common servants? Surely, you cannot think I should be so remiss in my duty as that. Why, as soon as I heard—"

"Just how did you hear?" Lady Celeste interjected impatiently.

"The vicar," replied Jordan, "and once we was here and had got our blacks on, we couldn't very well put them off again, so there seemed little point in going elsewhere."

"I must say," put in Lady Annis quickly, "that I am utterly shocked to see you both in colors. Though I have little right to speak on that head to you, Celeste, I should think that out of respect for your very own brother, Margaret, you might have seen fit to dress more conventionally."

"Foolishness," said Lady Celeste, moving now to warm her hands at the fire. "We'd no time for shopping before we left, let alone time to have anything proper made up, as anyone but a ninnyhammer might have realized without my having to explain the matter. Margaret can attend to such stuff now that she's home. Not that she don't look fine as she is.''

Mr. Caldecourt, lifting his quizzing glass to his eye, surveyed Margaret from head to toe and agreed. "Slap up to the echo," he said, nodding. "Dashed if she ain't, Mama. That sort of rig will be all the crack in London when the Season begins next month. I'm persuaded we shall see any number of fashionable ladies in just such a getup as that.''

Irritated to realize that he was making her self-conscious, Margaret smoothed the slim, slate-blue wool skirt of her traveling dress, then turned away from him to remove her bonnet and gloves. She was saved the necessity of making any reply to his observation by Lady Annis's assurance that she, for one, would see nothing of the kind.

"We shall stay quietly in the country this year, my pet. I am certain that my poor nerves would never survive the excitement of a London Season so soon after the shock of poor Michael's death. And we *are* in mourning, you know.''

"But dash it all, *we* ain't dead," objected her son. "Perhaps I shall have to live a bit more quietly, without the usual romp and rattle, but I needn't avoid London altogether. A man must live, after all.''

"You will do well, my dear, to be guided by me," Lady Annis said implacably, her dark brows beetling over her small dark eyes. "Do not forget that you have a duty to your little cousin.''

Jordan colored up to his side-whiskers, but Lady Celeste had become bored by their conversation. She cut in now firmly and in customarily brusque tones. "We should not wish to keep you longer from your bed, Annis. You are indeed looking peaked and must be longing to put off your stays. I'm persuaded they are much too tight. Pray run along if you have finished your tea. Margaret and I shall do very well on our own. Where," she added, glaring at the double doors leading to the gallery, "do you suppose Moffatt has got to with our supper?''

Lady Annis protested mildly that she knew her duty, but

she was easily routed by the stronger-minded Lady Celeste. Jordan likewise showed a tendency to linger, but he was no match for the old lady, who told him straight out to take himself off because she'd had quite enough of his airs and affectations for one evening.

Once they were alone Lady Celeste took the chair vacated by Lady Annis, removed her frothy bonnet, and tossed it inelegantly onto a nearby claw-footed settee, leaning back with a long sigh of relief.

Margaret, sitting upon a Kent chair with identical clawed feet, regarded her grandaunt fondly, waiting for her to recover her equanimity. Instead, to her surprise, Lady Celeste frowned.

"What is it, ma'am?"

"Why are they here?" The old lady lifted her pointed little chin and straightened, gazing directly at Margaret. "What keeps them about?"

"To be sure, ma'am, their being here is a nuisance, but perhaps if they came for the funeral and if her ladyship's health is truly precarious—"

"Fustian. They complain most who suffer least. There is nothing wrong with Annis Caldecourt that a little less idleness wouldn't cure. I wish I may see her doing her duty by young Timothy. If he's so much as laid eyes upon her, I'll wager it was none of her doing. And who asked her to interfere, anyway?"

"Mr. Maitland, according to Jordan," Margaret reminded her.

"That seems odd, very odd, indeed."

But Moffatt confirmed the information when he finally appeared, accompanied by Quinlan, carrying a tea service lavish enough to satisfy even Lady Celeste's wishes. "Aye, Mr. Maitland saw fit to apprise her ladyship of the master's death," he said when asked. His features were once again expressionless, but there was that in his tone which told Margaret, at least, that Moffatt thought the vicar had been guilty of a great piece of impertinence.

"But why are they still here?" demanded Lady Celeste as she helped herself from a platter of cold roast beef.

"Her ladyship insisted that it was for young Master Timmy's benefit," Moffatt said, taking a basket of hot bran muffins from Quinlan's tray and holding them out for Margaret's examination. "She would have it that you and young Miss Margaret was fixed in Vienna and wouldn't be able to come home."

"Nonsense," Lady Celeste said, waving Quinlan's services on to Margaret. "That woman wants something. Mark my words. She's a schemer, always has been, and though she may disguise herself, she will not deceive the wise."

Margaret had been listening to her ladyship but watching Moffatt. Now she was certain he wanted to speak, but she knew he would not forget himself so far as to put forth his own ideas on any subject without having been requested to do so. "What is it, Moffatt?" she asked gently.

Lady Celeste's head came up sharply and she directed her piercing gaze at the butler, who seemed for once to have lost some of his aplomb. "What is it, man? Out with it. That woman *is* up to something."

"I don't know that for certain, my lady, but I have heard it said the master failed to leave a will."

"Young men often do," her ladyship pointed out. "What has that to do with anything?"

"I don't know, my lady, but Mr. Jordan went down to London for the opening of Parliament the first of the month and returned only two days ago. He was closeted with her ladyship for long bits before and after. Young Melanie—the chambermaid, you know, Miss Margaret, though she came to us after your ladyship departed for foreign parts with Sir Harold—she said she once heard them speaking about a petition, whether it would be granted or not. Her ladyship said there was no reason not, so long as they were quick about it. I can tell you," he added quietly, "I've been that worried. Couldn't think what it was all about, myself."

Margaret frowned. No will and a petition to Parliament—

what could that all mean? "Has his lordship been to call, Moffatt? Perhaps he will know what is going on."

The butler grimaced. "Hasn't set foot in the house, Miss Margaret. Not even after the funeral."

"He did attend the funeral, though?"

"Aye. Stood at the back of the church a-scowlin' like he does. Saw him myself. But he never showed up for the buryin' or the baked meats after. And he ain't been next or nigh the manor since." Moffatt's strong feelings were clearly evident in his lapse of grammar. "Like as not he's dispensed with civility altogether," he muttered as he followed Quinlan out the door.

Margaret frowned. Such behavior didn't sound like Abberley, who had been, after all, her brother's closest friend. They had been housemates at Eton and had shared a study at Oxford. As a child, she had looked forward to their school holidays almost more avidly than they had themselves. No doubt she, being eight years younger, had been something of a pest, but neither of them had ever seemed to mind. They had taken her riding and had even allowed her to trip along behind them when they went shooting rabbits or wood pigeons in the large beech wood between the manor and the hall. She had been, at such times, the despair of her assorted governesses, but she had loved every moment, feeling as though she had two wonderful big brothers instead of only one. That his lordship had not done his best to keep an eye on the manor and on Timothy seemed very strange.

"I have it!" Lady Celeste had fallen into a brown study as she ate, but now she interrupted Margaret's thoughts, her expression worried. "They have petitioned the House of Lords for guardianship, I'll wager, and perhaps even for control of the property. Annis and that dreadful offspring of hers mean to live here!"

2

"Surely, you must realize that it was the only possible course for us to follow under the circumstances," Lady Annis said virtuously the following morning in the breakfast parlor when Lady Celeste demanded to know if she and her son had petitioned for guardianship. Then, before the older woman could respond, she spoke quickly to the stiff footman who served her. "A few more slices of that excellent Yorkshire ham, Archer, and perhaps one or two of those delicious apple turnovers. Really," she added, patting her round, black-bombazine-covered stomach, "Mrs. Moffatt's cooking has quite ruined my figure."

"Can't see that you've changed a jot since the last time I saw you," said Lady Celeste brutally. "That was after the typhus epidemic eight years ago that carried Sir William Caldecourt and your Stephen off within a week of each other, and you told us then that you were wasting away to a shadow out of grief."

"What circumstances, ma'am?" Margaret asked hastily. Lady Annis, her cheeks unbecomingly reddened, turned to her, bewildered. Margaret kept her patience with difficulty. "Why did you find it necessary to petition for guardianship?"

"Why, the Fates clearly intended that we do so, my dear." Her ladyship recovered herself quickly. "There was no will, you know—very remiss of Michael, I'm sure, but a common enough failing among younger gentlemen, who think they will never die. In any case, you must see that dearest Jordan,

22

who is practically your only remaining male relative and the heir apparent as well, is the natural person to take charge, both of dear Timothy and of the estate.''

"The *dear* estate," murmured Lady Celeste incorrigibly.

Margaret's lips twitched, but because she knew her grand-aunt was perfectly capable of repeating her words in tones more audible to Lady Annis if requested to do so, she quickly suggested that perhaps they had not searched carefully enough for her brother's will.

"Oh, but we did," replied Lady Annis, wide-eyed with sincerity. "Archer here can tell you that I did not begrudge the least exertion, in spite of my poor health. He, Jordan, and I quite turned out poor Michael's bedchamber, the library, and the estate office, looking for anything even resembling a will. There was nothing at all, I promise you. Where is your footman, by the by? I confess, we have felt the lack of a third manservant, though I did not think we would."

"I have given Quinlan leave to visit his family in Dorset for a month," Lady Celeste told her without apology. "I cannot think why you turned the others off."

But Margaret, uninterested in domestic problems for the moment, was still thinking about the missing will. "Perhaps Lord Abberley would know where Michael kept it," she said musingly.

"Lord Abberley," said Lady Annis with injured scorn, "has not seen fit to pay us so much as a civil visit of condolence. Not," she added with tightening lips, "that I should have been flattered to have received such a call from the likes of him."

"Why, whatever can you mean, ma'am? Lord Abberley has ever stood our friend."

"Then I shall say nothing against him," said Lady Annis primly.

"Nothing *to* say," said Lady Celeste, a warning note in her voice.

"That is as may be," retorted Lady Annis in tones which indicated that she, for one, could say a great deal if pressed to do so. "I do not forget that he is your grandnephew, although it is with difficulty that one realizes he stands as close to you as dearest Margaret does. But you clearly don't wish me to speak ill of him, so I shall say no more."

"Dreadful woman," said Lady Celeste an hour later when Lady Annis had departed at last to take her morning drive—a necessity for the good of her lungs, she had explained at length, and sternly ordered by her doctor. "Quacks herself," added her ladyship. "How your Uncle Stephen, a sensible-enough man by most standards, managed to bear with her long enough to produce that languid lackey she calls her dearest pet, I shall never understand."

"Papa said Uncle Stephen fell in love with one of Lady Annis's elder sisters who was already spoken for and that he decided Lady Annis would do as well. Papa said he learned his error, but not quickly enough, for they were already betrothed by then, and Uncle Stephen couldn't, in good conscience, cry off."

"And, of course, there were no more unmarried sisters by then, either," said Lady Celeste with a touch of sarcasm. "The Earl of Brundage had seven daughters, poor man, but I daresay he'd have had more if he hadn't cried 'Enough' after one look at Annis's sour face."

Margaret laughed, but intruding thoughts quickly sobered her again. "Aunt Celeste, I simply cannot believe that Michael failed to make a will. In fact, I'm quite sure he drew one up soon after he married poor Marjory. He had to because of the marriage settlements, I think, and surely he would have added to it or written another when Timothy was born or when Marjory died. He wasn't an irresponsible man, even if he *was* young."

"True enough," Lady Celeste agreed. "He never was the sort of loose screw so many young men seem to be these days. He was very like your father, Michael was, a kind and sober man. I was so pleased when your mama married Sir William, for she was quite my favorite niece. Always the toast of the Season in London, Julia was, before she cast her handkerchief—a diamond of the first water. There were so many men after her—even a duke—that I was afraid she'd be swayed by a title or some ne'er-do-well's charming words or handsome face. But Julia no sooner clapped eyes on your father than she decided he was the man for her. You are very like her, you know, just as Michael was like Sir William.''

Margaret had heard these words many times before, but although she still felt sad whenever she thought of her parents, her eyes didn't so much as mist now. Indeed, she had long since decided she had no tears left. She had not even cried after learning of Michael's sudden death. The last tears she had shed had been for Frederick Culross. ''I wonder,'' she said now, ''what would have become of Mama if Papa had been killed in battle before they were able to wed,'' she said quietly.

Lady Celeste had been lost in her own memories, but these sad words brought her head up with a snap, and she said flatly, ''Julia would have cried her eyes out and then got on with her life. And if you're thinking of young Culross again, let me tell you you should put all that behind you now. It has been three years since Waterloo, and you weren't even properly betrothed to the man, so that's time and more in which to bury the past. He wouldn't have done for you, anyway.''

''We weren't betrothed because Michael refused to allow it with Frederick leaving as he was to join Wellington, but he *had* agreed to allow Frederick to pay his addresses to me and I had agreed to receive them. Why, you never knew Frederick!''

''Well, of course not. It would have been a trifle difficult to effect an introduction when he was with Wellington, trying to catch Bonaparte, and your grandfather and I were in Vienna. Such a welcome change, too, after the Russian court. So gay and everyone having such a lovely time. Of course, no one knew until Bonaparte had been on French soil for over a week that he had even managed to escape from Elba. Then there was a deal of bickering, I can tell you.''

Margaret glared at her. ''Never mind that. Why wouldn't Frederick have done for me?''

Lady Celeste sighed. ''Shouldn't have said that, I expect. It slipped. After so many years in diplomatic circles one might expect I'd have learned to put a guard on my tongue, but I never did. And the fact is that when you talk about young Culross, you always tell me how kind he was, and thoughtful, how he was always exerting himself to please you.''

"He liked pleasing me. What's wrong with a man being thoughtful and kind?''

"Nothing, but you need a man who will cross you now and again, not one who trips over himself to please you.''

Margaret opened her mouth to insist hotly that her beloved Frederick had been made of sterner stuff than that, but honesty intruded. Perhaps Lieutenant Culross had been rather easily led. In order to keep her sharp-eyed companion from pouncing upon whatever truth she might see in her face, Margaret quickly turned the conversation back to her brother's will.

"Surely you must agree, ma'am, that Michael would have done his duty where Timothy is concerned. And he would never have named Jordan the boy's guardian or trustee.''

"No, certainly not. More likely to have named your grandfather jointly with his man of affairs. Who handled Michael's business?''

"Mr. Jeremy Swift in Royston, but I believe he had a man in London as well. Abberley would know. Aunt Celeste, even if Michael failed to make a will, we cannot stand by and see Jordan take control of Caldecourt Manor.''

"No, indeed. We must contrive a little, I think.''

"We must act,'' Margaret said decisively, "and we need help. I am going to ride over to the hall at once.''

"You mustn't go alone, dear,'' her ladyship said firmly. "I shall go with you.''

"Nonsense. You know you like at least a full day to recuperate after a long journey. I shall do fine alone. Moreover,'' she added when Lady Celeste stiffened slightly, "one of us must remain here to become acquainted with Timothy. He had scarcely turned four when I left to join you and Grandpapa in Vienna, so I daresay he won't remember me at all. And it won't help our cause if he treats us like strangers and appears to be well-acquainted with Jordan and Lady Annis.''

Although giving it as her opinion that if Timothy were indeed well-acquainted with his cousin and Lady Annis, he would express a preference for anyone else to stand guardian in their stead, Lady Celeste was much struck by Margaret's view of the matter and finally agreed that no great impropriety lay in visiting a second cousin whom one had been accustomed since birth to think of as a second brother. Thus it was that half an hour later, attired in a forest-green woolen habit with gold frogs and military epaulets, Miss Caldecourt set out for Abberley Hall, riding a neat black mare named Dancer from her brother's stables and accompanied only by an elderly groom.

The ride took the best part of another half-hour. As they rode through the thick beech wood, she was conscious of a damp chill in the air and found herself longing for the moment when they would emerge into open country again and pass through the gate into one of Abberley Hall's well-tended fields. She wondered idly if it had been possible to begin planting the barley yet or if the fields were still too hard-frozen to plow, but to her amazement the first field, when she reached it, was cluttered with dried stalks and early weeds. Not so much as the normal clearing off had been done the previous fall.

Her groom did not have to climb down from his saddle to open the gate, for it was already open—or half-open—lurching precariously from one rusty hinge. The fence surrounding the field to keep out deer from the forest was in a similarly dilapidated condition, with whole sections broken down.

The second field was in no better condition, and when they passed through the main gate to the hall, Margaret was distressed to note more weeds cropping up here and there along the broad gravel drive and throughout the once plush herbaceous borders. The borders themselves had run amok, and the lawn more nearly resembled a hayfield. Indeed, she found herself dredging her memory for a view of the hall as it should be, set amidst neatly trimmed borders and well-scythed lawns. Even the house seemed to have gone to seed, though it loomed before her now in much of its ancient splendor—a pile of imported stone and local flint, three stories high in the massive central block, with two-story wings flying off at odd angles everywhere. A regular honeycomb, Abberley had been wont to call it. A standing joke in the family, according to Lady Celeste, was that there had been no need for priest holes at Abberley, since Cromwell's men might have searched the place to their heart's content and in all the confusion of rooms have overlooked an army of priests. But the building, once so well-cared-for, needed a full-scale cleaning and refurbishing. Two of the windows facing the drive from the central block were cracked, and the woodwork was in desperate need of paint.

Margaret slipped from her saddle unaided at the stone steps sweeping up to the entrance, which was set under a broad, stone portico. She tossed her reins to the stoic groom:

"Go round to the stables, Trimby. I don't know how long I shall be, but I expect someone will be there to direct you and give you a mug of something hot."

The groom nodded, doubtful but obedient, and Margaret hurried up the steps to bang the heavy brass knocker. The house had a deserted air, and she had the feeling that if anyone were going to answer her summons, he would have to come up from the nether regions to do so. Thus, she nearly jumped out of her skin when the door was pulled open while she still had her hand on the knocker.

"Miss Margaret!" The neat, wiry man who stood there regarded her in amazement. "We thought . . . that is, Mr. Maitland was given to understand . . . that is, well, we're right glad to see you've come home, miss."

"Good morning, Pudd. I am very glad to be back, but news must travel a good deal more slowly than it did before I left Hertfordshire. I arrived at the manor last night and was certain you would have received word of it by now."

"No, miss." Puddephatt did not explain. Nor did he stand aside to let her pass.

"Pudd, it is chilly out here," she said pointedly.

"Yes, miss. Was you meaning to leave a message?"

"No, I was not," Margaret replied, speaking more sharply. "I wish to speak to his lordship. And not before time, either," she added with a sweeping gesture that included the overgrown lawn, the weeds, and the leggy, sprawling borders. "Whatever is he about to have let his servants neglect the place so?"

"There's pretty near only me and the rib left, Miss Margaret. So long as he gets fed and don't have to answer the door, he don't much care about nothing else."

"Then, he is here," Margaret said, certain the little man must be exaggerating.

Puddephatt hesitated. "Aye, miss, like as not."

"Well, for heaven's sake, take me to him, or tell him I am here."

Nervously the wiry man glanced over his shoulder toward a pair of tall oak doors in the near side of the ancient stone hall. "I'm thinking that it wouldn't be wise, Miss Margaret. I'll tell him you was here and that you be wishful to see him. More than that I shouldn't like to undertake."

Margaret looked hard at the manservant. She had known him since her childhood when he was a mere footman who could be counted upon to produce lumps of sugar for her to give her pony or to warn young mischiefmakers when to play least in sight. Now he looked careworn and rather anxious. She hadn't missed the quick glance over his shoulder either.

"His lordship is in his bookroom, is he not?"

"Aye, miss," he said unhappily, "but I daren't announce you. 'Twouldn't be fittin' for you to see him just now."

"Fustian," said Lady Celeste's grandniece. "Stand aside. You needn't announce me at all. I've not the slightest notion of what's what with his precious lordship that he isn't even of a mind to be civil, but I assure you I mean to see him now, at this very moment, and not at his convenience."

"Miss Margaret, no!" But Puddephatt might as well have spared his breath, for she pushed past him, crossed the stone floor of the hall with quick, angry steps and pulled open the doors to the bookroom.

Adam Fortescue, sixth Earl of Abberley—all six feet, three inches of him—lay sprawled in a tattered leather chair before a cold fireplace, snoring harshly, his light-brown hair more tousled than Margaret could remember ever having seen it before. But even before she had had time to register the sight fully, her nostrils were assaulted by the aroma of stale brandy fumes wafting through the air.

"Merciful heavens, Puddephatt," she exclaimed, wrinkling her nose, "how long has his lordship enjoyed this disgusting condition?"

"Nigh onto three months or so, miss," was the quiet reply.

Margaret stared at the manservant. "You're jesting!" He shook his head. "You are saying he has been like this since Sir Michael's death?"

"Aye, miss. Took it right hard, he did."

"But the land, this place . . ." She waved her hand in an all-encompassing gesture. "All this decay didn't set in over a period of a mere two months."

Puddephatt shook his head. "His lordship lost interest in estate management some time ago. Preferred London, the social scene, gaming, women—that is, parties and the like. When Sir Michael and Lady Caldecourt took you to London, you'll remember that he went down, too. But then you went off to Foreign Parts, and when her ladyship died in childbed soon after, Sir Michael withdrew into himself a bit. Not that he and the master weren't still close. They were. But Sir Michael busied himself with estate business, and the master began to care less about matters here and to go about even more than he had before, to house parties and such. He was hunting in Leicestershire when Sir Michael took ill and died. We sent word to him as soon as Sir Michael went sick, and he only just made it home in time for the funeral, on account of the warm spell we'd had went cold again, and the vicar wasn't wishful to risk the ground freezing solid. A full bottle of brandy his lordship had that night, and it's been much the same ever since."

Margaret nodded, then looked back at the figure sprawled

in the chair near the fireplace, his booted feet splayed far apart on the faded green-and-purple Aubusson carpet. Drawing in a long breath, she braced her shoulders resolutely, then spoke without turning her head.

"Fetch me a bottle of porter, a basin of cold water, and a cloth, Pudd. At once, if you please."

He nodded and went to do her bidding, soon returning with the bottle of that beverage best known for its excellent restorative powers under his arm, and the cloth over it. He held the basin in his two hands with an earthenware mug hooked over one finger beneath it. As he entered, Margaret was attempting to restore life to the fire.

"I'll attend to that, miss," he said, handing her the basin and cloth, and setting bottle and mug on a nearby table next to an empty brandy bottle.

Margaret watched Puddephatt move swiftly to the hearth, then turned her attention to Abberley. On closer inspection she saw distinct ravages of dissipation. His once-handsome face was pale, and crow's feet twitched at his eyes and mouth as he snored. There was likewise an unhealthy puffiness under the eyes, while a red-gold stubble around his lower cheeks and chin testified to the fact that he had not allowed himself to be shaved that day, nor possibly the day before. His neckcloth had become disarranged, and she noted that his linen—once a matter of great pride with him—was dingy. A sudden flash of anger overcame her at this last observation, and with scarcely a thought toward reason or consequence, she upended the basin of cold water over his lordship's tousled head.

Puddephatt's gasp of dismay was lost entirely as his lordship came sputtering to an upright position in the shabby chair and struggled unsuccessfully to get to his feet.

"What the bloody—" He dashed water from his brow with the back of his sleeve and saw Margaret standing over him, her eyes flashing, her arms akimbo. "Marget, what the devil are you doing here?"

"Attempting to bring you to your senses, my lord," she

said tartly. "Please do not attempt to rise on my account. You appear to be in no condition to attend to the civilities."

"Civilities be damned," he muttered wrathfully. "If I could get to my feet, it would be for the sheer pleasure of throttling you. I don't suppose you stopped to consider that the Aubusson will scarcely be improved by a wetting. Or this chair—one of Chippendale's masterpieces, my father always said."

"Well, Mr. Chippendale would scarcely be pleased to see how little you've cared for his masterpiece," she retorted, "and your precious Aubusson has seen many a better day as well."

"M'lord," said Puddephatt hesitantly, picking up the brandy bottle and bending to find the glass, which had somehow managed to roll under his lordship's chair, "I've taken the liberty of pouring out a mug of porter—"

"Well, pour it back again or drink it yourself, man, and fetch me another bottle of the brandy. Lord knows, I need something stronger than porter to sustain the shock of Miss Caldecourt's assault on my person. Yes," he added, looking morosely down upon his sodden state, "*and* to ward off pneumonia, I'm thinking."

"Fustian," said Miss Caldecourt. "You'll drink that porter and like it, my lord. Go away, Pudd. His lordship has no further need of your services at present."

"The devil he hasn't," growled Abberley, stopping the manservant midstride. "His lordship, may heaven help him, has the most urgent need of a dry shirt and coat at the very least, so hop to it, man, and don't forget the brandy!" Absentmindedly, he swigged from the mug of porter, frowned at the unfamiliar taste, then swigged again, eyeing Margaret malevolently over the mug's rim. "Thought you were fixed in Vienna," he muttered after a brief silence.

Having taken advantage of that silence to glare at Puddephatt in such a way as to make clear that it would be at peril of his own life if he were to bring his master that bottle of brandy, she turned her direct gaze once more upon his lordship.

"Surely you knew I would return as soon as I had word of Michael's death?"

"Had it from Maitland that you wouldn't."

"The vicar?"

Abberley nodded, then winced. "Aye, daresay he had it from that sour-faced aunt of yours."

"She is *not* my aunt. Merely Uncle Stephen's wife—more's the pity. Adam, you must collect yourself. I need your help."

"Not my help, you don't," he said more to the mug of porter than to her. "My help's not worth sixpence. Not worth tuppence, come to that. Not worth . . ." But words failed him. He could suggest nothing further that his help was not worth.

Margaret, staring at him as though at a stranger, felt the need of a chair. A trifle dazed, she reached behind her until she located the mate to the one Abberley sat in, and sank down upon it. He had made no further attempt to rise despite the fact that she was certain he must be sitting in a puddle. Nor did he speak, and since he had never before refused to help her out of a scrape, she could think of nothing further to say to him. Thus it was with a feeling of unmixed relief that she greeted Puddephatt's return a few moments later.

He entered the room quietly, carrying a pile of clothing over his arm and a bottle in his hand. Margaret noted with dismay that it was a brandy bottle exactly like the one he had carried away moments earlier. She opened her mouth in angry protest, but before she could voice the words leaping to her tongue, Puddephatt put a finger to his lips. Since it was the hand holding the bottle, the gesture was nearly lost, but Margaret understood his intent and kept silent. He set the bottle down beside Abberley.

"There ye be, m'lord."

"Ah, bless you, man." Ignoring the fact that his man had neglected to provide him with a fresh glass, Abberley fell upon the bottle and drank thirstily, swallowing almost convulsively several times before a black look crossed his face and he snapped the bottle to arm's length, glaring at it accusingly. "What the devil is this?" he demanded. Puddephatt was silent, watching him in a wary but measuring way. Scarcely a half minute passed before what little color was left in his lordship's face drained away. "Oh, my God, Pudd, what've you done?" he muttered, setting the bottle down hard upon the table and attempting once more, this time with a look of desperation, to get to his feet.

Puddephatt snatched up the basin from the floor where Margaret had put it after dousing the earl and said quickly over his shoulder, "If ye'r not wishful t' see 'im cast up 'is accounts, Miss Margaret, ye'd best wait a bit in the front hall."

Margaret fled.

In the hall she found herself remembering Abberley as he had been in better times, a young man given to the airs, graces, and general fastidiousness of a dandy. He had not gone so far as to employ one glovemaker to cut the thumbs and another to make the rest of his gloves as had the most famous dandy of them all, Mr. George Bryan Brummell, who was now—for his sins—a permanent resident on the Continent, but she had rarely seen Abberley before with an unstarched neckcloth or linen that was not immaculate. Indeed, she had hitherto scarcely ever seen him with a hair out of place or without that air of confidence he had been wont to wear so casually. What had brought him to this pass?

Her thoughts had produced no acceptable answer to the question before Puddephatt finally emerged from the bookroom, the basin in his hands discreetly covered by a pile of discarded clothing.

"He'll see you now, Miss Margaret," he said, for all the world, she thought, as though nothing remarkable had occurred.

"Whatever was in that bottle, Puddephatt?"

"Oh, just a bit of this and that," replied the manservant cryptically. "He's a mite weakish and not in the best of tempers," he added, "but he'll do now—for the moment, anyway."

Hoping that his pessimism with regard to Abberley's temper was misplaced, Margaret entered the bookroom once more to find the window open wide to a chilly breeze, the fire

burning determinedly upon the hearth, and his lordship looking paler than ever but more presentable. He glowered at her
when she stepped past him to close the windows, the brisk
breeze having already cleared the air sufficiently for her
comfort.

"Haven't changed, have you?" he growled. "Still tossing
the cat among the pigeons whenever the mood strikes you."

She turned from the window, glaring right back at him,
and retorted, "At least I don't fail when all that is needed is a
spot of resolution."

"Meaning that I did, I suppose." He looked away as if he
could no longer meet her eyes. "I expect you're right about
that. I certainly failed Michael when he needed me most."

"Failed him! How did you fail him?"

"By not being here when he needed me, of course," he
replied as if she ought to have known the answer.

Resentment welled within her. How dared he? By what
right did he take that particular blame unto himself? "Is that a
fact?" she demanded, moving angrily toward him. "You
think you were responsible for his death, so you drown your
stupid sorrows in a hundred brandy bottles and let the world
around you go to rack and ruin!" Suddenly the tears she had
long since decided she could not shed for Michael's death
spilled down her cheeks in rivers, but attempting to ignore
them, she continued to rip up at Abberley, calling him every
insulting name she could think of and accusing him, among
other things, of encouraging Lady Annis and her despicable
son to usurp control of Caldecourt Manor from its rightful
heir.

"And Michael trusted you!" she cried. "I trusted you! I
thought matters here were in safe hands because you were
here. But I was wrong, so wrong." Folding suddenly into a
chair, Margaret finally gave way completely to her tears,
hiccuping and gasping, her face buried in her hands, her sides
heaving with terrible, racking sobs, while Abberley, his ill-
usage completely forgotten, stared at her in dismay.

3

"Marget," the earl said gently, "please stop." For a moment he stared at her helplessly, but when she continued to sob, making no effort to regain control of herself, he finally thrust a hand through his hair and moved toward her more purposefully. "Marget, that's enough now," he said firmly. When she gave no sign of having heard him, Abberley leaned down, grasped her by her shoulders, and gave her a shake.

Margaret hiccupped again, but her hands fell away from her eyes and she gazed accusingly at him through her tears. "Go away," she muttered. "I don't wish to talk to you anymore. You're a beast, and a disgusting one at that. Go back to your brandy."

Abberley straightened, grimacing slightly as if his head were still aching, but when he withdrew a large handkerchief from his waistcoat pocket and handed it to her, his expression was stern. "Mop up, my girl, and mind your tongue. You've already tried my patience beyond what it would bear from anyone else. If you've a wish to be well smacked, just try me a bit further."

"You wouldn't." She dabbed at her eyes with his handkerchief.

"I would," he corrected, regarding her narrowly. "In a minute and with pleasure." His lips tightened when her breast heaved with another sob and she began to twist the handkerchief between her fingers. "Give me that thing. You're making a muck of a simple task, as usual. Come, stand up, because I'm damned if I'll kneel at your feet, and anyone can see you need help. Up, Marget."

Hauling her to her feet, he took the handkerchief from her and ruthlessly began drying her cheeks with it. She stood submissively enough, but from time to time there was still the suggestion of a sob, and despite the sophistication of her military-styled habit, she looked more like a bereaved child than a competent young woman. At the third heartbroken little sob, Abberley grabbed her shoulders again.

"Damn it, Marget, I won't have this! You mustn't. Please." Suddenly, with a barely suppresed groan, he snapped his arms around her shoulders and hugged her to him so tightly she could scarcely breathe at all. But he, too, seemed to have trouble, for his next words were muffled. "Ah, Marget, little Marget, I'm sorry I failed you. I made a mess of things, but you should never have trusted me. I'm not worthy of your trust. I'm not a man to be depended upon, little girl, and that's a fact."

His words, or perhaps his tone, had the desired effect at last, and after a moment's silence, Margaret murmured, "Adam, you're suffocating me." As she attempted to extricate herself, she realized that over the years she had forgotten how big and broad he was. And how strong he was. She wriggled again, but at the same time she experienced an odd reluctance to free herself from the confines of his embrace. Then, as suddenly as he had caught her up, he released her again, and she found herself regarding him somewhat uncertainly. "I must apologize," she said, the words finding their way to her tongue with difficulty. "I don't know what came over me. I quite thought I had no tears left."

"You've stored up rather a number of tears, I think," he said quietly, keeping his hands tightly at his sides. "The only time I've ever seen you cry before was after your mother died."

Margaret took a deep breath and stepped a little away from him, finding his nearness overpowering. "Fancy your remembering that," she said. Self-consciously, she blew her nose, then attempted a tiny smile. "You found me in the beech-wood thicket that day."

He nodded, still watching her closely. "We'd all been searching for you for hours. I remember it was spring and you were in a grassy little meadow surrounded by elder flowers, sobbing your heart out."

"You told me the flowers would die from overwatering," she reminded him.

"I was a lout even then. I ought to have held you and comforted you. After all, you were a little girl whose mother had just died. What age were you? Nine, you must have been nine, because Michael and I entered Oxford at Michaelmas term that year."

"I don't think I'd have responded as well to mollycoddling as I did to worrying about the elder flowers or to your promise of a ride on Falconer if I dried my tears. Do you remember Falconer?"

"Of course I do. A huge roan gelding, a gift from my father, and one of the finest hunters I ever had in my stables."

"What happened to him?"

"Pneumonia, two winters ago," he said, looking away, then moving abruptly to stir the fire. "He had gotten beyond hunting, but I liked him."

Margaret was silent, watching him, her tears forgotten. The room was quite warm now and heavy with the familiar scent of wood smoke. The fire didn't need his attention, and she wondered what he was thinking. No matter how much he had cared for the old horse, she couldn't believe he was reliving sorrow over Falconer's death. His attitude sprang from something else, something deeper, and she wanted to touch him, somehow to comfort him, but she could not bring herself to do so. Her own feelings were unfamiliar, and she wasn't by any means certain she wanted to sort them out. No doubt, she told herself, she was merely suffering some strange aftereffects of her emotional storm.

When Abberley turned back to her from the fire, his face clear of any particular expression, she was convinced she had been imagining things. He looked only as if he were attempting to determine if she was entirely recovered or not.

She straightened her shoulders. "I am truly sorry to have subjected you to such a scene," she said. "It was patently unfair of me to blame you for anything that has happened."

"No," he replied, giving her look for look. "You had every right to expect more from me. I assumed that Lady Caldecourt and your cousin had everything in hand, but you used the word *usurped* a moment ago. Do you mind explaining that more clearly?"

Margaret felt warmth invade her cheeks as she recalled that she had said a great many more things to him—had shouted them at him, in fact, in a very unladylike fashion. She could not meet his eyes for a moment until her memory provided her with a sharp vision of the way he had looked when she first entered the bookroom. Squaring her shoulders again, she fought down her blushes and shot a glare at him from under her lashes.

"Perhaps I had better sit down," she said. "I daresay there is a good deal you do not know."

Abberley chuckled. The sound rolled forth and seemed to fill the air. His dark-blue eyes sparkled and his white teeth gleamed when he grinned at her. "Ah, Marget, you haven't changed. Not a jot. I can still tell what you are thinking just by heeding the changing expressions on your face. No sooner did you begin to remember some of the very rude things you shouted at me and to be properly ashamed of yourself than you also remembered why you lost your temper in the first place." His expression gentled and he took a step toward her. When he didn't take another, Margaret felt a surge of disappointment. His chuckle had stirred a host of good memories and a glow of warmth besides. She smiled at him, but he didn't smile back. His expression was serious again. "Foolish girl," he said, "you've no need to be ashamed. I do not doubt that I deserved to hear every word and more. But please explain about your aunt—that is, Lady Annis—and that countercoxcomb son of hers. I was given to understand that they had taken charge of young Timothy and assumed they had the right to do so, that Michael had specified such an arrangement in his will.''

''Michael left no will.''

''Nonsense, of course he did.''

Margaret's eyes lit with hope. ''Were you a witness to it, Adam?''

''No, but I assumed that was because I was mentioned in it somehow. He'd always said . . . But that is of no consequence now,'' he amended with a shrug. ''Look here, do you want a glass of ratafia or some wine? I could certainly do with—''

''Nothing, thank you,'' she interrupted tartly. ''You don't need anything either, Adam. You've got to help me.''

''All right,'' he conceded, taking a seat not in the Chippendale chair but in another nearer the window, ''but you can have no notion what that concoction of Pudd's did to my insides. I need a settler.''

''Then ring for tea if you must.''

''Tea! Lord, I don't drink tea. Doubt if there's a tea leaf in the house unless Pudd springs for a bit for his missus now and again when he's feeling flush.''

''For his rib, you mean?''

Abberley chuckled again. ''She'd fetch him a good clip on the ear if she knew he'd said that to you.''

Margaret awarded the sally a slight smile, but her thoughts had wandered again. ''Adam, if Michael had drawn up a will, where would he have kept it?''

''Either in the library or in the estate office,'' he answered promptly. ''I'd plump for that big oak desk of his in the library.''

''Would he have hidden it? Is there a secret drawer or a false bottom or something in that desk?''

''No, I'm certain Michael would have told me of any such device.''

''Perhaps it was a family secret, handed only from father to son, and he hadn't handed it on to Timothy yet.''

Abberley grinned at her. ''Michael still would have told me, and I'm quite certain there was no such thing, because we do have something of that nature here at the hall, and he knew about it and said only that the notion was an archaic one and foolish to boot.''

"Here?" Margaret was diverted. "What sort of secret?"

"Just a tricky panel in the master bedroom. One of the ancient Abberleys back of beyond had it installed, learned the trick, then did away with the fellow who contrived it.''

"Dear me, what a charming ancestor. Is his portrait in the gallery?''

"No, he was the second Baron Abberley, the one in the drawing-room tapestry, clutching at all the jewels round his neck. He was a friend of Brother John's while King Richard—the lionhearted one—was off enjoying his crusade. One of our wealthier ancestors. He built the first bit of the pile here, this bit, as a matter of fact, though it's been renovated a time or two since then.''

"I know the gentleman you mean," Margaret said. "All jewels and duck feet. But your great grandmother stitched that tapestry, I thought.''

"Right, but she copied it from an ancient example that was falling apart," he said. "I'm glad you noted the duck feet. In the original, the baron's ankles were crossed, as they are on his tomb, but Great-grandmama knew for a fact that he'd never set foot on any crusade, so she made the correction.''

Margaret laughed. "Aunt Celeste has told me about your great-grandmother before, of course, but she never told me that tale. Still, even though the baron wasn't a nice man, I don't think you ought to have told Michael about the secret panel.''

"Didn't. My father showed both of us. He agreed with Michael, you see, that more than one person should know about any secret of that nature, lest the secret be lost. After all, if the family jewels were kept there, it might make matters a trifle awkward for any heir who hadn't yet been told the secret. That's why I'm certain Michael would have told me of any odd hiding place he might have had.''

"But, Adam, he must have written a will.''

"Of course he did. Like as not, your charming relatives

discovered that it didn't benefit them quite so much as they'd anticipated and destroyed it, hoping for better treatment from the House of Lords.''

Margaret stared at him, knowing he had just voiced thoughts she hadn't wanted even to formulate. "Would they dare?''

He shrugged. "Others have. Did you write to Jensen?''

"Jensen?''

"Michael's solicitor in London. Marjory died there, after all, and Michael must have had a number of legal matters to contend with afterward. Stands to reason he'd have turned everything over to Jensen. The man would at least know if a new will was drawn up at the time.''

Margaret gave a sigh of relief. "Of course. I did know he'd employed someone in London, but I had forgotten he and Marjory were still in town when she died. I was in Vienna by then, you know.''

"I know. I thought you would come home.''

"When Michael wrote to tell us of her death, he said not to come, that there was nothing we could do. I should have done so anyway, perhaps, but I wasn't really ready to face England again so soon.'' When Abberley didn't say anything, she returned to the subject of Mr. Jensen. "I meant to ride into Royston today to speak with Mr. Swift, in any case. I shall ask him to go to London at once.''

Abberley straightened in his chair. "I'll attend to it for you. I can go and be back before Swift—who, despite his name, is no speedier than any other man of law—gets his papers organized. I've a notion I ought to have looked into the matter before now. It just never occurred to me that Lady Annis or Jordan Caldecourt would play at ducks and drakes where young Timothy's fortune is concerned.''

Margaret's eyes lit. "Would you, really? Oh, Adam, I should be so grateful if you would attend to the matter. Only . . .'' She regarded him doubtfully.

"I know. I said you mustn't depend upon me. And ordinarily you mustn't, Marget. I'll only let you down. But I'll fix this business for you, you can count on me for that much.'' He got to his feet. "It's the very least I can do.''

She thought he looked tired. One light-brown lock had fallen forward over one bushy eyebrow, giving him a rakish look. She considered the thought. No doubt he was a rake, at that. She had heard such things said of him more than once, and certainly his name had never been linked to any female's for longer than a month or so, which no doubt would explain Lady Annis's self-righteous sniffs and knowing looks. Margaret knew from his expression now that he was going to send her away, and she didn't want to leave. She wanted to speak to Mrs. Puddephatt to make sure he would get a nourishing dinner, and she wanted to warn Puddephatt himself to hide the brandy. But she had no right to do either, so she smiled at Abberley and let him help her from her chair.

"I shall depend upon you, my lord," she said then, quietly. "I hope such dependence does not prove to be overly burdensome."

Abberley grimaced. "You've a barbed tongue, my girl, but your point is well taken. Did you ride over alone? You must not do so again."

"Trimby came with me," she informed him, "but if you prefer, I shall bring Aunt Celeste along next time."

His sardonic smile acknowledged the hit. "Thank you for sparing me that much." The accompanying shudder was only half mocking. "I daresay she would have dealt with me more harshly than you did."

"She would have combed your hair with a joint stool, cousin dear. You'd be well advised never to allow her to see you in such a condition as I was privileged to see."

"I believe I directed Pudd to tell visitors I was not at home," he replied, looking down his nose.

"Put a sock in it, Adam," she retorted rudely, "and don't you dare to blame poor Puddephatt for admitting me. You'd have been well served if I *had* allowed Aunt Celeste to come with me."

He smiled then, ruefully. "I shan't blame Pudd. I just wish you had not seen me in such a state, and I hope you never do so again."

"There is a way guaranteed to prevent such an occurrence, my lord."

He nodded soberly. "Next time I shall forbid Pudd to *open* the door."

She gasped, then realized he was waiting for her to rise to the bait. Her lips twitched, but she shook her head at him and turned toward the door. "I have accepted your apology, sir, but I don't think you ought to press the advantage. I am still not altogether pleased with you."

He yanked the bellrope, then held the bookroom door open for her. "You're entirely justified, Marget. I shall have to mend my ways."

Outside a few moments later, with Puddephatt watching benevolently from the open doorway and Trimby holding both his own horse and the little black mare, Abberley tossed her into the saddle. In clear daylight he looked worse than ever, Margaret thought, but a decided twinkle leapt to his eye when she complimented him upon his great strength. It faded a moment later, however, when she began to upbraid him for the condition of his lawns and borders.

"And the drive is a disgrace, Adam. There are weeds everywhere. Moreover, there are fences down in the eastern fields, and the fields themselves—"

"Enough, brat," he said with a warning look that told her more sternly than his words that he had heard all he wanted to hear in front of Trimby. "You attend to matters at the manor and leave the hall to me. I'll bring whatever information I receive from Jensen directly to you. You may look for me at the end of the week." He smiled wryly. "And please convey my regards to Aunt Celeste. You may tell her I was sorry not to see her today."

Her own eyes danced then. "I shall tell her no such plumper as that, sir. I shan't betray you, but neither will I protect you from her wrath if you persist in your foolish behavior. You are strictly forbidden to touch so much as a drop of brandy until you return from London, do you hear?"

He glanced quickly at Trimby, but the groom had moved tactfully forward to adjust his stirrup and was paying them no heed. "You mind that tongue of yours, my girl," Abberley said in an undertone, "or you and I will have a falling-out."

She bent toward him, unintimidated by his scowl. "I meant what I said, my lord. I am perfectly willing to fall out with you if it becomes necessary. One look at your condition tells me I shall win any such encounter easily enough."

He glared more savagely than before, but she met his look without a blink, and a moment later he stepped away. "Till the end of the week, Margaret," he said stiffly.

"Indeed, sir. Have a safe journey."

As she urged her mare to a canter in the weed-choked drive, she was conscious of feeling let down. Abberley rarely called her Margaret, only Marget, the name she had called herself as a child, so when he called her Margaret, she knew he was seriously annoyed with her. Perhaps she ought not to have favored him with the rough edge of her tongue with Trimby and Puddephatt as an audience. That had not been well done of her. Still, Abberley had deserved to hear the words from someone, and the condition of the property was scarcely a secret. He was, furthermore, accustomed to her bursts of temperament and had always tolerated them well enough in the past. He would get over his annoyance.

No doubt he saw her now as he had always seen her, no more than a pesky younger cousin who spoke her mind more often than was comfortable for the peace of his. She was no more than that to him, certainly, despite the fact that, in his arms, she had felt protected and comforted, more so than she had ever felt anywhere else. Even Michael had never been able to make her feel as safe as Abberley did. Probably, she told herself, it had something to do with the size of the man. Surely, there was nothing romantic about it. His gesture had come merely from habit. All her life he had rescued her from scrapes of one sort or another, generally of her own making, and had protected her from the dangers of the world around her. Of course, Michael had done so, too. Tears welled into her eyes again at the thought of Michael, and she brushed them away, resolutely turning her thoughts homeward, not wishing at the moment to think of either her brother or his best friend.

Abberley was away for a full week, but Margaret scarcely had a moment free during that time to wonder what was keeping him. What with taking up the responsibilities of running a large household (for despite Lady Annis' oft-mentioned sense of duty, she seemed quite content to leave everything to Margaret) and renewing her acquaintance with her young nephew, Margaret had little time for anything else. Then, too, as soon as word got around the neighborhood that Lady Celeste and Miss Caldecourt had returned to Caldecourt Manor, they began to receive callers. Among the first were the vicar and his daughter, who were received in the blue-and-white drawing room by Margaret and Lady Celeste, Lady Annis having gone out for her daily drive and Jordan being occupied elsewhere on private business of his own.

The Reverend Mr. Maitland was a spare gentleman in his fifties, with thinning gray hair. A pair of wire-rimmed spectacles perched upon his bony nose, and through these he surveyed the world with a birdlike alertness. The air of alertness, however, as both Margaret and Lady Celeste were well aware, was misleading. More likely than not, Mr. Maitland, rather than attending to what was being said to him, was thinking of something altogether different, such as an interesting passage he had read in one of the classics the previous evening. At the moment, he was faithfully doing his duty.

"A dreadful business," he said as he accepted a cup of India tea from Margaret's hand, "that even men as young as Sir Michael should so utterly fall. But," he added more cheerfully, "they that wait upon the Lord shall renew their strength and shall mount up with wings of eagles and not be weary. They shall—"

"Papa, you are not in the pulpit now," said Miss Pamela Maitland softly from her chair near Lady Celeste. He blinked at her, and she smiled back at him, a singularly sweet smile. Blond and blue-eyed but long of face and lacking much in the way of a figure, Pamela Maitland was not a beauty. She was, however, one of the most popular young ladies in northern Hertfordshire, for her sweet nature and her many kindnesses had long since made her welcome everywhere, from tenants' cottages to the great houses. She was Margaret's age and one of her dearest friends. When the vicar, quite unoffended, began to sip his tea, she turned to Lady Celeste. "We are truly pleased to see you home again, ma'am."

"Can't deny it's good to be back in Hertfordshire," acknowledged her ladyship with a bright smile. "There's much to be said for the gaiety of Vienna, but there's naught amiss with a bit of peace and quiet, either."

Pamela smiled again. "I believe we can promise you quite as much peace and quiet as you can tolerate, ma'am. Nothing untoward ever happens hereabouts, unless it's young Timothy up to mischief."

"Sir Timothy," corrected her father gently, proving that, upon occasion, he did listen to what others said.

"Indeed," Pamela said with a laugh, "though he is rather small to suit one's notion of a baronet. How is he faring, Margaret?"

"Well enough for the most part," Margaret told her. "You're right about the mischief, though. He's already had more than one turn-up with Jordan just since our arrival, and I'm given to understand that such incidents are by no means unusual. His nanny seems to have taken a pet over something Jordan said to her about her methods of raising children, and she left a day or two before we arrived. I haven't really thought about what to do with Timothy now. He's too young to send to school, but I don't know if a new nanny is the answer or not." She didn't want to mention that, until she had word from Abberley, she dared not take the initiative herself where her nephew was concerned, but Pamela seemed to understand her predicament well enough.

"Have you thought about sending him to Papa for lessons?" she asked. "No one could object to such a scheme, surely."

"The very thing," agreed Lady Celeste before Margaret could speak. "What do you say, Mr. Maitland?"

The vicar looked at her blankly. "Say? What do you wish me to say, my lady? A fool's voice is known by a multitude of words; thus, I should not wish to speak without knowing the subject upon which I am to discourse."

"I expect that means you weren't listening," said her ladyship sagely, "but 'tis deeds, not words, we want from you, sir. Can you undertake to tutor my great grandnephew?"

"Sir Timothy?"

"Of course, Sir Timothy. He should be well-grounded in Latin and numerous other subjects before he goes off to Eton next year, after all."

"Indeed, yes," agreed the vicar, much struck. "Does he not have a governess?"

"No," replied Margaret. "Could you do it, sir? We should be much obliged."

"We must all do that which it is our duty to do," replied the vicar, from which Margaret was rightly given to understand that he would be pleased to have Timothy as his pupil.

The relief she felt over having that particular problem solved was tempered, however, by a more immediate difficulty. When she went in search of Timothy to inform him of his good fortune, the boy was nowhere to be found. That situation, in and of itself, was not distressing, for she had quickly discovered that Timothy saw no reason to disclose his intended whereabouts to any of the adults with whom he lived. He had been friendly enough to both Margaret and Lady Celeste. Indeed, he seemed to regard her ladyship with something approaching awe, making Margaret wonder what tales his father might have told him about their grandaunt. But Timothy recognized no one's authority, least of all Jordan's or that of Lady Annis. His attitude toward both was little short of contempt. During one contretemps between Jordan and the boy, when Timothy had flatly refused to obey some arbitrary command and Jordan had threatened to thrash the boy soundly, Margaret had intervened without so much as a thought. To her astonishment, Jordan had agreed, albeit sullenly, to let him off. It had not astonished her a jot afterward, however, when Lady Annis had a good deal to say—and none of it to Margaret's credit—on the subject of spoiling young boys.

When she had looked in the nursery, questioned the maids and Archer, the taciturn footman, and had searched most of the rooms on the upper floors, Margaret turned toward the stairs, intending to walk as far as the stables to see if any of the grooms might have seen him. She knew his dearest wish was for a pony of his own and that his father had for one reason or another not yet provided him with one, but there were animals he was allowed to ride, and Margaret had already learned that young Timothy had little difficulty persuading one or another of the stable lads to take him out whenever he wished to go.

She was halfway down the main stairs leading to the hall when the front door was flung open and Jordan strode in, looking furious.

"Where the devil is that young scamp?" he demanded. His airs and affectations for the moment deserting him, he sounded only like an angry man.

"You are looking for Timothy?"

"You're dam—dashed right I'm looking for Timothy, and this time, sweet coz, there's not a thing you can say that will save that lad from the hiding of his young life."

"You haven't the right to thrash him, Jordan. Not yet." She hadn't told him about Abberley's quest, nor did she intend to tell him. She knew perfectly well that if she did, their relationship would become more strained than it was already. If Abberley discovered that Sir Michael actually had not drawn up a will, then Jordan and Lady Annis would gloat. If, on the other hand, he discovered a will . . . Well, there was time enough to consider the ramifications of such a discovery if, indeed, it ever took place. She held her ground now as Jordan approached her, taking the stairs in angry strides.

"You won't stop me, Margaret, not when you see what that brat did to my new Wellingtons."

"Your boots?"

"Aye, not that they're worth a split farthing now. Your

sweet Timothy filled them with mud and set them near the fireplace to bake. My man didn't find them until the mud had hardened inside. When I lay my hands—"

"Oh, Jordan," Margaret said, stifling laughter, "how dreadful. Were they very expensive?"

"They aren't even paid for yet," he muttered, glaring at her. "You may well laugh, but I daresay you wouldn't if they were your boots."

"No, I wouldn't," she admitted, frowning, "but I don't think he would do such a thing to my boots. Why does he dislike you so, cousin?"

4

Jordan made no reply. With a near growl of anger he passed her, continuing his way up the stairs.

Assuming that further search would prove useless, Margaret made her way to the kitchen to request that the cook inform her when the upstairs maid who was looking after Sir Timothy until other arrangements could be made had sent for his supper.

"Really, Aunt Celeste," she said some moments later when she encountered that lady in a small upstairs sitting room, "that child could disappear for days with no one the wiser, I believe."

"Don't waste your pity upon the scamp," advised her ladyship, correctly interpreting Margaret's tone. "Young Timothy wants discipline."

"Well, I shan't allow Jordan to beat him," Margaret said hotly.

"Nor shall I," agreed the other. "Not that he don't want beating, for he does. He's been let to have his own way far too long, and it isn't a bit good for him. But although Jordan Caldecourt is scarcely the man to teach him manners, the boy oughtn't to be allowed to get away with such pranks as that boot business."

"No, of course not, and I mean to speak very severely to him," Margaret said, "but I cannot help feeling pity all the same."

"Pity won't help him. He wants his world turned right side

up again. Do you think Michael would have tolerated such an attitude as the one he displays toward Annis and Jordan?''

"Michael didn't like either of them very much," Margaret said slowly.

"Nonetheless . . ."

"Of course, you're perfectly right. Michael would have torn a good strip off him the first time he saw that little chin tilted up and heard that arrogant tone in Timothy's voice. But Michael is gone, and Timothy must be feeling very lost and lonely without him. Why, I can remember—''

"Which did you more good," Lady Celeste interrupted ruthlessly, "people feeling sorry for you and trying to comfort you or people treating you normally and expecting you to behave yourself?''

The memory of Abberley scolding her for overwatering the elder flowers with her tears and promising that if she ''dried up'' he might, just *might* allow her to ride his horse flashed through her mind. When he had apologized only the other day for being a lout and failing to comfort her properly, she had called the sort of comfort he'd had in mind ''mollycoddling.'' Had people been mollycoddling Timothy? Had even his father perhaps been guilty of that after Marjory had died? Suddenly, she was seeing the boy from another viewpoint. If he was an object for pity, it was because he had been allowed to run wild, not because he had lost his parents. He was like an unbroken colt and could scarcely be held accountable for his actions until someone took him in hand. And that someone, she decided then and there, would not be Jordan Caldecourt.

Consequently, as soon as she had word from the cook that Sir Timothy's supper had been sent up to the nursery, she excused herself to the others without explanation and hurried upstairs to the second floor.

The nursery was a cheerful room overlooking the back gardens of the manor and the low, greening chalk hills beyond. A healthy fire blazed behind the barred grate, and the room was comfortably warm. Timothy, neatly dressed in fresh nankeens, a well-starched white shirt, and a short blue jacket with large brass buttons, sat in solitary splendor at a small table before the fire, nibbling disinterestedly at the simple food upon his plate. He was a wiry child, small for his age, with straight chestnut hair that was as undisciplined as he was himself. Though it had been ruthlessly brushed back from his forehead only minutes before, several strands had fallen forward over bright blue eyes very reminiscent of Lady Celeste's.

When Margaret entered, he pushed the hair back again as he looked up at her warily. He said nothing at all.

Margaret smiled at the rosy-cheeked maidservant, who was pouring out a mug of milk from an earthenware pitcher. "You may leave us, Melanie. I'll bear Sir Timothy company while he eats his meal."

"Very good, miss." Melanie returned the smile with a broad grin, placed the mug beside Timothy's plate, dropped a brief curtsy, and left the room with a faint rustle of her blue camlet skirts.

Margaret pulled a small straight-backed chair up to the table and sat down opposite the boy, regarding him seriously. He pretended to ignore her and continued eating, showing more interest in his food now than when she had first entered the room.

"Timothy, I wish to speak to you," she said quietly, "but you may continue to eat your dinner. I only want you to listen."

He shot a glance at her from under his straight brows, but the glance was a brief one. His attention went immediately back to his plate.

Margaret thought for a moment, then thanked him as though he had answered her properly. "You will be pleased to know," she added, "that I have arranged for you to take lessons from the vicar, beginning tomorrow morning. You are quite a big boy now and must no longer be treated like a baby."

The boy straightened in his chair and shot her another of those under-the-brow glances, this time a measuring one.

She nodded, again as though he had spoken. "I see you realize you have been let to behave badly because everyone believed you were too young to know better. I do not believe that myself. You are quite old enough to know the difference between right and wrong."

"I ain't been let off so much," the boy muttered.

"Haven't, dear," Margaret corrected automatically. "You haven't been let off."

"That's what I said."

"A gentleman doesn't say *ain't*, Timothy. I daresay you mean that Jordan has often scolded you."

"Aye, and more besides." He set down his fork, watching her now more openly. "I don't like Jordan."

"You must call him Cousin Jordan," she said gently, "and I'll tell you a secret, Timothy," she added before he could protest. "I don't like Cousin Jordan either." She smiled at him, and the boy smiled back, a quick grin that showed his relief and was likewise full of mischief. It lit his narrow face, erasing the arrogant look as though it had never been and making him look more like a child than a little old man.

"Did you hear how I fixed his boots?" he asked conspiratorially, clearly thinking he had discovered an ally.

"I did," Margaret said, letting her smile fade. "That was not well-done of you, Timothy, though I can understand some of the feelings that prompted you to do it."

"Jordan is a wicked man," Timothy said hotly.

"Nevertheless, you cannot play such tricks, my dear. You must apologize to him. I wll go downstairs with you once you have finished your supper."

"I won't." The black look descended again, and he glowered at his plate.

"Yes, you will. A proper gentleman always apologizes when he has behaved badly. Only babies are too cowardly to do so."

"I ain't a coward," he muttered.

"Well . . ." she said doubtfully, ignoring the lapse of grammar this time, "if you say so, I must believe you, of course, but I have not yet seen you behave bravely, you know."

The blue eyes glared from under beetled brows, but when

Margaret said nothing more, the boy relaxed slightly. "Like as not, he'll thrash me," he said, still muttering.

"No, that he shan't," she promised. "I won't allow him to do anything of the sort. That is precisely why I mean to accompany you this time."

Again the measuring look, followed by a period of silence. Though she wanted very much to press harder, Margaret held her tongue. She was rewarded several moments later when Timothy straightened again and pushed his plate away.

"I expect the sooner it's done, the better," he said, scraping his chair back and standing. The napkin, one corner of which had been carelessly tucked into his shirt beneath his pointed chin, fell to the floor, and he moved as though he meant to leave it there. But then, with an oblique look at Margaret, who was also getting to her feet, he bent and picked it up, dropping it onto the table. As he stepped beside her toward the door, Timothy shot another of his quick looks upward at her, then said carefully, "It isn't only grown gentlemen who apologize, you know. Papa made me do so even when I was quite small."

Releasing a small breath of relief, Margaret said lightly, "I thought that was very likely the fact of the matter, for I knew your papa very well."

Timothy nodded. "He was your brother. I know, for he told me so himself." He paused thoughtfully. "I don't have a sister."

"I know, Timothy." They had passed into the corridor and now reached the head of the stairs. Margaret stopped and turned, bending to a half-kneeling position, to face the boy eye to eye, her hands gentle upon his thin shoulders. "You must have been very lonely, all these long weeks since your papa died. But you aren't alone any longer, my dear. Aunt Celeste and I are here, and we shan't leave you."

His lower lip trembled and his eyes were suspiciously damp, but he did not turn his gaze from hers. Instead, he stared at her unblinkingly, as if he would know the truth of her words from something he might see in her eyes. Margaret said nothing at all and made no attempt to rise, though her

knees and thighs began to ache before he finally blinked the
tears away and gave himself a little shake as though he were
returning from some distant place. Then his eyes narrowed,
and he said in a matter-of-fact tone, "Aunt Celeste is rather
old."

Not misunderstanding for a moment, Margaret said in exactly the same tone, "But I am not, Timothy, and the ladies
in the Fortescue family, as you can tell by Aunt Celeste, tend
to live long lives."

"Your mother did not," he said flatly.

"Ah, but she died in a carriage accident," Margaret pointed
out, "and if I have not met a similar fate already with all the
traveling I have done, I expect it is because I am not meant to
die in that fashion."

He nodded, moving once more toward the stairs, and
Margaret hoped he was satisfied for the moment, though from
her own experience, she knew the doubts would return again
and again until the terrifying fear that he would be left
entirely alone had faded into memory. Even then, of course,
the fear would return from time to time, but if she could help
ease it now, she believed it would never be so strong again.

The boy faltered once, outside the drawing-room door.
Knowing that Jordan was inside with Lady Annis and Lady
Celeste, waiting for their dinner to be announced, he glanced
doubtfully at Margaret.

"You've nothing to fear, Timothy. He has no right to lay a
hand on you, so I shall be able to stop him easily. But you
must make your very best apology, and you must never do
such a thing again. Do you understand me?"

He nodded, his lower lip gripped firmly between his teeth.

"Then, come along, my dear. It will soon be over."

Dealing with Jordan, even in the face of a properly repen-
tant Timothy, took longer than Margaret had anticipated, but
with Lady Celeste's staunch support and the added assistance
of Moffatt's timely announcement that dinner was served, she
carried the business off with a high hand and sent Timothy
back to the nursery a quarter-hour later, unscathed.

At the dinner table Jordan waxed bitter. "I see that you

mean to coddle the brat," he said, helping himself liberally from the platter of well-done roast beef Moffatt held for him. Margaret, noting the color of the meat, made a mental notation to speak to Mrs. Moffatt. Though she had said nothing before now, it was clear to her that the cook had forgotten over the years that she and Lady Celeste preferred their beef rare. When Moffatt had served the other two women and moved toward her, Margaret shook her head, serving herself from a bowl of broccoli in cheese sauce that Archer held at her right hand instead. As she replaced the spoon in the bowl, she realized that Jordan was repeating her name in an impatient tone.

She looked across the table at him. "Are you still annoyed, Jordan? You will achieve little by berating me, you know. Until Parliament grants your petition—if indeed the Lords see fit to do so—you have no right to maul Timothy about. And whether the petition is granted or not, you will still have no authority over me. This is my home. You can scarcely order me to leave it."

"To be sure," he returned hastily, his cheeks flushing, "I have no intention of doing such a thing. That is . . . Will you not be returning to Vienna?"

She favored him with a thin smile. "No, Jordan, I will not. Grandpapa very kindly invited me to visit him when it suited me to do so, and I have taken full advantage of his hospitality for nearly three years, but I have no wish to return."

Lady Annis sniffed. "I don't say you are not welcome in your own home, Margaret, for I am sure that is a thought far from my mind; however, I hope you do not expect me to play the part of companion or"—she shuddered dramatically—"chaperone. I should think you might have recognized by now that my health must prevent my playing such a role. And it would not be at all suitable for you to remain under this roof with just Timothy and Jordan if I were forced to repair to one of the watering spots for the benefit of my health, you know."

"I am not yet underground, Annis," Lady Celeste said

tartly. "Margaret knows that she can depend upon me to remain with her."

Margaret laughed at the look of dismay on Lady Annis's face, but she spoke as if to Lady Celeste. "Yes, of course, I know I can depend upon you, ma'am. That was all settled before ever we left Vienna. For you must know, Annis, that Aunt Celeste agrees with you that I must not be left to my own devices, though despite what both of you believe to the contrary, I am quite capable of looking after myself, and Timothy, too, if that were necessary."

"But, surely, Sir Harold has need of your services in Vienna, Celeste," Lady Annis said, her voice rising into a whine. "Whatever will he do without you? He must be feeling quite bereft."

"Fustian," retorted the old lady. "Harold put off his short pants long ago and is perfectly well able to take care of himself. He has an excellent housekeeper, and if he finds himself in dire need of a hostess, he's certainly young enough to take a second wife. We rub along together tolerably well, but he won't demand my return when he knows Margaret has need of me."

"I had forgotten that he is several years younger than you are," Lady Annis said with what Margaret felt was pure maliciousness. "No doubt he believes it would not be good for you to make that long journey again at your advanced age."

Lady Celeste's bright-blue eyes snapped, but she smiled sweetly. "One must show gratitude where gratitude is due, and that was kind of you, Annis. I am persuaded that that is quite the first time you have put yourself to the effort of considering someone else's health. I must be flattered indeed that you have selected mine for the exercise."

Lady Annis gaped at her for a full five seconds before turning her attention strictly to her plate. Margaret choked on her broccoli, but Jordan turned a deaf ear to the exchange. Perfectly satisfied and still smiling angelically, Lady Celeste signed to Moffatt to serve her a helping of breaded fish.

The following morning, attended by the chambermaid Melanie, Sir Timothy went off to the vicarage for his first lessons. There were more callers in the days that followed, but with the first days of April came more temperate weather, and everyone seemed to relax into the new routine. Despite her household responsibilities, Margaret was often able to enjoy a morning ride on Dancer and even managed to find a private moment or two during the day or early evening in which to indulge her love for music at the pianoforte in the little parlor adjoining the blue-and-white drawing room.

She had arranged for a seamstress from Royston to call at the manor the day after Abberley's departure, and she and Lady Celeste had quickly been provided with mourning gowns to wear when they received their visitors. A complete wardrobe would take longer, but Lady Celeste had managed to convince her that since more than three months had now passed since Michael's death, they could avoid full mourning for their daily attire and make do in private with more somber colors than they would otherwise wear. Thus, Margaret had selected materials of gray, soft lavender, and dark blue, all of which were more becoming to her than the uncompromising blacks she had earlier determined to wear.

By the following Tuesday a full week had passed since Abberley's departure, but Margaret scarcely had a chance to consider that fact, for no sooner had she finished her breakfast that morning than a guilt-ridden Melanie burst into the breakfast parlor. Their first day notwithstanding, they had quickly discovered that Lady Annis rarely came down to breakfast and that Jordan didn't come down until long after everyone else had left the table, so Margaret and Lady Celeste were alone, indulging in second cups of chocolate. Both turned, startled by the maidservant's uncharacteristically precipitous entrance.

"Good gracious, Melanie, what are you about, girl?" demanded Lady Celeste. "Is the house afire?"

"Oh, no, m'lady. Beg pardon, m'lady. Oh, Miss Margaret, he's done gone!"

"Who's gone?"

"Master . . . I mean, Sir Timothy, miss! He's done a bolt, 'e 'as, an' wi'out 'is breakfast, as well!"

Lady Celeste merely raised her eyebrows, but Margaret had to force herself to speak quietly. "Calm yourself, Melanie. Sir Timothy has not run away, you may be sure of that. He is merely up to his old tricks, I daresay, and the last thing we must do is to panic. Tell me exactly what happened, if you please."

"Nothing 'appened, Miss Margaret, and that's a fact. He don't like me t' 'elp 'im dress. Says 'e's a big lad, 'n all, and that 'e kin do it 'imself, so I don't do more than take 'im a tray at sunup like a gennulmun, with chocolate. Then I goes back at nine o'clock to take 'im a proper breakfast in the nursery afore we walk to the vicarage. Only when I went back this morning, 'e was gone. I searched 'igh 'n low, miss, thinking 'e was only playin' least in sight, but 'e's gone." Melanie ended on a near wail and began to twist her cambric apron between her hands. "Oh, Lord, 'er ladyship and Mr. Caldecourt 'll want me turned orf, sartain, miss."

Lady Celeste said coldly, "Since neither her ladyship nor Mr. Caldecourt has anything to say to anything *yet*, their wants need not concern you, Melanie. Pray, take control of your emotions. Such behavior is most unhelpful."

Melanie stared at the old lady, but the tone was sufficient to steady her. "Yes, m'lady. Beg pardon, m'lady."

Lady Celeste's tone also had its effect on Margaret. She turned to Melanie with a smile. "We have both allowed ourselves to worry unnecessarily," she said. "Simply because Timothy has behaved well for two or three days is no reason for us to think he has mended his ways so quickly. I am quite certain he has determined to disappear for the day in his old fashion."

When the matter was put to her in that way, Melanie relaxed noticeably. "Do you know, miss, 'e's been such a lamb, I'd plumb forgot. It's remarkable, that is. I'm blessed if that young limb o' Satan ain't jest took to 'is old ways again. Do we just let be, miss?"

"No, we don't," Margaret said with quiet determination,

pushing back her chair and getting swiftly to her feet. "I warned him that his naughtiness would no longer be overlooked out of pity for his bereavement. You must go to the vicarage, Melanie. There is a slight chance he has decided merely to dispense with your escort, but if, as I expect, they have not seen him, you must explain to the vicar that he will not be burdened with Timothy today. It would not be fair to leave him wondering what time the boy will arrive. Then you must come back and help search for him."

"He usually goes into the woods some'eres, miss."

"I believe you're right, and I will search the woods between here and the hall. When you return, you must get Archer and the maidservants to help you search the manor. Wherever he is, I want him found, and quickly. This must stop now."

"I'll attend to the indoor servants," Lady Celeste said quietly.

Margaret shot her a grateful look, then hurried up to her bedchamber to ring for her tirewoman to help her change into her riding habit. She had not thought to have a new one made up and realized as she dragged the dashing, green, military-styled habit from her wardrobe that she would have to do so. Her dresser, a gawky, gray-haired woman who had served her in that capacity since the days of her come-out and who had accompanied her to Vienna without fuss as though that were a commonplace enough thing to do, thus earning Margaret's eternal gratitude, entered to find her struggling to pull her morning dress over her head.

"That dress is easier got out of if you step out, Miss Margaret," she said grimly, coming to the rescue, "and if you'd said you was meaning to ride this morning, I would have put out that habit in the first place."

"Oh, Sadie, I wasn't meaning to ride, as you know perfectly well," Margaret said, emerging at last from the gray folds of the morning gown and reaching for her boots, "but that wretched child has disappeared again, and I mean to find him."

"Well, I daresay you know what you're about, missie, but

if you want a spot of advice, you'll warm that lad's backside
for him when you do lay hands upon him. A proper varmint,
by all I hear.''

"Indeed, he can be," Margaret acknowledged, allowing
Sadie to assist her into her silk shirt and then into the woolen
skirt of the habit, "but I think he can be managed well
enough without resorting to violence if we but put our minds
to it. He has been allowed to go his own road too long, is
all.''

Sadie's sniff said more than the words that, privileged
though she might be, she could not bring herself to utter.
When Margaret only grinned at her, she grimaced and shook
her head. A few moments later, having helped her mistress
into the elegant spencer with its gold frogs and epaulets, she
handed her a gilt-handled riding whip with a wry twist of her
lips. "Don't forget this, Miss Margaret. I'm thinking you
could put it to good use, if only you would.''

But Margaret laughed at her and hurried to the stables,
where Dancer awaited her. Trimby helped her into the saddle,
then swung up into his own. "Where be we headed, miss?''

"Toward the hall, Trimby. We are searching for Sir Timothy, however, so I do not want you to ride beside me, for we
can search more territory quickly if we separate. If I need
you, I'll shout.''

"As you wish, miss," he said, nodding. "The woods be
the most likely place, I'm thinking.''

"My thoughts, exactly.''

The sun was shining brightly, and although the day was
crisp, it was born of spring, not winter, for the seasons had
turned in a matter of days. Shoots of new grass showed green
in the meadow between the stables and the woods, and new
leaves decked the trees and shrubbery. Crocuses and tiny
lilies that looked too fragile to survive in the chilly air pushed
their heads up through the manor's lawns. Margaret smiled.
This was her favorite time of year in Hertfordshire.

Trimby took the lead until they had entered the woods, but
then he turned to the right, guiding his horse among the
thick-growing oaks and beech trees. Margaret kept to the path

a while longer, then turned off to the left, intending to ride back and forth to the edge of the woods, where the ground began to move up across the downs and into the chalk hills. There were patches of thick, impenetrable shrubbery in some places, but since much of it was dotted with nasty thorns, she didn't think it necessary to investigate such places too thoroughly. The few lingering, slow-melting snowdrifts showed no sign of a boy having crossed them, so these too she passed without a second thought. She had been crisscrossing her patch of woods for nearly an hour when, upon nearing the path again, she heard hoofbeats. Thinking it must be Trimby coming to find her, she urged Dancer to a more rapid pace, intending to cut him off, but even before she emerged onto the path, her keen ears informed her that the hoofbeats were coming from the wrong direction.

Swinging toward the sound, she heard the sharp, screaming whinny of an indignant horse before the hoofbeats ceased abruptly. What seemed to be a full moment's silence was followed by an equine snort and a scrabble of movement on the path. When Margaret's eyes finally focused upon a flurry of activity in the shadows just beyond a brightly lit clearing ahead, she realized that the quickly moving horse had been wrenched to a halt and that his rider had dismounted. Setting a heel to Dancer's flank, she rode forward in an attempt to see more clearly and recognized Abberley just as he bent forward and yanked a disheveled young Timothy from beneath an alder bush.

"Here! Lemme go!"

Margaret opened her mouth to call to them, then snapped it shut again in astonishment when Abberley pulled the struggling boy close enough to deal him one sharp smack on his backside before setting him back on his feet. Timothy yelped but went silent immediately when Abberley demanded sternly to know if he wanted something to make him yell properly.

"Well," repeated his lordship implacably, "do you?"

"No, sir."

"Then don't let me catch you playing such a trick ever again."

"No, sir."

"Abberley," said Margaret, close enough now to look down at the pair of them, "whatever are you about?"

His lordship, looking a deal healthier and rather handsome in buckskins and a sleek brown leather coat, glanced up at her without surprise, indicating that he had been aware of her approach. "Whatever are *you* about, Miss Caldecourt, to allow this child to run loose like this, popping up under horses' feet and nearly getting himself killed?"

Margaret was aware of a sudden knot in her midsection and a dizziness that convinced her that all the blood must have rushed from her head. "Killed?" Her voice had little of its usual strength. "Surely, you exaggerate, sir."

"I am not in the habit of exaggerating," he assured her grimly. "If it were not for Apollo's aversion to trampling on living creatures, young Timothy here would be mincemeat. He dashed out of the shrubbery directly in front of me, then froze long enough to have been killed. As it was, he startled Apollo and I was nearly thrown." He paused, glaring at her. "This is scarcely a safe place to play hide-and-seek."

Margaret saw the boy swallow carefully and knew he was expecting more trouble. She met Abberley's glare, saying only, "We were not playing, sir." Then, before he could ask for an explanation, she added, "And you have no right to be smacking him."

The earl's eyes glinted. "I have the right of any man startled out of his wits by an idiotish act," he said, turning to the tall, bay horse and steadying it with gentle movements of his hand along its graceful neck. Margaret turned her eye upon Timothy, thinking he meant to do another bolt, and nearly missed his lordship's next words. "But I also have more right than you know."

She turned back as he swung into the saddle. "What do you mean by that, Adam?"

He smiled at her, then leaned down to the boy. "Up you come, young fellow. No need for you to walk back."

Timothy hesitated for only a moment before allowing himself to be hoisted up before Abberley. As they turned back toward the manor, Margaret took a good look at the earl. Though he did indeed look better than he had the last time she had seen him, he still looked tired. They had ridden beside each other for some moments before she realized he had not yet answered her question.

"What right have you, Adam?" she repeated. In the flurry of the near accident, she had forgotten his quest. "What did you discover in London, sir?"

Turning slightly, he smiled at her again, this time ruefully. "I fear your brother's wits had gone begging, Marget. He managed to delude himself into thinking that I would make a proper guardian for young Timothy here."

5

"Then you found the will!" Margaret's eyes lit with triumph. "I knew Michael would never be so daft as to chance letting Caldecourt fall into Jordan's hands."

"There was a will at the manor, too, I suspect," said Abberley, "but I think it would be more diplomatic not to inquire too closely into what must have become of it, don't you agree?"

Margaret grimaced. "My inclination is to tell them both what I think of their machinations, but I shall be guided by your decision, sir. I hope you mean to tell me exactly what you discovered in London."

"I do, certainly, but not, I believe at the present moment," he said with a meaningful glance at the boy seated on his saddlebow. "Do you understand, young man, what I have just told your aunt?"

"No, sir," said Timothy meekly, keeping his eyes on the shady trail ahead, where Trimby appeared just then, having ridden out from beneath a particularly large beech tree some twenty yards beyond.

Abberley paid no heed to him, speaking to the boy. "It means that I stand in the place of your father now."

"You are not my father," Timothy said grimly.

"No, I am not," Abberley agreed, unoffended, "but by law I stand in his stead, which means I am responsible for seeing that you grow up to be a gentleman. Because of that, it is my duty to stop you from doing foolish and dangerous things." He paused. "I would like to know what you were doing back there just now when you frightened my horse."

"I wasn't doing anything," Timothy muttered.

"I should not like to have to ask your aunt what you were doing," warned Abberley. "I believe, since she was not playing a game, that she must have been searching for you, which is a thing she should not have to do, you know."

Timothy dared a small shrug and, when there was no response, said with more than a touch of defiance, "I didn't want lessons today."

"Lessons?" Abberley quirked an eyebrow at Margaret.

She smiled. "The vicar has kindly undertaken to give him lessons for a few hours each morning," she said.

Abberley nodded. "That is indeed kind of Mr. Maitland. You are quite old enough to begin lessons, Timothy. Surely, you wouldn't prefer to spend the whole day with your nanny now that you are so grown up?"

"He hasn't got a nanny," Margaret interjected, a note of irony in her voice making the earl look at her sharply.

"Routed?"

"Indeed, though you mustn't blame Timothy. There were other forces involved."

"I see." There was a moment's silence. "I begin to believe you have been making a nuisance of yourself, young man. Perhaps, once I have had the opportunity to speak at length with your aunt, it will be necessary that you and I have a long chat together. What do you think about that?"

Timothy shot a slanted look at Margaret, half daring her to say something, half frightened that she would.

She smiled at him. "I do not believe such a conversation will be necessary, my lord. Timothy has behaved very well this week. His only lapse has been his neglecting to inform me this morning that he meant to come into the woods instead of going to Mr. Maitland."

The boy relaxed, but a twist of Abberley's lips showed her he wasn't fooled for a moment. And once they had arrived at the manor, where she was able to turn Timothy over to Melanie, the earl led her straight into the downstairs parlor, a little-used room just off the front hall, where they could be assured of at least several moments of privacy.

"That lad's been leading you a dance, or I miss my guess," he said without preliminary. He stripped off his riding gloves and laid them beside his whip on a side table.

Margaret made no attempt to deny the charge. "This has been a difficult time for him, sir. What do you mean to do with him?"

"Do with him?" He stared at her, bewildered.

"Well, you said Michael had appointed you his guardian. Does that mean you intend to take him back to the hall with you?"

"Good Lord, no!" He pushed a hand through his hair, staring at her in astonishment, his earlier commanding attitude gone completely. "What on earth put such a notion into your head? What would I do with him at Abberley?"

"Well, if you are his guardian—"

"Look here, Marget, you're not thinking of going back to Vienna, are you?"

"No, but what has that to do—"

"That has everything to do with the point at hand. I haven't the least idea of how to raise a boy. That's woman's work, at least until he's of an age to go to school. It never occurred to me for a moment that Timothy would live anywhere but here. I frankly admit that if you were returning to the Continent, I should be at a standstill, for I am certainly the last person he should be forced to depend upon, but if you are willing to remain here and look after him, that seems the most logical way to deal with the problem. I shall see to it that the property is properly looked after, of course."

She shot him a sardonic look. "Will you, my lord? As properly as Abberley has been looked after, I suppose."

He grimaced. "Michael's bailiff knows what he's about, you needn't worry. I'll see he has full authority. As you will have full authority over the management of the house. I daresay," he added quickly, "that it will give you pleasure to rout certain of its present inhabitants."

"It will, at that," she agreed, more in charity with him at

once. "Tell me what you discovered. Did Mr. Jensen actually have the will in his possession?"

"Pretty nearly. He had a complete duplicate in his files. It is his policy always to make two copies of important papers, and the copy was properly signed and witnessed, exactly like the original."

"Then, why on earth did he not make its existence known?"

"He didn't realize there was any need to do so. He assumed that everything was properly in train here, that someone would have made contact with him had any difficulty arisen. He knew nothing about Jordan Caldecourt's efforts in Parliament."

"Merciful heavens!" Margaret exclaimed. "I'd quite forgotten. Can the will be overturned by that dreadful petition?"

"Of course not. I put a stop to the petition before I left London. Just explained that an error had been made, that the will existed, after all. I had to produce it before witnesses, but everything is settled now. There are still certain formalities to be attended to, regarding probate, but you have nothing to worry about where the Caldecourts are concerned."

When he moved as though to take his departure soon after making this blithe statement, Margaret shook her head at him. "Oh, no, you don't, my lord. You are going to tell this tale to Jordan and Lady Annis yourself. They'll never believe it, coming from me. They'll probably demand to see the will."

He patted his jacket. "In my pocket."

"Well, take care you are not set upon by thieves on your way back to the hall," she warned with a small shiver.

"Lord, it's not the original, just a fair copy that one of Jensen's clerks made out for me. The original's in London, where it will remain until probate is completed. You've nothing to fear."

He followed her obediently to the drawing room, where they found the others.

Lady Celeste beamed upon him. "How nice to see you, dear boy. Have you brought good news?"

"I have," he replied, taking her outstretched hand and

giving it a squeeze as he bent over to kiss her powdered cheek. "You are looking marvelously well, ma'am."

"Why is it that people always say that to me as though they are much surprised to find me so?" demanded her ladyship, laughing at him. "If I were twenty years younger, they would tell me I was in good looks or that my dress was particularly becoming. Instead, they comment upon my health as if they had been expecting me to cock up my toes before they'd had the chance to lay eyes upon me again."

"Exactly so, ma'am," said Abberley, his tone serious but his eyes twinkling merrily.

"Odious boy. Make your bow to Lady Annis."

He turned, the merriment fading. But his tone was perfectly polite as he greeted Lady Annis, who languished with her cut-crystal vinaigrette in a deep armchair, and Jordan, who had risen from his lounging position on the settee to greet Margaret.

"You say you have brought news?" the younger man inquired, watching him closely. "From where?"

"London," replied Abberley briefly.

Lady Annis drew a sharp breath. "London? You went to London, Abberley? We are in daily expectation of news from London ourselves, though I daresay you could not have known that."

"Indeed, ma'am, I know exactly what you were waiting to hear, and I am sorry to disappoint you. Your petition has been withdrawn."

"Withdrawn!" Jordan took an angry step forward. "If you have been interfering in matters which do not concern you, Abberley, I'll have you know that—"

"Dear me," interjected his lordship, bored, "such vehemence quite distorts your image, Caldecourt. After striving to appear blasé, one must never resort to bursts of temper. I have interfered only in that which concerns me very much. I have been sadly remiss in my duties, but after seeing Miss Caldecourt last week I was reminded of them. I merely went down to London to arrange for Sir Michael Caldecourt's will to be entered for probate."

"Sir Michael's will!" Lady Annis sat up, her ill health forgotten. "But surely you mistake the matter, Abberley. Sir Michael left no will."

"I fear 'tis you who mistakes the matter, ma'am. There is indeed a will, and it names me young Timothy's guardian and cotrustee with Sir Harold, which is rather a nuisance since he is out of the country, but I daresay I shall contrive well enough." He said the words casually, as though he had not the slightest notion of the effect they would have upon his listeners, but it would have been an insensitive man indeed who failed to realize that Lady Annis and her son were dumbstruck.

Lady Celeste was not. "I daresay you counted your chickens before they hatched, Annis," she said cheerfully. "Never a wise thing to do, you know. I am persuaded you will wish to return to Little Hampstead as quickly as possible, now that you know you will not be burdened with Timothy's affairs after all."

"Can't," said Jordan, not without a glint of triumph. "Let the house till the end of the year. We'll have to go to London."

"London!" Lady Annis was betrayed into a squeal of dismay. "How can you even think of such a thing, Jordan, when I am well nigh prostrate now? You know I am never well in London. The noise, the excitement, the constant bustle—my poor nerves would never stand it. No, my dearest," she continued, calming herself with apparent difficulty, "much as it goes against the grain to throw ourselves upon Margaret's gentle mercies, we must do so. She could not be so heartless as to make us leave when she knows she might well be sending me to my death."

Margaret carefully avoided meeting either Abberley's eyes or Lady Celeste's. Her voice was devoid of expression. "You must stay as long as you like, of course, Annis."

Lady Celeste was indignant and didn't scorn to show her feelings then or to express them to Margaret once they were alone. " 'Tisn't her health at all, as you must know," she said tartly then. " 'Tis simply the shock of thinking even for a single moment that she might have to tip over the ready to pay for lodgings in town.''

"Tip over the ready, Aunt Celeste? Really, Timothy should hear you.''

The old lady chuckled. "I did scold him for using slang, didn't I?''

"You did.''

"Well, best he learn now that he should do as he's told, not what he learns from others.''

"You are a fraud, Aunt Celeste.''

"You are attempting to change the subject, miss.'' her ladyship retorted. "You know perfectly well that Annis wants to remain only to avoid spending any of her own money. If they have hired out that great barn of a house Stephen bought in Little Hampstead, she must be making a pretty penny on the deal. Let her spend it to quack herself and to provide a roof to cover her head.''

"You don't mean that, ma'am,'' Margaret said quietly. "You would be the first to condemn my actions if I were to turn them out. We don't like them, but they are still family. They have the right to stay at the manor as long as they like.''

Lady Celeste sniffed, but she presented no further argument.

Timothy, on the other hand, waylaid Margaret less than an hour later—first, demanding to know how soon Lady Annis and Jordan would be leaving; and second, wishing to know if she had told Lord Abberley anything to his discredit.

"I didn't tell him anything,'' Margaret began, then, blatantly taking advantage of the opportunity, added in pointed tones, "this time.'' Noting that she had the boy's full attention for once, she continued, "I trust you will give me no reason to bear tales of your behavior, Timothy.''

"You wouldn't cry rope, would you, Aunt Marget?'' His eyes were wide, innocent, those of a child in desperate straits.

"Ah, Timothy, you still don't understand about guardianship,'' she said sadly. "You see, his lordship has the right to know if you are not behaving, and I would be in deep trouble if I tried to protect you from him. I am persuaded there must be a law that says I cannot do such a thing."

"Would they take you to prison, Aunt Marget?"

She grinned at him. "No, you unnatural boy, so you needn't sound so hopeful of such a thing coming to pass. You'd just best behave yourself."

"And will his lordship make them leave soon if I behave?"

Margaret's grin faded. "They wish to stay, Timothy, and it is our duty to make them comfortable. They are part of our family, you see, so we cannot simply send them away."

"You don't want them to stay."

She sighed. "I want you to behave properly toward them, young man. You will only make matters difficult for me if you do not."

He favored her with a long look, then said, "Very well, but when I am a man, I shall tell them they cannot stay here anymore."

"Goodness, I hope they won't be here so long as that," she said, laughing.

Later that afternoon she accepted Lady Celeste's invitation to accompany her on a drive through the countryside in an open landaulette. The day had warmed up considerably. The sky was clear and deeply blue, and the Ermine Street roadbed was dry though badly rutted as usual. Tall hedges lined the way for a mile or so as the carriage rattled its way southward, but then they entered open country that provided fine bursts of scenery.

Margaret turned to her companion with a delighted smile. "I'd nearly forgotten how beautiful Hertfordshire can be. This was a splendid idea, ma'am."

"Needed fresh air to strengthen my lungs," returned Lady Celeste, straight-faced.

Margaret chuckled. "I daresay you've a pair of the strongest lungs in Britain, ma'am."

Lady Celeste smiled, well pleased with the compliment, and they fell silent again to enjoy the scenery.

Shortly afterward, the coachman turned west toward the village of Mayfield. After fording a small stream that flowed

from the mighty Cam River, situated some miles to the east
of them, they entered the quiet white and gray village, where
the road forked. Several cottages nestled around the small
flint church on the western fork, but most of them occupied
one side or the other of road leading north. Their walls were
of flint or of plaster, sometimes decorated with patterns in
lines, and there was abundant thatch. Here and there the line
of cottages was interrupted by a gateway opening into a
farmyard. Sunlight beamed brightly on the neat little village,
and sparrows chirped in the trees at the farmyard gates.

Taking the northern fork, they soon left the village behind.
There were more copses of trees now, and the country seemed
to rise on all sides of them. Eventually the road would take
them past Caldecourt and Abberley to Therfield Heath, though
it was commonly traveled only part of that distance. They
passed between newly plowed fields that would soon be tall
with corn, clover, or barley. White bryony grew in the low
hedges lining the fields and even sprawled over the still-damp
rabbity mound by the wayside. The grassy borders between
the roadbed and the hedge showed new green shoots. At first
the road was rough, but hard and white. Soon it became
practically green and then wholly so, but it was level, and
after Ermine Street, the carriage seemed to be fairly skim-
ming along. As they passed by fields Margaret knew to be
part of Caldecourt Manor, the road was lined for a time by
lime trees. Then there was a spread of elder flower and lady's
slipper. Everywhere they heard the chatter of young birds.

She was surprised when Lady Celeste directed their coachman to drive past the road leading the back way to the manor,
for beyond the lovely group of sycamore and hornbeam trees
at the crossing, the road might have been no more than a series
of cart tracks between tenant farms, rarely with a hedge on
both sides, more often with nothing separating track from
field or thicket. Here there were no newly-plowed fields but
only weeds and scrub, so there was at once a sense of privacy
and of freedom. They were on Abberley's land now, and
before long they came to a cottage.

Margaret vaguely remembered that there had once been

two cottages here, comprising a single tenant farm. Now there was only the one cottage and a tumbledown shed. The thatch on the cottage was black with mildew, and the walls were filthy. There was none of the feeling of neat cheer that had met them in Mayfield village. Spring seemed not to have touched the farm either. Lady Celeste signaled their coachman to draw up in the weedy yard.

"Aunt Celeste?" Margaret watched her, wide-eyed.

The old lady's eyes glinted with anger. "That young man wants a good thrashing," she muttered.

"What young man?"

"Abberley. He should be flogged for letting matters come to this. A man's land is his heritage. He has a duty, damn him."

"Aunt Celeste!"

The old lady merely glared at her, and since they had no footman accompanying them, she pushed open the door and let down the steps for herself. A moment later she stood in the middle of the yard, surveying the scene through narrowed eyes. Just then the door of the cottage opened, and two women —one elderly, the other middle-aged—peered at them from the threshold.

"Mrs. Muston?" Lady Celeste raised her voice slightly to make herself heard. "Is that you, Mrs. Muston?"

"Aye," the older woman replied cautiously. Then the younger whispered something hurriedly in her ear. "My lady? Bless my soul, ma'am, is it yerself, indeed?"

Lady Celeste stepped briskly toward her, holding her skirts up to keep them from catching at the weeds. More slowly, fascinated, Margaret descended to the hard ground.

"Where is your son, Mrs. Muston?" her ladyship demanded.

"Gorn t' Mayfield," replied the old lady, dropping a low curtsy and yanking at her daughter-in-law to follow her example, "an it please ye, ma'am."

"Well, it does not please me, for I wished to speak with him," said Lady Celeste. "I wish to know why this farm, which was always the best-kept farm on the estate, has been let to fall to rack and ruin."

The older woman shook her gray head. "There's been naught to plant, m'lady. The master b'ain't to 'ome fer the most part, 'n there be no bailiff these past two years an' more. Times be 'ard all round since the war be over 'n done, but 'is lordship plain don't care fer the place, 'n that's a fact."

"Are the other farms in a like condition?"

"Worse," said the younger woman quietly. "If my husband weren't able to find work in the village from time to time, my lady, we would starve. Some of the farms have been abandoned, but my husband's family has farmed this land for several hundred years. He won't leave. Says things are bound to improve."

"Aye, they will if I have a say in the matter, which I daresay I shall," said Lady Celeste tartly. She eyed the younger woman searchingly. "You're mighty well-spoken for a farm woman, Mrs. Muston."

"Thank you, my lady. I was the assistant housekeeper at the hall for several years before his lordship reduced his staff. Mrs. Puddephatt, who, as you probably know, was a lady's maid in town before she married her husband, taught me a great deal."

"She did, indeed. Look here, Mrs. Muston, we're very shorthanded at the manor, thanks to my nephew's wife's nipcheese notions. Do you present yourself to Mrs. Moffatt in the morning. I daresay she can find a position for you."

The woman's gratitude was painful for Margaret to see. In that moment she thoroughly agreed with Lady Celeste. Abberley deserved to be flogged.

But Lady Celeste wasn't finished. "You tell that husband of yours that I say he is to draw up a list of his needs," she said imperiously. "That roof needs rethatching, for one thing. I can see that myself. He will also need seeds and perhaps some new tools as well, but I haven't the slightest notion what is required, so he will have to help me. Once I know what is needed, I can see that the things are ordered from Royston or from London, if necessary. For the present, until I can find a proper bailiff, we shall make use of Mr. Farley at

Caldecourt. I am told that he knows his business. The reckoning, of course, will go to his lordship.''

"Aunt Celeste—"

"Not a word, miss. I'll attend to this. You get back in the carriage. I want to visit more farms. There's work just crying out to be done here. I intend to see it gets done.''

Two hours later, they had seen enough, and Lady Celeste had passed her message to several more farmers. As the landaulette turned past the sycamores onto the road leading the back way to the manor, Margaret let out a long sigh.

"He will have ten thousand fits, Aunt Celeste. You have no right to be pledging his purse right and left as you've done today.''

"Nonsense," the old lady said, straightening her bonnet, which had tilted forward over one bright blue eye. "The hall's my home, too, is it not? Didn't I live all my life under that roof until my brother Harold said he needed a hostess after your grandmother died? Wouldn't I be living there now if I hadn't agreed to come to the manor with you instead? I say," she added, struck by a sudden unpalatable thought, "he's *got* a purse, hasn't he?" She glared accusingly at Margaret. "Not rolled up, is he?"

"No, of course not. He's always had more money than he knows what to do with.''

Lady Celeste pounced on the phrase. "Precisely. Well, I know what to do with it, and if Abberley don't like it, may Heaven protect him.''

Three days passed before Margaret could discover whether Abberley liked the arrangement or not, and she lived in daily expectation of an explosion of some sort or other. But when he rode up to the front entrance of the manor early in the afternoon of the third day, leading a small black pony, he did not appear to be in a temper. Margaret, observing his arrival from the drawing-room window with a surge of pleasure that seemed disproportionate to the sight of a tall, broad-shouldered gentleman dismounting from a large bay horse, thought it remarkable that he should look cheerful. In view of the fact that Lady Celeste had been very busy indeed during those three days, his smile when he turned both horse and pony over to an accommodating stableboy seemed nothing short of miraculous.

Margaret was alone when he was announced, but she had scarcely finished welcoming him when her nephew burst into the room.

"Whose pony is that?" he demanded, skidding to a halt with one of the Oriental carpets bunched between his feet.

Abberley's bushy eyebrows shot upward and Margaret's hands flew to her hips. "Young man," she said in a dangerously calm voice, "you will leave this room at once, and you will not return until you can do so in the manner of a gentleman."

Timothy's mouth opened and words of sputtering protest tumbled over one another as he looked to Abberley for assistance.

"Straighten the carpet on your way out," the earl advised with a smile.

Outraged but left without a choice, Timothy turned, dragged the carpet back into place with his heel, and left the room. Neither Margaret nor Abberley spoke. They merely waited. A moment later, the boy reappeared, containing his emotions with difficulty but managing nonetheless to present an appearance of civility.

"How do you do, sir?" he inquired politely, facing Abberley.

"I am well, thank you," replied the earl, straight-faced, "but you should greet your aunt first, you know."

"Good afternoon, Aunt Marget," Timothy said with more haste than sincerity, turning back to Abberley before the last word was out. "Please, sir, I-I saw a pony, a black pony, being led to the stables."

"Did you, indeed?"

"I did, sir. Is he . . . that is, will he live here, sir?" Timothy seemed scarcely able to breathe.

"He will," the earl replied, his eyes beginning to dance.

Timothy released his breath in a long sigh. "He's mine?"

"He is. You may go and see him, if you like."

The boy turned on his heel, ready to race for the door, but

he stopped himself with a huge effort and turned back, blushing fiercely, to say, "Thank you, sir. Thank you!" He turned again, took a step, then looked back over his shoulder. "Has he got a name, sir?"

"Not yet. I thought perhaps you might be able to think of one."

"Yes, I believe I'll call him Theodore." With that he was gone.

Margaret grinned at the earl. "Whatever possessed you? Now, we'll never know where he is."

"Yes, you will because you will give orders both to Timothy and to your stable people that the pony is not to be saddled unless there is a groom to go with him. And that his lessons must be finished before he rides."

"My, you're very paternal today," she said, teasing him.

He frowned. "I know Michael meant to get him a pony long ago. Somehow he just never got around to it. I learned that this one was for sale and decided the time had come for the boy to have his own. I hope you are not distressed."

"Of course not. I think it was a fine idea." She paused, watching him, then said carefully, "You seem to be in excellent spirits today."

"Why not? Spring is in the air."

She realized then that he could not yet know of Lady Celeste's activities. He was too relaxed, too amiable, and she knew from past experience that he would not welcome the old lady's interference in his affairs. Nor would he contain anger beneath a mask of cheerful unconcern. Briefly, Margaret wondered if she ought to tell him what their grandaunt was up to, but before she had thought the matter through, Lady Celeste herself entered the room.

She was dressed becomingly in flowing pink silk, an afternoon frock nipped in just under her small breasts, and cut high to the throat and long to the wrist. The upper part of each sleeve was slightly puffed, and there was a narrow ruffle edging the neckline. Lady Celeste greeted the earl with an easy smile, but Margaret realized she was watching him measuringly, as though wondering if he meant to take her to task.

"His lordship has brought Timothy a pony, Aunt Celeste," Margaret said, her eyes twinkling. "Wasn't that kind of him?"

Lady Celeste looked at the earl. "Uncommon kind," she said slowly. "Turning over a new leaf, Abberley? Thoughtfulness don't seem to be your long suit."

He refused to be offended by her words. "I merely fulfilled an intention the boy's father had," he said. "It is nothing."

Lady Celeste seemed about to agree with him, before an arrested look in her eye told Margaret that she had remembered there might be shoals ahead. Instead, she muttered something nearly amiable, then asked if he would care for tea.

"His lordship doesn't drink tea, ma'am," Margaret said with a laugh. "Perhaps Moffatt can find some of Michael's sherry if Jordan hasn't drunk it all."

"I'd prefer Madeira," his lordship said when the order was relayed to Moffatt.

"At once, sir."

When they had been served, the conversation continued desultorily, but nothing was said about the tenant farms or the condition of the Abberley estate. His lordship took his leave half an hour later, promising to give the orders regarding the new pony at the stables, and Margaret looked accusingly at her grandaunt.

"You ought to have told him, ma'am."

"Fustian, he'll find out soon enough. I've placed a number of orders in Royston in his name. Someone will send him a reckoning soon enough."

They saw nothing of his lordship the next day or the next. Nor yet the next. But on Friday, just as Lady Annis was wondering what was keeping Moffatt with her tea and Margaret was beginning to become bored by both her ladyship's conversation and the bit of embroidery in her own lap, his lordship entered the drawing room in such a way as to remind her forcibly of the way in which Timothy had burst into the same room some days earlier, demanding to know about the pony.

Before the earl could speak, Lady Annis snapped, "Good gracious, Abberley, where are your manners? And where is Moffatt?"

"I didn't wait for him," Abberley retorted in the same tone before turning his fierce gaze upon Margaret. "I want to speak to you and to Aunt Celeste. Right now," he added harshly, making it clear that he would brook no argument.

6

"Aunt Celeste has gone for a drive," Margaret said more calmly than she felt. Her heart was pounding, for he looked furious, and she was a little afraid of that look. Even Lady Annis had not dared to say another word in the face of it.

Abberley glowered. "Gone for a drive, has she? Meddling again, no doubt."

"What on earth is he talking about, Margaret?" Lady Annis asked, reaching for her salts. "Abberley, I wish you will not speak so loudly. You have already startled me so that I'm sure it will be hours before my nerves recover. Not that you consider that, of course. You do not even have the civility, sir, to inquire after my health."

Abberley ignored her, so Margaret said with more gentleness than she might otherwise have employed, "Pray, do not distress yourself, Annis. Clearly, his lordship is annoyed about something, but it has nothing to do with you. Of that I'm quite certain."

"And so you should be," muttered his lordship wrathfully. But he turned at last to Lady Annis and made an effort to redeem himself. "I beg your pardon, ma'am. If Miss Caldecourt will be so kind as to escort me downstairs to the front parlor, there will be no further need to impose upon your solitude."

"That is out of the question, Abberley," Lady Annis said irritably. "You cannot take an unmarried young woman into a private room. Whatever can you be thinking about?"

Seeing that his lordship's patience—what there was left of

it—was being sorely tried, Margaret interposed. "Do not trouble your head about such trivialities, Annis, I beg you. I have been accustomed to looking after myself in all manner of situations for some years now. Matters are not quite the same on the Continent, you know, as they are here in England."

"More's the pity," said her ladyship with a dignified sniff. "I suppose you will do as you please, whether your behavior offends me or not. I shall say no more."

"Let joy be unconfined," said his lordship sourly once they were safely on the other side of the door. "How do you tolerate that woman?"

"I don't tolerate her particularly well," Margaret told him, "but fortunately her uncertain health prevents her from interfering much with the household. She would have been less offended if you had inquired after her palpitations, you know."

"Good Lord, has she *got* palpitations?" he asked, disgusted.

"Well, of course she has," Margaret said, allowing him to take her elbow and guide her toward the stairs. "She has got every disease or disorder she has ever heard about. Just ask her. Or don't, she'll tell you anyway, given half a chance, and she'll tell you as well how the Fates have decreed that she suffer all these ills without benefit of the slightest sympathy from anyone else."

He was betrayed into a chuckle, and Margaret was glad to hear it, although their progress toward the front parlor was undelayed. "Thank you for the warning," he said as he pushed the door open and waited for her to precede him into the room. "I shall bear it in mind." He shut the door.

"Adam," she said, turning, "I hope—"

"I know perfectly well what you hope," he retorted. "Just answer one question. Was it your idea or Aunt Celeste's?"

"You ought to know the answer to that without asking," she said with a smile.

He nodded. "Aunt Celeste. I had hoped her tour of foreign capitals might have cured her of her more outrageous starts, but I see it has done nothing of the kind."

"During the Congress, she told Count Talleyrand that he ought to take passage to London at once in order to consult with Sir William Knighton about his clubfoot," said Margaret demurely.

"She didn't!"

Margaret nodded. "She sets great store by Sir William's wisdom, you know."

"Good job she didn't recommend Sir Richard Croft," he said dryly. "Poor man killed himself last month, you know."

"I know. They say he blamed himself for Princess Charlotte's death in childbed," Margaret said, "but even Aunt Celeste would scarcely recommend an accoucheur to Count Talleyrand."

" 'Tis a wonder to me she didn't set the whole Congress by the ears."

"Well, I daresay she very nearly did upon occasion. I know Grandpapa was most annoyed with her when she told Prince Metternich to his face that he would get a deal farther in diplomacy if one could but trust his word."

"Good Lord!"

"I know. He was furious, but she didn't let his wrath deter her in the least. Just said he ought to have been taught from the cradle that it didn't behoove a man to blow hot and cold in the same breath."

"Why did Sir Harold put up with it? He ought to have sent her home."

Margaret shook her head, grinning. "He didn't dare. They liked her."

"Liked her?" He sounded disbelieving.

"Very much. Even Metternich. He said she was a woman in a thousand. Not most original statement, by any means, but I think he was a bit in love with her, which would account for a lack of creativity, don't you think?"

Abberley made a sound perilously like a snort. "Rubbish. The woman is a menace. Do you know she has ordered farming tools from London, not to mention seed from Royston, flint and plaster from God knows where, and that she's had the nerve to order a number of my tenants to rethatch their cottages?"

"If she's ordered flint and plaster, it sounds to me as though she has plans beyond a bit of thatch, sir."

"Well, you needn't look so damned pleased about it. It's my estate, not hers."

"If I were you, sir," Margaret told him roundly, "I shouldn't puff that fact off to anyone who's had a look at the place lately."

"I know things are not in prime twig at present, but that scarcely gives her the right to make free with my purse strings. In case you are unaware of the fact, there has been an agricultural depression in England since the end of the war," he added defensively. "The state of affairs at Abberley cannot be set entirely at my door."

"Fiddlesticks," Margaret retorted, unimpressed. "If you have suffered such financial reverses as all that, this is the first I've heard of it, and I cannot see that penury has curtailed your raking. You've neglected the estate shamefully, and you know it. Furthermore, if you wish to give your head to Aunt Celeste for washing, just try telling her she hasn't any right to give orders at Abberley. She thinks of it as her own home, and justifiably so. No one else has questioned her authority to set things right."

"And you believe I would be a fool to do so now," he said with a grimace, looking first down at the carpet then up at her from beneath his brows. "Well, you're very likely in the right of it, but I don't like it."

"Your liking it hasn't got much to do with anything," she said flatly, not missing the fact that he had made no further effort to protest a lack of funds. "Either you've got to take matters in hand yourself or let Aunt Celeste have her head. I believe she's found you a bailiff."

"The devil she has!"

"Mr. Farley has a cousin, you see," Margaret began, but she got no farther.

His eyes flashed. "I'll choose my own bailiff, damn her! If I'm expected to work with the man, she can at least allow me to have a say in who he will be."

"I don't think she trusts you, Adam," Margaret said calmly,

watching for signs of further fireworks. When he smoldered
but remained silent, she added, "You haven't exactly ex-
pressed an interest in your people before now, you know."

"My people are fine," he said stubbornly.

"Mary Muston told us the three of them would have
starved if Jake hadn't managed to find odd jobs in Mayfield," she replied, her voice quiet now and gentle because
she was certain he had known nothing about the Muston's
plight.

"Starved?" There was sudden pain in his eyes. "I never
thought . . . For God's sake, why didn't they tell me?"

"Mary said you were never around to tell, that you were
mostly in London or visiting friends. After your last bailiff
left—"

"I see," he said, not letting her finish. He straightened,
pushing his hand through his hair, then turned away from her.
"Tell Aunt Celeste to do as she pleases. I won't interfere."

"Adam, that's not—"

"Well, here you are," said Lady Celeste, pushing the door
open with a bang. "I heard you were here, Abberley, and
I've been searching high and low. Farley has a cousin named
Will Clayton, whom I'd like you to meet. Capable man. I
like him. Sure to make you a fine bailiff. You need a bailiff,
you know. Too much to be done to try to handle matters
yourself. Come along and meet him. He's down at the estate
office with Farley now. I told them I'd bring you straight
along."

Abberley shot an enigmatic look at Margaret. "Tell Clayton to visit me first thing in the morning, Aunt Celeste," he
said, his voice carefully even.

"But he is here now, dear boy."

"Then you will know precisely where to find him to
deliver my message." He turned toward her, his dark eyes
meeting hers in a direct gaze. "I'll see him in the morning,
ma'am. Right now, I have other business to attend to."

Lady Celeste moved as though to protest, but after a look
from one to the other, she seemed to think better of the

notion. "I'll tell him you are looking forward to making his acquaintance," she said confidently.

"As you will, ma'am." When the door had shut behind her, he turned back to Margaret, but instead of the anger she had expected to see in them, his eyes were filled with laughter. "Was that an example of attack being the best defense?"

Relieved, she chuckled. "I believe it must have been something of the kind. She must have heard that you were in a temper and decided to bluster it out. She certainly blew in like a dervish."

"She used to be a devil to go in the hunting field, you know. Learned at a tender age to get over rough ground as quickly as possible. Now I suppose I shall have to hire the damned fellow."

"If Farley vouches for him—"

"He's his cousin, didn't she say? He'll vouch for him. I only hope Clayton is half as good as Farley is, so he won't let her down."

"Don't you mean to take hold yourself, Adam? Surely, it's time and more for you to do so."

"I hadn't meant to," he replied, moving toward her, his gaze locking with hers, "but I begin to think I may have more reason to do so than I had believed."

Margaret's breath caught in her throat when he reached for her. His hands were gentle upon her shoulders. Her lips parted slightly, and she felt as though her body had suddenly come awake after a long sleep. When his right hand moved along her shoulder in a small caress, tiny chills raced away from it in every direction, only to be replaced immediately by a radiating warmth. She reached to touch the moving hand.

He bent toward her, his expression gentler than she had seen it in a long time. "Perhaps I might indeed find reason now to put my affairs in better order," he said quietly.

"Might you, sir?" she whispered.

His lips were only inches from hers now. Margaret waited, every nerve focused upon the slow movement of his head toward hers.

Again the parlor door opened with a bang. This time the intruder was not Lady Celeste but Moffatt.

"My lord," he said quickly, "Miss Margaret, you must come at once. There's been an accident."

As they whirled to face him, Margaret felt warmth rushing to her cheeks, but any thought of embarrassment at being found in such a position with Abberley faded at once in the face of Moffatt's clear distress.

"Aunt Celeste?" Margaret demanded tensely.

"No, miss, it's Master Timmy. Mr. Farley's already sent one of the lads for Doctor Fennaday, but I think you should come at once."

"Farley? Then, the accident occurred outside somewhere!" All color drained from her face, and she turned in near panic to Abberley.

He was curt. "What the devil happened?"

"The pony, m'lord. Master Tim jumped into the saddle like he always does, and Mr. Farley says the pony near leapt over the stableyard fence, kicking and carrying on like he was demented. Master Tim never had a chance to get his seat, I'm told."

"How badly is he hurt?"

"I wouldn't like to say, sir. I haven't seen him, and you know how those lads are prone to exaggerate. I came for you and miss at once."

"Well, don't worry anyone else until we know the worst," Abberley ordered, striding toward the door with Margaret right behind him.

"Begging your pardon, m'lord, but the only one who don't know is Lady Celeste."

Abberley stopped short. "You told Lady Annis before coming to us?"

"No, m'lord. Her ladyship was just leaving the yard in her carriage when the accident occurred. Mr. Caldecourt was with her, and Archer, of course."

"Jordan's accompanying her must be a first," muttered Margaret, already pushing past the earl in her haste to discover how badly Timothy had been hurt.

Abberley followed her without another word to the butler, and they reached the stableyard several moments later to discover that quite a crowd had gathered around poor Timothy.

At an order from Abberley, the group divided, letting them pass, and Margaret soon saw the boy lying in a crumpled heap, with Mr. Farley, a thick-chested man of middle height, kneeling beside him. Timothy's face was scraped and bruised as though he had slid along the ground, and his right arm was bent at an odd angle. She hurried forward to kneel beside him just as his eyelids flickered. Farley let out a breath of relief.

" 'E's cooming round, miss."

"Heaven be thanked," said Lady Annis, behind them. She turned to her footman. "Archer, I shall return to the carriage. Jordan, you must lend me your arm. I must sit down. My nerves. That wicked boy, to give me such a dreadful jolt."

"Mother, don't you think we might wait at least to see if Timothy is all right?"

"Do as you please," she snapped. "Archer, your arm!"

"Why haven't you done something to make him more comfortable?" Margaret demanded, ignoring everyone behind her.

"Didn't ken 'ow bad off 'e be," the bailiff answered brusquely. "Happen 'e didn't ought ter be moved."

"He's right," Abberley said, squatting down beside her. "Wait until the boy moves for himself or Fennaday arrives. Otherwise we could do further damage." As he spoke, he reached toward Timothy, then pulled his hand back uncertainly.

Hearing an unfamiliar note in his voice, she glanced at him. The earl's face was dead-white, lined with anxiety. Margaret wanted to touch his arm, to tell him Timothy would be all right, but she wasn't by any means certain that was true. Just then Timothy groaned, and everyone's attention riveted upon him.

His eyes opened, and he looked up in bewilderment. "Where's Theodore?" he asked, then closed his eyes again with a moan.

Abberley looked at Margaret with the same bewildered air.

"The pony," she reminded him, realizing he must have forgotten what Timothy had said he would name his new pet.

" 'E's gorn," said Farley. "Bolted, 'e did. We'll fetch 'im along later."

"Lie still, Timothy," Margaret said. "Where does it hurt?"

"My arm," the boy said, his voice little more than a whisper, his brow now wrinkled in pain.

"Happen it's broken, Miss Margaret," said the stableman. "If that's all that's wrong, I can help him, but I didn't want to move him without I was sure."

"Does anything else hurt, darling?" she asked.

"I hurt all over," he said weakly, "but nothing else hurts so bad. I'm cold," he added, prompting Farley to bellow at Trimby to fetch a blanket along double-quick.

"Straighten your legs, boy," Abberley said, "but do it slowly and stop if anything hurts."

Timothy obeyed, grimacing but game. Moments later he was laid out straight upon the ground with a blanket tucked up to his chin, and the bailiff had rigged a splint to keep his arm steady until the doctor could look at it.

Dr. Fennaday, a young, redheaded gentleman with wiry curls and bushy side-whiskers, arrived fifteen minutes later in his gig. By that time Lady Annis had had recourse several times to her salts bottle, her whining demands carrying easily across the otherwise nearly silent yard. When the doctor jumped down from his gig, she hailed him with relief.

"Doctor Fennaday, how good of you to come. You must know how dreadful this has been for me."

"I'll attend to you as soon as I've dealt with the boy," the doctor called to her cheerfully. "Mr. Caldecourt, you must take your mother straight up to the house and order her a nice cup of tea." All this was said over his shoulder as he walked straight toward Timothy. "Well, now, young fellow, me lad," he said, effecting a broad Irish brogue, "what's this ye've gone and done t' yerself, might I ask?"

"I fell off my pony," said Timothy, watching him warily despite his pain.

"A pony, eh? Dreadful beasts, ponies are. The scourge of

mankind." He glanced around at the numerous people standing about. "Do you think we might dispense with the audience, Farley?"

The bailiff gave a few brisk orders, and the yard cleared of all but the doctor, Margaret, Abberley, and himself. "Happen ye'll need some'un t' carry the lad, sir," Farley said then.

Dr. Fennaday had put the blanket aside and was skillfully testing Timothy's unbound limbs. Without a word, he then began carefully prodding at the boy's midsection. Once Timothy let out a sharp yelp.

"Sorry, lad, did that hurt?"

"Tickled," Timothy said with a pained smile.

The doctor nodded, turning his attention to Timothy's right arm. A moment later, he stood up. His first words were for Farley. "You did a neat job there, man. We'll take him into the house now."

As the bailiff moved to pick Timothy up, Abberley stepped forward. "I'll take him," he said grimly. With the doctor's help, he picked the boy up carefully, then waited until Fennaday had arranged the injured limb across Timothy's stomach before leading the way back into the house and up to the nursery floor.

"If you'll just ring for a maidservant, Miss Caldecourt, to help me undress him," the doctor said then, "I'll set the arm and bandage it. Then all the boy will need will be some rest."

"I'll help you, Doctor," Margaret said firmly.

He looked at her measuringly but seemed to approve of what he saw. "Very well," he said.

Undressing Timothy proved to be a painful thing for him, and after he had cried out for the second time, Abberley muttered, "You've no need for me. I'll just go see if they've begun a search for the pony."

Margaret glanced at him, but he had already turned away and her attention was quickly reclaimed by the doctor. He had tipped a dose of laudanum down Timothy's throat as soon as Abberley had laid the boy down upon his bed, and by the time they had his shirt off him, Fennaday decided the opiate had begun to work sufficiently that he could start setting the arm. By the time he had finished, Margaret found herself wondering if the state of Lady Annis' nerves might be contagious. She felt wrung out. The doctor looked her over again, this time with a twinkle in his gray-green eyes.

"I recommend a glass of Madeira, unless you're partial to brandy, Miss Caldecourt."

"Is he going to be all right?"

"He'll be fine," he assured her. "I want him to stay quietly in bed for a few days. The less he moves about, the better. I'll leave you some medication for the pain. Give him a dose at bedtime and then as he seems to need it. Just don't overdo it. The worst of the pain will disappear in a couple of days."

When he had taken his leave, she looked for Abberley to tell him what the doctor had said, but the earl was nowhere to be found. In the stableyard, she was told he had ordered his horse and it was believed he had returned to the hall. She had no further chance to pursue the matter, however, for Lady Celeste had learned of Timothy's accident and Lady Annis was annoyed that the doctor had forgotten to examine her.

"My nerves," she whined. "I am persuaded he ought to have listened to my heart, which is quite leaping about in my breast. But no one cares that I am ill. Oh, no, even my son has deserted me. And I have missed my drive, which is essential for my health."

"Good gracious, Annis," said Lady Celeste in disgusted tones. "Have you no thought for anyone but yourself? That poor boy upstairs—"

"Well, of course I was worried about Timothy. It is no longer my duty to worry about him, however, and Margaret has said the doctor is unconcerned. He is scarcely like to die, Celeste, though I may tell you that when I saw him part company with that dreadful pony, I am certain my heart absolutely stopped beating. I felt so faint—"

"Fustian," retorted the old lady. "You've never had room in your head for a thought about anyone but yourself, Annis, and don't try to tell me you aren't glad Margaret is here to take charge of the boy, for I shouldn't believe you." Before the younger woman could open her mouth to defend herself, Lady Celeste turned back to Margaret and asked. "Is the doctor quite certain Timothy will survive?"

"Oh, yes, thank heaven. He was bruised and scraped up a bit, you know, but his worst injury is the broken arm. When I think how easily he might have been killed, I feel ill."

"Then don't think about it," advised her ladyship with strong good sense.

But Margaret couldn't avoid thinking about what a near miss Timothy had had. She had begun to care deeply for the boy, and consequently, she blamed herself for the accident. It was sheer luck he hadn't been killed. By all rights, he should have been. Certainly, if she allowed herself to care too much for him, something dreadful would happen. Experience had shown her that. It didn't do to love anyone, not if she didn't want to lose him.

She didn't see Abberley again until late the following morning, and she knew the moment she laid eyes upon him that he had been drinking heavily again. It didn't show in his general appearance, for he was dressed neatly and precisely in buckskins, a snowy-white shirt and dark jacket, and shining, tasseled Hessian boots. Clearly, either he or his valet had taken pains with his dress. His hair was neatly combed, too, but his eyes were bleary and nearly hidden in dark pockets, and his complexion was pasty again. He also seemed to have the headache, she noticed, for he grimaced when Lady Celeste, sitting with Margaret and Lady Annis in the morning room, greeted him cheerfully.

"Did you see Farley's cousin this morning, Abberley?"

"I did. Seems a fine chap. I've given him *carte blanche*."

Margaret cocked her head. "Does that mean you don't intend to take the reins in hand yourself, sir?"

"Can't," he returned brusquely. "I'm leaving for London first thing tomorrow. I've a number of engagements there I cannot put off." He refused to meet her gaze. "Just stopped by to tell you I was going and to inquire after the boy."

"Timothy will be fine, sir. Must you go?"

He nodded. "They find the pony?"

"Not yet," she told him. "Farley thinks he must have wandered into the woods. There's good grazing there and the weather's warming quickly, so he must not be feeling a need for his stable. They'll no doubt find him today."

"Well, when they do, you tell Timothy I've said he's not to ride him again. He's not to ride at all until his arm is completely healed, but even then I don't want him on that damned pony. Shouldn't have bought him in the first place."

Margaret began to protest, but he cut her off and took his departure soon afterward.

Lady Annis remarked indignantly that he seemed to take little interest in his ward. "Seems to me he might at least wait until the boy is recovered," she said.

For once Margaret agreed with her. "I'm afraid he's overreacting to Timothy's accident, but I do wish he were not going away just now," she said wistfully.

Lady Celeste said nothing at all. She merely pursed her lips, and her eyes narrowed slightly as she turned her attention to the pile of blue knitting in her lap. She was working a carriage robe, for she rarely did fancy work, saying she had little patience for such stuff. Still, she enjoyed having something to keep her hands busy and to which she did not have to pay a great deal of attention.

Soon afterward, Margaret went upstairs to visit Timothy and found the boy tossing and turning, unable to get comfortable because he was in pain again. She had given him a small dose of his medicine after his breakfast, but she had not given him quite as much as the doctor had said she might for fear of overdosing him. Now, she wished she had given him the full amount.

"Poor boy," she said gently, ringing for Melanie to help her and change his bedding. Pouring the full amount into the glass this time from the bottle kept on a high shelf away from the bed, she held his head and ordered him to drink the stuff.

"It's nasty," Timothy muttered, but he swallowed obediently. Once they had made him as comfortable as possible,

Margaret sat by the bed to read to him until he was able to sleep. After that she was careful to give him his medication as soon as he began to complain of the pain again, but she left strict orders that no one else was to give it to him. She was afraid that if two people began dosing him, the results might be disastrous.

The little black pony wasn't found until the following day. One of the stableboys led him into the yard just as Margaret and Lady Celeste were leaving to drive over to Abberley's estate so that Lady Celeste might inspect the progress being made there and to make certain that the new bailiff had indeed been given a free hand.

"I'm so glad they found Theodore," Margaret said, leaning back against the squabs. "Timothy has been beside himself with worry."

"Did you tell him Abberley said he wasn't to ride the little beast again?"

"No, for I don't want to upset him before he is entirely well. He still suffers from pain much of the time, you know. I gave him a full dose of his medicine before we left the house, or I shouldn't feel right about leaving him to his own devices just now."

"Nonsense, you don't want to coddle that young man," said Lady Celeste crisply. "He'd be better served if you were to ride over to the vicarage later this afternoon and ask Mr. Maitland if he would consider visiting here to give the boy his lessons."

"Lessons! He's scarcely well enough for lessons."

"Fustian. He's merely broken his arm. It will do him good to have something to take his mind off it. He'll turn out to be the sort of complainer Annis is if you don't mind your step."

Margaret gurgled with laughter. "You don't believe that for a moment," she said. "I'm more worried about him deciding to ride before his arm is healed than I am about turning him into a hypochondriac."

Lady Celeste nodded. "Very true. You'd best relay those orders as soon as we get back. I've a notion he won't flout Abberley's authority."

"What authority? The man's gone to London, and he's done very little to make Timothy aware of any authority. He leaves him to me."

Lady Celeste shook her head with a sad grimace. "I've known that rascal Abberley since the day he was born, and I've always had more cause to complain of his arrogance than of his being shy to take a lead. Until now," she added. "Now he don't seem to wish to take hold of anything."

"I thought he was beginning to," Margaret said slowly, marshaling her thoughts, "but I think now he blames himself for the accident and can't face up to anything else because of that. Absurd, of course, that he should think himself a poor guardian just because Timmy's pony gave him a toss. Abberley had nothing to do with it. It just happened."

Though Lady Celeste said nothing, there was a penetrating look in the bright-blue eyes that brought a rush of color to Margaret's cheeks. Had she been asked to explain the cause of her discomfort, however, she would have been hard-pressed to do so.

When they returned to the manor an hour and a half later, Lady Celeste was beaming with satisfaction, well pleased with the progress they had seen. In place of weeds, rundown shacks, and other signs of neglect, there were trim yards, new thatch, neatly mended fences, and newly plowed fields. They had also encountered a gratifying number of smiling faces.

"Your Mr. Clayton seems to be quite as capable as Farley," Margaret said as they drove around to the front of the house.

"Indeed, I was particularly pleased to note that work has already begun on the Mustons' second cottage," said her ladyship complacently. "Old Mrs. Muston always preferred her own place."

But Margaret's attention had been distracted by the sight of Farley himself coming around the corner of the house. Seeing that he had caught her eye, he motioned subtly to her, his attitude causing her to insist that Lady Celeste go into the house without her.

"I shall be along directly, ma'am," she said, "but I see

Farley, and now is as good a time as any to be certain that Abberley explained the rules he laid down for Timothy's riding.''

"An excellent notion," said her ladyship approvingly. "I shall order us some tea."

But moments later, Margaret wasn't by any means certain she had an appetite for tea. Farley, after drawing her to one side and glancing around as though to be sure they could not be overheard, said succinctly, "Happen mischief's afoot, Miss Margaret."

7

Margaret stared at the bailiff, a knot of fear making her voice shake when she demanded to know what he was talking about.

"This, miss," he replied tersely, opening his big hand to reveal a long, sharp thorn of the type commonly found in the beech wood resting in the palm. "Trimby found it thrust through the pony's saddle blanket. When the lad leapt up as he did, his weight fair shot the thorn into the little beast. Don't wonder he carried on so. Some'un meant mischief, miss."

"Couldn't the thorn have got there by accident?" Margaret asked hopefully.

"Not in my stables, miss." He was offended, and she apologized quickly, but she still hoped he might be wrong. Who would want to play such a dangerous prank on Timothy? She considered the matter as she went into the house and up to join Lady Celeste in the drawing room. If it had been Jordan, now, who had taken a toss, she would know immediately where to lay the blame. That thought gave rise to another. Timothy still made little attempt to disguise his contempt for his cousin. Indeed, since Margaret had forbidden Jordan to thrash him, that contempt had been, if anything, more openly displayed. Was it possible that Jordan might have chosen such a method to wreak his vengeance upon the boy?

Briefly she considered discussing the possibility with Lady

Celeste, but she could not do so at once, because Lady Annis was also in the drawing room; and, by the time that lady left them, to attend to some vaguely described chores, Margaret had decided not to mention the matter. More than likely the old lady, strongly disapproving of Jordan anyway, would merely repeat her suggestion that Margaret should send both him and his mother packing.

Shortly after Lady Annis' departure, Margaret also excused herself and went upstairs, intending to look in on Timothy. She met Melanie emerging from the nursery. The maidservant was frowning.

"Is Sir Timothy awake yet, Melanie?"

"No, miss, and 'e ought ter be, I'm thinkin'. 'E's breathin' funny like, too."

Instantly the tension Margaret had felt with Farley returned with a vengeance. She pushed past the maidservant and rushed to Timothy's bed. The boy was breathing raspily and his face was pale, nearly gray. Margaret knew just by looking that something was wrong. She shook him gently. There was no response other than a faint moan.

Ordering Melanie to send someone for the doctor, Margaret shook Timothy harder, hard enough, in fact, that she ought to have been causing him a good deal of pain. But it was some moments before she got any response at all. Finally, however, the boy's eyes opened and he looked at her blearily, his eyes glazed as if he didn't recognize her.

"Timothy, wake up!"

His eyes closed again, but Margaret shook him, demanding that he wake up. By the time the doctor finally arrived, Timothy was awake, although still bleary-eyed, and Margaret was exhausted. Dr. Fennaday came in cheerfully and maintained his smile while he examined the boy, but after he had him comfortably settled, he requested a private word with Margaret.

On the landing, he was no longer smiling. In fact, his expression was decidedly grim. "How much medication have you given him today?"

"Just the normal dose, Doctor, nearly three hours ago."

"Well, his reaction is not normal. Has anything like this happened before?"

"No, of course not. I should have sent for you if it had."

He nodded, grimacing. "Might the boy have taken more of the medication himself? Or might someone have given him a dose not knowing you had already done so?"

She shook her head and explained that the bottle was out of Timothy's reach and that orders had been given that no one was to give him his medicine except herself.

"In that case, I have to ask if anyone means the boy any harm?"

Margaret gasped. "What possible reason could there be?" But her thoughts turned immediately to the thorn lying in Farley's palm.

"I don't know that, Miss Caldecourt, but I can tell you his reaction is that of an overdose. In fact, if I didn't know better, I'd say he had been given something much stronger than what I prescribed. I've taken the liberty of replacing that bottle of medication just in case it somehow became contaminated. I suggest you put it where others have no access to it."

"I will," she said meekly.

He left soon afterward, though not before having been waylaid by Lady Annis, who had evidently experienced some strange symptoms that she wished to discuss with him.

Margaret, after a final look in on Timothy, who seemed to be resting comfortably, went in search of Lady Celeste. She found her still in the drawing room, knitting the blue carriage robe. The old lady had heard only that Timothy had been taken ill and that the doctor had been sent for. She explained that she had thought she would help best by staying out from underfoot.

"I knew he was in good hands, my dear," she said gently.

"We must send to London for Abberley at once," Margaret informed her, not mincing matters.

"Good gracious! I just assumed the boy had done something foolish and injured his arm again. Is it more than that?"

"I think someone is trying to harm Timothy," Margaret replied without roundaboutation. "Do you know Abberley's direction in town, ma'am? He has a house in Berkeley Square, does he not?''

''Whether he does or not does not signify in the slightest,'' stated her ladyship calmly.

''Aunt Celeste, you cannot have understood what I have been saying to you. Someone in this house may even be trying to kill Timothy. I know that sounds absurd, but there was a thorn under his saddle and just now I have been told that someone tampered with his medicine. If I had not been at hand—''

''I am not in my dotage, whatever else I may be,'' said her ladyship tartly. ''I understood you perfectly well, and when you have lived as long as I have, you will know there is rarely anything absurd about attempted murder. Usually the absurdity is the greed behind the attempt.''

''Greed?''

''Of course, my dear. Sir Timothy is a very wealthy man, and his heir is right here in the house, or as near as makes no difference.''

''Good heavens, you cannot think Jordan would—''

''Why not? He don't dote on the boy, as far as I can see.''

''Well, even if it is so, we have no way to prove it, and I have no wish to cope with such a problem alone. Abberley is Timothy's guardian, and for once I agree with Annis. His duty lies right here.''

''To be sure, but there is no reason to send all the way to London.''

''But he left for town three days ago, did he not?''

Lady Celeste did not reply at once, and suddenly Margaret realized the old lady was looking a trifle conscious. Indeed, she looked guilty.

''Ma'am, what are you trying to tell me? Did Abberley go to London, or did he not?''

''Not, I'm afraid.''

''Aunt Celeste, he had every intention of going!''

''Well, you said you did not wish him to go, and I must confess I agreed that it was irresponsible of him even to consider going at such a time, so I arranged for him to stay here instead."

"Arranged? What on earth did you do?"

"I spoke to Jake Muston, and he arranged for Abberley's coach to be waylaid. They were all masked, of course, so he don't know who's responsible."

"Where is he, Aunt Celeste?" Margaret demanded, her emotions spinning. She didn't know whether to be delighted or dismayed, but she was certainly astonished—though not for the first time—by her grandaunt's audacity.

"He is in the north tower room at Abberley," said Lady Celeste calmly, "and I cannot conceive of why you should be so surprised. When a thing wants doing, 'tis best to do it."

Shaking her head in bemusement, Margaret left the old lady to her knitting and hurried up to change into her habit, sending orders to the stable at the same time to assure that Dancer would be awaiting her pleasure. By the time she was mounted and on her way through the woods to the hall, she had begun to see humor in the situation, and more than one chuckle escaped her lips as she drew nearer to Abberley. Trimby looked at her as though he were wondering if her mind had turned.

"I am quite sane, Trimby," she said as she dismounted at the broad front steps and tossed him her reins, "but I do not know how long I will be. I shall send for you when I am ready to return."

"Aye, miss," he returned, not meeting her eyes.

She chuckled again and turned toward the steps.

Puddephatt answered some two or three minutes after she first began banging the knocker. He was surprised to see her.

"I wish to see his lordship, Pudd," she said, grinning at him.

"His lordship has gone to London, miss," said the butler, staring carefully at a point beyond her shoulder.

"No, he hasn't, you old fraud," Margaret said. "I know precisely where he is, in the north tower room. Aunt Celeste said you had the key. I trust you haven't been starving him."

"No, miss, though the food ain't been what he's accustomed to, the missus not having been told he was there."

"Because she'd have had your head on a platter and Jake Muston's as well, and you know it."

"If ye please, Miss Margaret, ye'll not be telling the master 'twas Jake and the others. He might guess it for himself, but 'twould be best to be naming no names."

"Very well, though I am persuaded he will think it only a good joke on himself."

"Not he, Miss Margaret. He's been in the devil of a temper these past few days. First drinking himself into a stupor the night young Sir Timothy took his tumble, then determined to go to town for no reason in particular that he could name, and now . . . well, let me tell you, miss, if you think to find him in a good humor, you'd best be thinking again. I know her ladyship meant well, and I'd not want to be the one to go against her orders, especially not once the deed had been done. I'll not say I'm not glad to see you either, miss, because I can tell you I wasn't looking forward to being the man who let him out."

In the face of the butler's anxiety, Margaret felt her own good humor fading. It was one thing to be amused by Lady Celeste's bland air of having done nothing more than what was practical. It was quite another to think of facing Abberley in one of his fouler tempers. Her courage ebbed, but she knew she had to tell him about the thorn and the doctored medication. He had a right to know. Besides, now that she knew where he was, she couldn't justify keeping him there. Drawing a long breath, she turned to the butler.

"Perhaps you'd better give me the key to the north tower room, Pudd. Does he even know you are involved in this business?"

"I don't know, miss. He hasn't seen me. I made up a big packet of food from the larder—bread, cheese, beef, wine, and whatever else I could find—and simply left it and a chamber pot in the room before the others delivered him. He was blindfolded clear up until they shoved him into the room and slammed the door behind him. Her ladyship had come to tell me what I might expect, you see, and to make sure my missus was busy elsewhere. She knew right well that Marthy'd never stand for such a stunt.''

''Then, you may be perfectly safe. I'll not tell him where I got the key, and if I know Aunt Celeste, she'll take the blame for the whole.''

''Well, he won't believe she abducted him all on her lonesome,'' Puddephatt pointed out, not without a glimmer of a smile on his thin face.

Margaret chuckled. ''Leave it to her. Before she's done with him, he'll believe anything.''

Her smile faded again once she was on her way, unescorted, to the north tower. The room in question was a small round chamber at the top of the ancient tower, and was reached by climbing a great number of winding stone steps. She was not looking forward to the climb. Even less was she looking forward to facing the earl's wrath. After three days of nothing but bread and cheese and probably a bottle or two of wine, she would not be astonished to discover him raving. When she realized what the sanitary conditions must be, she grimaced, biting her lower lip.

The key fit the door at the bottom of the tower and also that of the room at the top. When Margaret had made her way to the second door, she paused to catch her breath, then stepped forward, key in hand.

''Who's out there?''

She could hear him clearly despite the thickness of the tower walls and the thick oak door between them, and she quickly realized that there were spaces at both top and bottom of the door to account for the fact that he had heard her coming.

''It is Marget, Adam. I've come to let you out.''

''Have you, indeed? And just how did I come to be locked up here in the first place?'' he bellowed. ''Was it your doing, my girl?''

''No, and that is of no import now,'' she said, fitting the key into the lock.

''The devil it isn't! You're going to tell me who is responsible for this outrage, and when I get my hands on the guilty party, I'll bloody well make him wish he had never been born.''

Margaret removed the key from the lock. "Adam, are you quite dreadfully angry?"

"Dammit, girl, this is no time for a comfortable coze. What are you waiting for? Open this door at once.''

"Answer me, Adam. How angry are you?"

The reply came in a low growl. "Angry enough, by God, that if you don't open this door immediately, I'll soon make you wish you had.''

"I see. Then I am persuaded that I shall do better to leave the door locked, for I wish to talk with you, but you don't sound as though you are at all in a mood for conversation.''

"Damn you.'' He sounded completely exasperated. "Of course I'm not in the mood. Didn't I just say that? The only thing I want to hear from you is the name of the person responsible for having me abducted. Unless, of course, you arranged the matter yourself.''

"No, I didn't, but I'm glad someone did, for I need you. Something has happened which—''

"Open this door!'' he bellowed in furious but measured tones.

"I won't,'' she replied just as loudly. "Not until you promise to listen to what I have to say.''

"I'll listen, all right, just so long as you tell me what I want to hear.''

Margaret bit her lip. She was quite certain he would pay no heed to anything else she said until he knew who had arranged to have him waylaid. And so long as he was safely locked up, there seemed to be no reason not to tell him.

After a moment's silence, she said quietly, "Aunt Celeste arranged it.''

There was a longer silence. Then he said grimly, "I see.''

"I don't think you do, sir.''

"Let me out, Margaret.''

Knowing from the fact that he called her Margaret that he was still in a fury, she hesitated. "Aunt Celeste meant no harm, Adam. I had told her I wished you wouldn't go to London just when Timothy was ill, and she decided it would be better for you to remain in Hertfordshire.''

"She failed to discuss the matter with me," he said with a touch of sarcasm.

"I know. She didn't discuss it with anyone."

"Not so," he said, his tone gentler now. "She discussed the matter with at least four large, rather rough men. I recognized Jake Muston's voice. Who were the others?"

Not deceived in the slightest by the gentle tone, Margaret chuckled. "I'm thankful to say I haven't the least notion, sir. And it doesn't matter, for I'm certain you would never be so unfair as to blame them for following Aunt Celeste's orders. You know perfectly well that your tenants, each and every one of them, would ride into hell for her."

There was another long silence. Margaret was sure he had not liked hearing such a home truth from her, and she had no wish to say more. She merely waited for his response. At last he muttered, so low she almost didn't hear him, "I am their master. Their loyalty should be to me."

She said nothing.

"Are you still there, Marget?"

"Yes. Are you still angry?"

Silence.

"Adam?"

He chuckled. At first she wasn't sure she was hearing correctly, but the sound grew louder, and she knew she wasn't mistaken after all. It never grew quite to a full laugh, but she knew everything would be all right. The key was still in the lock, and she turned it, opening the heavy door.

He stood just inside the door, framed by rays of sunlight from the small windows behind and on both sides of him. As the door opened, he put his hands to his hips and favored her with a stern look.

"I ought to put you across my knee," he said evenly.

"You wouldn't be so ungentlemanly," she told him, smiling. "I might just as easily have left you here, you know."

"I might still go to London," he said, but she thought she detected a twinkle in his eye.

Ignoring it, she said flatly, "You won't. Someone has tried twice to injure Timothy, perhaps to kill him." She turned to lead the way down the winding stone steps, but he stopped her with a hand to her shoulder.

"What's this? Tell me."

So she told him then and there. And when she had finished, she looked him straight in the eye and said, "You won't go away, will you? We need you here."

His expression was grim again, and there was pain in his eyes. "I'm not going anywhere," he said, giving her shoulder a squeeze. Then he sighed deeply. "Ah, Marget, what you must think of me, even to ask such a question after all you've told me. I've behaved despicably and I'm not proud of that. My behavior might well have been responsible for Michael's death, and now Timothy is in danger."

"That is not your doing," she said hotly. "Nor was Michael's death."

"Not directly, of course," he agreed, "but I did little to avert disaster either time. When Michael fell ill I was too far away to help, not because I had pressing business, but merely because I am an idler, a do-nothing, a wastrel. And if I had taken Timothy into my own custody, as you suggested the moment I discovered Michael had appointed me his guardian, neither the accident nor the business with the medication would have occurred."

"My, my," Margaret said dryly. "I had no notion you had such a powerful influence over Fate. I might have suggested the possibility of your bringing Timothy here, but I'd have fought you the minute you attempted to remove him from the manor. I'll fight you if you attempt it now. I have taken steps to assure his safety, and I shall make certain nothing happens to him. As for your belief that others depend upon you only at their peril, I take leave to tell you to your head that that is a result, not a cause. You can certainly take steps to become more dependable, if you will but do it. In the meantime," she added swiftly, noting a harder look in his eyes, "now that we are warned, Aunt Celeste and I can take whatever precautions are necessary at the manor.''

''Aunt Celeste.'' He said only the two words, but his mood lightened considerably as he said them.

Relaxing, Margaret grinned at him. ''If she thinks it practical to remove him to the hall, sir, I daresay you will find him on your doorstep whether either of us wants it or not.''

He laughed. ''I'll certainly think twice before attempting to remove him without her approval.'' Then he grew serious again. ''Marget, I want you to know that I'll do all I can to help. I have no intention now of going to London. Instead, I shall remain here and occupy myself with the land. You were quite right to point out to me that my tenants have more loyalty to that crazy old lady than they have to their rightful master. I have no right even to label myself in such a fashion when I have done nothing to earn the title.'' He sighed, eyeing her ruefully. ''I believe I have come to my senses, little girl.''

Margaret smiled at him, but she took his words with a grain of salt, believing that though he meant them at the moment, his habits were too strongly rooted to respond to mere good intentions. She would reserve judgment. Still, she was glad she had managed to stir him into a better humor, and she was more than glad that he would not leave at once for London.

In the days that followed, Abberley seemed to wish to prove to the entire county that he had taken the reins into his own hands at last, and with a vengeance. He was everywhere to be seen on the vast estate, and Lady Celeste pronounced herself well-pleased with him. He also made a point of visiting the manor at least once each day to look in on Timothy and to discuss the boy with Margaret. Timothy clearly looked forward to his visits, and she found herself beginning to watch for Abberley's arrival and to feel an odd leaping in her breast whenever his name was announced. She told herself it was no more than pleasure in the fact that he was exerting himself to keep his promise to her, but there could be no denying the warm glow or the rush of color to her cheeks whenever he entered the room, holding out both hands to greet her.

Timothy's condition improved rapidly and by the third day after the incident with his medication, he was able to leave his bed, although sharp twinges of pain kept him from his normal activities for some days longer. Until it became possible once more for the boy to tolerate the walk to the vicarage, Mr. Maitland visited him every afternoon and seemed to enjoy the visits. The vicar informed Margaret and Lady Celeste quite seriously that he was not boggling the boy's mind with real lessons but was reading to him instead from improving works. Timothy's descriptions of those same works did not bear repeating in formal company, but Margaret knew the sessions would do the boy no harm and might even do some good.

Pamela Maitland often accompanied her father and whiled away the hour of his visit in pleasant conversation with Lady Celeste, Margaret, and Lady Annis. Jordan, when present, paid the young woman broad compliments, but his lack of sincerity was so obvious that Margaret finally told him without roundaboutation that his attentions to Pamela were offensive. His cheeks reddened painfully at the rebuke, but from that day forth, he took care to be otherwise occupied when Miss Maitland accompanied the vicar.

Abberley often paid his call at the same time and seemed not in the least put out by the need to await the vicar's departure before looking in on his ward. He would enter the drawing room, accept a glass of Madeira from the hovering Moffatt, and seat himself to enjoy the company. His attentions to Miss Maitland were charming. He never failed to compliment her upon her gown, her hairstyle, or perhaps her excellent color. Margaret thought, rather grimly, that Jordan ought to take a lesson or two.

Nothing further happened to reinforce their worries about Timothy's safety, and there was no other indication that anyone wished the boy harm. Still, Abberley and Margaret agreed that a close eye should be kept upon him in future.

Therefore, Abberley had a stern talk with him, informing him that it would be at the risk of severe punishment that he would resume his private rambles about the countryside.

"You are to have someone with you at all times until I tell you otherwise," he told the young man, and Margaret nodded approvingly. They were walking to the stables together at the time. Nothing having been said to Timothy about the thorn under his saddle, Abberley had allowed the boy to convince him that it would be all right to ride Theodore again once his arm had healed completely, despite the pony's one-time show of bad manners. The three of them were going now to inform Theodore of his good fortune in being forgiven his lapse.

"I don't need a nursemaid," Timothy said, carefully keeping any note of impertinence from his voice. "I don't like having people with me all the time."

"I know that," Abberley said, "but since your accident, your aunt and Lady Celeste worry about your safety. This precaution is for their benefit as much as for yours. A gentleman does not purposely worry the ladies of his family when he can avoid it."

Margaret caught the earl's gaze over Timothy's head and smiled at him. "That is very true, Timothy. That is why his lordship wants you to be certain to take a groom with you when you ride and not to go off on your own without at least telling Aunt Celeste or me where you intend to go. And Melanie will continue to accompany you to the vicarage each day, although I know you are a big boy and can easily find your way alone."

"I *am* a big boy. I am not a baby."

"Which is why you will be very careful to do as you are asked," said Abberley cheerfully, "so as not to worry anyone."

"No," said Timothy, glancing up at him with a sardonic twist to his thin lips, "I 'spect I shall do it 'cause you said you would make me wish I hadn't been born if I don't."

Margaret chuckled, ruffling the boy's straight hair. "As good a reason as any, brat. Now, where is Theodore hiding himself, do you suppose?"

When the boy had run off to find his pony, she turned to Abberley with a warm smile. "Thank you, sir. I doubt I could have gotten him to agree to such strictures without a much more strenuous battle."

He returned her smile. "My pleasure. I believe he will obey me, but the danger seems to have passed, don't you think?"

She couldn't agree with him. Something deep inside her warned against complacency. Still, she couldn't deny that she felt safe when he was nearby, just as she always had from the days of her childhood. There was an intimacy growing between them again that had been lacking for some time, and she enjoyed it. It was good to be back on close terms with Abberley. With Michael gone, she told herself, she had more need than ever of a protective big brother to take her problems to and to discuss even minor difficulties with. Having Abberley so close at hand was comforting. But just as she had convinced herself that life was moving along nicely, the day came when Abberley failed to put in his expected appearance. Not until the following day did Margaret learn that a number of guests had arrived at the hall.

Mary Muston was her informant. Mary had been working at the manor as a parlormaid since the day after their visit to the Muston cottage, and Mrs. Moffatt had been very glad to have her. But once Abberley began putting his affairs in order, he had begun to renew the strength of his household staff, and one of the first requests from his housekeeper had been a near demand for her erstwhile assistant's return. Though Mary had agreed, Lady Celeste, aghast at the reductions the parsimonious Lady Annis had made in the manor staff, refused to part with a single servant unless someone else could be found first. So it was that the morning after Abberley failed to put in his appearance Mary approached Margaret somewhat hesitantly in the drawing room.

"Begging your pardon, Miss Margaret," the maidservant said, dipping a brief curtsy, "but Mrs. Puddephatt has sent to learn if I can be spared immediately. Mollie West, from near the village, is to come here tomorrow, so it will only be the one day, and there seems to be a small crisis at the hall.''

"Indeed, Mary, what has occurred?'' Margaret asked quickly, fearing something dreadful might have happened.

"A number of his lordship's friends—both ladies and gentlemen—arrived early yesterday afternoon, miss. Mrs. Puddephatt believed she could cope with the new staff alone, but it seems it's one of his usual rowdy parties, you know, and things often get out of hand. I'm asked to go at once if it won't inconvenience you too much.''

8

Margaret was annoyed, but her annoyance had nothing to do with Mary, and she willingly gave the woman permission to leave. Abberley sent his excuses later in the day in the form of a brief note delivered by a six-foot-tall footman in gleaming silver-gray livery.

"Goodness, how handsome he is!" exclaimed Lady Celeste when that worthy had taken his departure. "I've a mind to move back to the hall, Margaret dear. We have nothing like that here."

"Celeste, really," admonished Lady Annis, "you should not say such outrageous things, you know. It is not at all becoming in a woman your age."

"Fustian. Just saying what you was thinking yourself, Annis. Or what you ought to be thinking if you haven't already got one foot in your grave. Why are there no handsome menservants here, I ask you? That Archer fellow, who's the only one left but for Moffatt, is downright muffin-faced."

"I certainly had nothing to do with that, Aunt Celeste," Margaret said, laughing despite her ill humor. "There were a number of good-looking chaps here before I left for Vienna. I don't know Archer. He certainly wasn't one of them."

"Archer accompanied me from Little Hampstead," said Lady Annis grimly, "and anyone who has ever run an efficient household will tell you that one can get ten times more work out of a maidservant who isn't making sheep's eyes at a handsome footman."

"Ah," said Lady Celeste wisely, "there's the answer. You turned them all off so that mush-mouthed son of yours would have a clear field."

When Lady Annis returned an indignant denial and, shortly thereafter, left the room, offended, Margaret said gently, "That was not very kind, ma'am."

Lady Celeste grimaced. "Very true. I deserve a scold, I suppose, but there's no denying young Jordan has made his mark among the maidservants, and Annis knows it."

"Very likely, she does, but I think the maids can take care of themselves, you know. It isn't as if he wields any power over their lives. If he were master here, it might be different, but as it is, he's harmless, don't you think?"

"Makes a nuisance of himself, whatever the case." Lady Celeste turned a sharp eye upon her grandniece. "What has annoyed you, my dear? Surely not the fact that I have distressed Annis again."

"No, of course not. I think if I were honest with myself, I'd admit that I'm hoping one of your sharp remarks will send her back to Little Hampstead in high dudgeon."

Lady Celeste's lips twitched in appreciation, but she kept to the point for once. "Then, what is it, my dear?"

"Oh, Abberley, of course," admitted Margaret, frowning. "Just when I believed he was really turning over a new leaf, here he is raking again and no doubt falling into bed as dawn is breaking, reeking of brandy."

"I doubt the dawn reeks," said Lady Celeste demurely, surprising Margaret into a near smile. "That's better, dear. It don't do to allow oneself to be swayed too much by the doings of others. Abberley will reap the rewards of his naughtiness just as surely as Timothy does, mark my words. If he does swill brandy all night, his morning head will make him rue his excesses."

"He deserves a sore head," said Margaret vehemently. "Who do you suppose his guests are, anyway?"

"Such curiosity is unbecoming in a young lady of quality, my dear," said her ladyship virtuously.

"Pooh," retorted her undutiful niece. "You would like to know as much as I would."

"Very true," sighed Lady Celeste, "but then, as Annis so rightly says, I often behave in an unbecoming fashion. That does not mean that you should do so."

"Do you suppose he invited a party and then forgot he had done so?" Margaret asked, ignoring both the sigh and the observation that followed it.

"No, of course not, for he was meaning to go to London not long since, you will recall. Unless he invited them before then and has had no word from them since, which is very unlikely in such a case, then they must have arrived unannounced. It is the sort of thing members of his set frequently do when they are bored, you know. Most likely, they heard he was fixed at Abberley for a time—and he is likely to have written to tell someone that much, isn't he?—and they decided to surprise him, to liven up what they must have believed to be a dreary country existence. Since we have not been invited to take part in the festivities, we must assume that his friends are not suitable company for us and must await his next visit to discover if their arrival was indeed unexpected."

They did not see the earl, however, for four long days, and Margaret quickly came to realize how much she had come to enjoy his visits. She had become accustomed to being able to ask his advice about everything, from truly important matters to questions that might better have been put to the bailiff, as well as some that were of small importance to anyone. In point of fact, she missed Abberley's company. Despite his newborn interest in his own estate, he had spent part of each day at the manor, and four days without sight of him proved to be four very long days, indeed.

When he did ride over at last, he was not alone. The gentleman with him was dressed elegantly in a bright-blue, brass-buttoned riding coat with wide lapels and a rolled collar, buff breeches, tall white-topped boots, and a curly-brimmed beaver hat. The earl was dressed as usual in his buckskins and a dark coat. Margaret was surprised, but pleased, too, to note that he seemed none the worse for four days of carousing with his friends. The stranger's hair was lighter than Abberley's and his eyes were brown instead of blue. They sparkled merrily as the earl performed the introductions.

"May I present Lord John Kingsted, Aunt Celeste? He is Morehampton's younger son, you know, and has decided to hunt for a rich wife in Hertfordshire." The earl shot a grin at his friend. Standing side by side, they were almost the same height, though Abberley appeared to be a shade taller and a good deal broader in the shoulders.

"Seems to me Morehampton ought to have enough to settle between two sons," said Lady Celeste dryly as she acknowledged Kingsted's bow.

"He does, ma'am," that young man informed her with a twinkling grin. "I can't deny I'm looking to settle down—nearly thirty, y' know, n' high time to put childhood aside, as m' father says. But I can keep a wife in proper style, stap me if I can't. Can't say I wouldn't welcome an heiress as quickly as any other gent would, but one ain't necessary to m' comfort."

Margaret glared at Abberley, who returned her gaze blandly. He was pretty pleased with himself, she thought. Did he look to see her married off to a marquess's younger son? Not that young Kingsted wasn't well-mannered and pleasant looking. But he wasn't her style. Not at all, and if Abberley thought for one moment that he could carry this big brother business to such a pass—

"Margaret, dear, you have not answered Lord John," Lady Celeste said gently. "He has been saying all that is kind."

Margaret realized she had not paid the slightest attention to anything the gentleman had said. She had simply stared malignantly at the earl. Blushing furiously, she turned to Kingsted. "I beg your pardon, sir, my wits must have gone begging."

"No need to apologize, Miss Caldecourt. I merely said I was sorry to have heard of your brother's death and that I hope things have not been found to be in too much of a tangle here at the manor. We all liked Michael very much, you know.''

His eyes were kind now, the twinkle gone, and she felt more ashamed of herself than ever. Her rudeness had been inexcusable. To her surprise, Abberley came to her rescue.

"At first," he said calmly, "matters were a bit confused, but Michael's affairs have been found to be in good order. I am one of the trustees, as I believe I may have mentioned to you."

"Indeed, you puffed it off once or twice," retorted Kingsted with a grin. "How Michael came to make such a mull of things as to give you control of his estate beats me all hollow." Still grinning, he actually winked at Margaret.

"A fine attitude to take after driving all the way here from London merely to ask my advice," Abberley told him roundly.

So, Margaret thought with another sidelong look at the earl, Lord John had sought advice, had he? And no doubt Abberley had brought him straight along to make her acquaintance. Well, matchmaking from his lordship was the last thing she wanted, but she could handle Kingsted. There was no harm in being kind to him.

She smiled at him and said sweetly, "Abberley has been very helpful."

Kingsted leaned toward her and said confidentially, "You could do a deal worse than to follow his advice, you know. Got a good bit of intelligence in his cockloft, has Abberley."

"Will you stay to tea, gentlemen?" Lady Celeste asked. "I am persuaded that Lady Annis will wish to meet Lord John, and she is out driving just now."

The gentlemen stayed willingly, and by the time Lady Annis had returned from her sedate drive round the countryside, Pamela Maitland had also come to call. She was introduced to Kingsted and greeted him with as much poise as she would greet a friend of her father's or the gardener's boy, unawed by his high estate. She inquired after his journey from London, and soon everyone was trading tales of harrowing mishaps upon the road. Though Miss Maitland had rarely journeyed more than ten or twenty miles from her own home, both Lady Celeste and Margaret could easily match any tale told by the gentlemen, thanks to their extensive travels.

When Lady Annis arrived at last, Margaret took the opportunity provided by Lady Celeste's performing the necessary introductions to ask Abberley if he had left all his other guests at the hall.

"Only John remains," he said, smiling down at her. "The others left this morning."

"Was it a large party, sir?"

"Large enough. About fifteen persons, I believe, but enough to throw Mrs. Puddephatt off her stride a bit. I haven't entertained here in Hertfordshire for some time, and although the household staff is back to full strength now, a number of the servants are inexperienced. It was good of you to allow Mary Muston to come back to us on short notice."

Margaret regarded him closely. In the past weeks his old color had returned. He was looking tanned and much more healthy than that first day, certainly, and even now she could see little evidence that he had used his visitors as an excuse to return to old habits. She didn't dare to ask him whether he had done so, of course, nor did she wish to let him know how much she had missed him. One always resented change, she told herself firmly. That was all that had distressed her. She had merely grown accustomed to his visits. Nothing more. She glanced toward Lord John Kingsted, now engaged in polite conversation with Lady Annis.

"He seems perfectly charming," Margaret said, looking down at her hands so that Abberley wouldn't see the glint in her eyes. "Have you known him long?"

"Many years. Michael and I knew him at Eton. Then he went on to Cambridge, poor fellow, but we still managed to see him now and again. I'm surprised you haven't met him before."

"No, I know the name, of course, but I don't believe I've had the pleasure of an introduction before. To be sure, one meets so many people during the Season that it is possible to forget a face or two, but I am persuaded I should have remembered him."

"Yes, ladies generally do," Abberley said with a small chuckle. "He purchased a set of colors not long after leaving school, which may account for it."

"Oh, was he on the Continent?"

"Not he. Coldstream Guards, assigned to St. James's Palace, if you please. Spent his time doing the pretty for the queen and that lot. Soft work."

He raised his voice slightly upon noting that Kingsted had excused himself to Lady Annis and now approached them. That young man's eyes narrowed in mock anger. "Watch what you say, Abberley. Soft work, indeed. I'll have you know there's no duty so hazardous as looking after royalty. One never knows what to expect from one moment to the next. Assassination attempts, young whippersnappers accepting dares and trying to invade her majesty's bedchamber, others wishing to win bets by seducing a princess—one never knew, that's all. And no soldier on the Continent ever came to grief through failing to polish a button, I can tell you."

Abberley grinned at him, but Pamela Maitland, rising to take her leave, said his duty sounded most interesting to her, and surely it must have been very exciting to be at the center of things as Lord John had been. His lordship, grinning appreciatively, made her a profound leg.

"Have you brought a footman with you, Miss Maitland?" Abberley inquired, chuckling.

"Oh, no, sir, for the distance is not at all great. I walked over with Sir Timothy and Melanie when they returned from the vicarage, you know. You needn't worry about my safety. I shall be quite all right."

"No doubt, but it would give me pleasure to see you home. You needn't come, John," he added, "if you would prefer to remain here and visit a bit longer. You know your way back to the hall."

"Yes, indeed, but it would give me pleasure, also, to accompany you," said Kingsted with that twinkling smile.

"Perhaps you would all honor us by coming to dinner tomorrow evening," Lady Celeste said quickly as the group prepared to take their departure. "We would be pleased."

"Celeste," hissed Annis, "this is a house of mourning." Realizing the others must have heard, she turned a deprecating smile toward Kingsted. "Not that we would not greatly enjoy your company, sir. 'Tis merely that my health is so uncertain, you know, that I find it difficult to exert my mind to other things when I am overset by grief."

Lady Celeste shot her a look of displeasure. "I had not forgotten, Annis, but there is nothing amiss with having friends in to dine. Indeed, it would add levity to what are increasingly dull meals. We will have no dancing, although perhaps a tune on the pianoforte would not come amiss," she added, glancing at her grandniece. "You all must know that Margaret plays excellently well, and no one can say that music is frivolous, after all."

"We would be honored, ma'am," said Kingsted promptly. The others agreed, and Pamela was asked to invite her father as well. After they had gone, Lady Annis repeated her strictures on the wisdom of entertaining in a house of mourning, but Lady Celeste told her roundly that she didn't want to hear any more about the matter.

"They are coming, and even you, Annis, would not suggest that I rescind the invitation now that it's been accepted. You would do better to concern yourself with that son of yours."

Margaret gasped, fearing that Lady Celeste meant to put into words their belief that Jordan had been responsible for Timothy's fall and for tampering with his medication afterward. Lady Celeste heard the gasp and folded her lips together. But Lady Annis wasn't about to allow her to fall silent after making such an observation.

"Just why should I fret about dearest Jordan, Celeste?" she asked dangerously. "I can assure you that he hasn't given me a moment's distress since the day he was born."

"Then he is either cleverer than I give him credit for being, or you are a zany," retorted Lady Celeste, taking up the gauntlet with enthusiasm. "If you haven't seen him pinching the maids, I have. I daresay he's running rampant in the villages hereabouts, as well, for he struts whenever a female is present. Even Margaret and poor Miss Maitland have been annoyed by his attentions.''

''Nonsense, Margaret has said nothing to me.''

''No, Annis, I haven't,'' Margaret said quietly. ''I have not needed your assistance to deal with his advances. But neither do I welcome them.''

''Well, you would do better to reconsider before you make up your head on that score, my dear. You are nearly three-and-twenty, and that puts you well upon the shelf. I hope you do not think you will see another Season in London. You would look a hag next to all the seventeen-year-old chits.''

Lady Celeste snorted. ''Annis, you clearly need spectacles. Margaret's light would outshine any number of those young things. And even if it didn't, she would have no need to settle for the likes of Jordan. She's a wealthy young woman. Not a great heiress, by any means, but very few gentlemen would scoff at her portion, I assure you. She is hardly on the shelf yet.''

''That is as may be,'' said Lady Annis stiffly, ''but she had several Seasons in London without achieving a successful connection, and if you are about to remind me of young Frederick Culross, I beg you will not. Eligible he may have been, but he was scarcely a brilliant match.''

Margaret felt herself beginning to tremble with anger at being discussed in such a fashion. She wanted nothing more than to turn on her heel and leave the room. She saw Lady Celeste grimace with annoyance and believed her ladyship was about to pull out all the stops. ''Please,'' she heard herself saying in a strangled voice, ''I do not wish to hear any more. I am not interested in forming any connection, I assure you. I wish only to be left alone to pursue my life in my own fashion. So please do not bicker over what is best for me. I shall decide that in my own good time.''

''Well, really,'' said Lady Annis huffily, ''I cannot approve of your speaking to your elders in such a way, Margaret. It is not at all becoming to you.''

''I am sorry that you disapprove, Annis, but I felt I had to say something. Jordan does not worry me, but I hope you are not imagining a possibility of a match between us, for such a possibility does not exist."

"So I should hope," muttered Lady Celeste. Then, when Margaret caught her eye, she added with a grimace, "Oh, very well, I shall say no more. But, Annis, you would do well to discover where that precious son of yours spends his evenings, instead of always shutting your eyes to what you don't wish to see. If he isn't out seducing some tenant's daughter, I shall be surprised."

Lady Annis replied indignantly that Jorden would never do such a low, common thing as that, that he was a gentleman, a Caldecourt. Nevertheless, Margaret noted with amusement when her cousin was present for dinner the following night that he seemed to be at the dining table only under protest. No doubt, Lady Annis had insisted upon his presence so that their numbers would not be uneven, but it was also possible that she had taken Lady Celeste's warning to heart.

The gathering was a merry one. Margaret had arranged the seating, placing Jorden at the head of the table, facing Lady Celeste. As guest of honor, Lord John Kingsted occupied the seat at her ladyship's right, while Pamela sat to her left. After that, it had been a matter of simple precedence, except for one detail. By rights, Margaret ought to have been seated between Kingsted and Abberley, who as the highest-ranking male guest should have been to Jorden's left, but she hadn't believed she could be comfortable in such a position. Thus, she put Abberley across from herself, seated between Pamela and Lady Annis, and placed the vicar next to her.

It wasn't long before she realized she had made a mistake. Nearly every time she looked up from her plate, it was to find his lordship's dark-blue eyes upon her, and it was difficult to avoid his gaze. She was therefore more aware of his presence than she would have been had he been seated beside her. One had to turn one's head to catch the eye of the person directly to one's right or left. And in an informal setting such as this was, one's conversation was not confined to those persons.

The conversation was general and merry. Even Lady Annis seemed to be enjoying herself for once, and Jordan grew positively jolly. After the meal, the gentlemen refused to be isolated with their port and readily agreed to Lady Celeste's suggestion that they allow themselves to be served in the drawing room instead. And as soon as they had adjourned to that chamber, Pamela reminded Margaret that they had been promised a tune or two on the pianoforte.

Grateful to have reason to separate herself, if only briefly, from the others, Margaret pushed open the tall doors separating the drawing room from the adjoining parlor and repaired at once to the instrument, opening it and then reaching for a candelabrum, meaning to move it nearer to the music. A masculine hand reaching past her at the same time startled her. It was Abberley's hand, and he apologized at once for making her jump.

"I thought you might allow me to turn the pages for you," he said. "I read music tolerably well."

"Thank you, sir," she said breathlessly. "That would be very kind of you."

Once the others had settled into chairs, she played a sparkling song by Franz Schubert, then one of Mozart's lighter pieces. Margaret was not by any means a great pianist technically, but she had a keen ear and a memory for note and tone that served her well. She played, therefore, with exceptional sensitivity to the music, and her performance clearly pleased her listeners, who refused to be satisfied with merely two selections.

"Pamela plays very well," she said, pleased by their response but not wishing to overshadow her guest.

"Not so well as that," said Miss Maitland with a laugh. "Did you learn those pieces in Vienna, Margaret?"

Margaret shook her head. "No, they were part of my repertoire during my come-out Season," she said. "I do have several from Vienna. There is one in particular." She began thumbing through a stack of music on the low table beside her. "Ah, here it is."

Setting the sheet of music before her, she placed her hands upon the keys. Moments later the room was filled with the soft, mesmerizing notes of a haunting sonata. The tune created a mood that was at once relaxing and fulfilling, a mood that continued to increase even as the notes grew softer. There were several moments of stirring music played at greater volume, then soft rippling notes that faded at last into silence. The silence lengthened until it was broken by the sound of Pamela's sigh of contentment.

"My, that was beautiful," she said quietly. "Who is the composer?"

Abberley had been staring at the music, and it was he who answered her, his tone one of surprise. "The music is hand-written and signed," he said. "The composer is Ludwig van Beethoven."

"Gracious, is he in Vienna now?"

Margaret nodded, and Lady Celeste said, "We actually met him. He has been visited by musicians from everywhere, you know, led by their veneration for his genius and a desire to profit by his remarks. Sir Harold was much impressed by Margaret's skills and thought she would enjoy meeting so great a composer, so he arranged for us to do so."

"A great honor," said Abberley solemnly.

Margaret twinkled up at him. "It was, sir, and I was flattered to be given a bit of music, even though he scorned to accept a compliment, saying it was not a particularly good piece."

"Merciful heavens," said Pamela, "it is wonderful."

"He was not in a good mood," said Lady Celeste. "Sir Harold told us that shortly before we arrived, Herr Beethoven's physician had called to attempt to convince him to accept a *carte-blanche* offer from an English gentleman to write a number of symphonies. Unfortunately, the Englishman had ventured to describe, as a model for the symphonies he required, Herr Beethoven's own first and second symphonies, which Margaret says are in a plainer style than his others."

"Grandpapa said that it was only with great difficulty, despite the fact that he rarely has two coins to rub together, that Herr Beethoven could even be got to listen to the proposal," Margaret said with a laugh. "When he heard the condition that was tacked to it, he said very dryly to the physician''—she lowered the tone of her voice, imitating the composer—'' 'When I am unwell, I take your advice; when I compose, I take my own.' He would not pay any further heed to the proposition.''

Her audience laughed appreciatively and then Pamela demanded to know what the composer had been like in person.

''Well,'' Margaret said, ''he is about fifty years old and in excellent health, although he is unfortunately afflicted with deafness.''

''Not to such a degree as accounts of the man had led us to suppose, however,'' Lady Celeste put in. ''He is able to converse readily with the assistance of an ear trumpet, and an ingenious artist is contriving an apparatus of the same nature to be affixed to his pianoforte, which will facilitate his musical studies by enabling him to hear more distinctly the sound of the instrument.''

''Nonetheless, I have never so much appreciated my own exceptionally good hearing as during the few moments we were privileged to spend with him,'' Margaret said. ''He has never married, you know, and his habits are retiring.''

''I think his habits are uncouth,'' Lady Celeste said, wrinkling her nose, ''but much may be forgiven a man so passionately devoted to his art.''

''He sounds a dashed fool to me,'' said Jordan, bored. ''If he hasn't got a sou to his name, he must be all about in his head to send a man packing who offers him *carte blanche* merely for continuing to do what he likes to do. I can tell you I'd never be such a zany.''

''No, indeed,'' agreed his mother. ''If Mr. Beethoven were very wealthy, of course, that might be altogether different, but sometimes it is necessary to do things one might otherwise not do, merely to discover if the fates are willing to assist one to a better life. I cannot hold with allowing one's pride to interfere with the necessity of providing for one's comforts.''

''That is perfectly evident,'' said Lady Celeste pointedly.

''Shall I play something else?'' Margaret asked quickly, fearing that her outspoken grandaunt would take this opportunity to suggest that Lady Annis would be just as comfortable in a house of her own, "or would you prefer to hear Pamela now?"

"The hour advances," said the vicar gently. He had been nearly dozing in his chair until disturbed by the comments of Jordan and Lady Annis. Now he hitched himself up purposefully. "The day is now far spent, and the time is far passed."

"I daresay that means you wish to go home," said Lady Celeste.

Kingsted chuckled. "I believe you've got the right of it, my lady, but the vicar ought to have thought some before quoting that bit from Saint Mark. If my memory serves me, what follows is something about rushing away into the village to buy bread, for they have nothing to eat, and he can scarcely hold that to be the case here tonight after such a fine dinner as we had."

To Margaret's astonishment, Mr. Maitland actually blushed, but the look he turned upon Lord John was one of dawning respect.

Abberley also turned to his friend, his countenance expressing both suspicion and astonishment. "Where on earth did you learn anything out of the Bible?" he demanded.

Kingsted gave a sheepish shrug. "Not my fault," he said defensively. "Every time I was sent to the headmaster's study at Eton, he gave me verses to learn."

"That's not all he gave you, as I recall," retorted Abberley. "Look here," he added after a look from Kingsted promised retribution, "what do you all say to an excursion to Periwinkle Hill in a day or two?"

"You go in for picking periwinkles in your advancing years, do you?" inquired Lord John sweetly.

"No, of course he doesn't," Pamela said. "The drive is a lovely one, and the site boasts some very interesting ruins, sir. If you've never seen them, I daresay you'll find the excursion amusing."

"Will Miss Caldecourt accompany us?" asked Lord Kingsted, turning to Margaret, then adding hastily, "And the other ladies, and Mr. Caldecourt, of course?"

9

Both Lady Celeste and Lady Annis disclaimed any interest in jauntering about the countryside, and although Jordan, with a leering wink at Pamela, declared that such an excursion might be jolly fun, by the agreed-upon date he had changed his mind, insisting that he had an important appointment that could not be missed. The others concealed their disappointment admirably. Margaret, in fact, upon hearing that Jordan would be unable to accompany them, decided that the day would prove to be a fine one, indeed.

Pamela Maitland arrived in time to share a cup of tea with Margaret and Lady Celeste in the morning room, and the two gentlemen arrived a half-hour later. Since neither Lady Celeste nor Lady Annis would accompany them, it had been decided that the group would have greater freedom of movement on horseback than if the young women were confined to a carriage. Miss Maitland therefore wore a simple but very becoming habit of lightweight russet-colored wool with dark-brown braided trim. Her hat sported a dainty half-veil to protect her eyes both from too much sun and from the dust of roads that were rapidly losing their winter dampness.

Margaret's new riding habit of dark gray with black grosgrain edging had been delivered by the seamstress only the day before. Its very somberness accented the glow of health in her cheeks and the sparkle in her eyes. She wore neat black half-boots, a brimmed hat tilted rakishly over her right eye, and she carried black leather riding gloves and her slender, gold-handled whip.

Both gentlemen wore buckskins today, and both boasted snowy-white shirts, well-starched, intricately tied neckcloths, and stiff hats. Abberley wore a brown leather coat, however, while Kingsted sported a dashing bottle-green frock coat of the latest fashion with exaggeratedly wide lapels and a high, rolled collar. His shirt points and neckcloth were both so high that Margaret thought he would find it difficult to turn his head, but she had to admit that he looked very dapper. She and Pamela both exclaimed over his appearance.

"The man's a dashed coxcomb," said Abberley with a twinkle in his eyes.

"Up to every rig and row is what he means to say," said Kingsted, laughing. "Good day to you, ladies. You both put us into the shade, you know. Very becoming rigs, I must say."

Coming from one who was clearly well-acquainted with the rigors of fashion, this was praise indeed. Margaret saw that Pamela appreciated his words quite as much as she did herself, and if the warmth she felt in her cheeks was anything to go by, she was blushing just as much as the other girl. Really, she thought, it is not as though I've never received a compliment before. She glanced at Abberley to find that he was watching her, his eyes still twinkling. Feeling her cheeks grow warmer than ever, she turned hastily back to Lord John.

"It is kind of you to say so, sir. Would either of you like a stirrup cup, or shall we go?"

They denied any need for refreshment, and so it was that the foursome was mounted and away within the quarter-hour. They rode northward at first along Ermine Street, toward Royston. There was no longer anything to remind them of winter, for the fields were green and wildflowers bloomed everywhere. They were not the only persons to decide the day was a fine one for an excursion, either, for they met numerous persons on horseback and in carriages, traveling in both directions. It was not long before they realized there was a reason for the traffic other than the weather.

"Good Lord," Abberley said as they drew in to the shoulder to allow the passage of a heavily laden farm wagon, " 'tis market day in Royston. How on earth did we forget?"

Margaret laughed. "I knew it was, for I conferred with Mrs. Moffatt only this morning about what produce she would need to purchase there, but I never once thought about the fact that we would be riding directly through town."

Pamela agreed. "Our maid-of-all-work went to market. She was saying last night that it would be necessary for her to go into town today. But, like Margaret, I didn't think."

"Well, I for one don't mind a bit," said Kingsted. "I like bustle."

"You'll find it in Royston," Abberley promised him. "Market day is like a circus."

And so it was. The town was filled to its boundaries with carriages, carts, traps, and gigs, not to mention the people who rode in them or walked along the roadway. Making their way through the narrow streets proved a difficult task, for pedestrians took little care to remain on the flagways and were wont to step off in front of unwary riders or coachmen without the slightest sign that they intended to do so. The nearer the four riders came to the market square, the denser the crowds became. When a clearing appeared ahead of them, Margaret spurred Dancer, only to rein the mare in again quickly when Abberley's shout warned her that the people were stepping aside not for the road traffic but to make way for two men leading a huge black bear on a chain. Once the bear had passed, the crowds closed in again. When Margaret glanced back over her shoulder, the earl was scowling.

She grinned saucily at him, but fearing they would never find each other again if they became separated, she reined in next to Kingsted's big black, then looked around once more to be certain Pamela and the earl were still right behind them. A wagon loaded nearly to overflowing with children and chickens, as well as the farmer and his fat wife on the bench seat at the front, pulled in ahead of them, and for some moments they were able to ride faster as people moved casually out of the path of the four horses pulling the wagon.

"Seems a pleasant little town," said Kingsted to Margaret once they had emerged from the narrow, crowded streets onto the Icknield Way, still traffic-laden, but not so confining. "I wouldn't mind exploring a bit on a quieter day."

"Indeed," agreed Margaret, smiling at him, "it is a very historical town, sir. It even has its own royal palace, you know."

"No, by gad, I didn't. A royal palace? Surely, you're jesting, ma'am."

Abberley and Pamela had drawn abreast of them as they rode out of the town, then had pulled ahead so as not to block oncoming traffic. The earl called back now over his shoulder, "No, she's not jesting. Royston Palace is a symbol of one of our greatest claims to fame, the fact that James the First, who was hunting-mad, spent a good deal of time here."

"The Scottish bloke, you mean, the one that trotted down to take over London after Elizabeth stuck her spoon in the wall?"

"That's the one," the earl told him, nodding.

Pamela laughed. "He took over a bit more than London, sir," she said, looking back over her shoulder at him as Abberley had done. "My father enjoys reading history, you see, so I have heard the stories many times. James Stuart, on his southward progress from Holyrood to assume the crown after Elizabeth's death, took a great fancy to the high Chiltern heathlands around Royston. Very soon afterward he acquired two old inns in Kneesworth Street to which he added a series of new and spacious buildings that were known then as the King's Lodgings and which are now called Royston Palace."

"By gad, ma'am, you're as good as a guidebook," exclaimed his lordship appreciatively.

"Oh, no, I'm not so good as that," denied Pamela, still laughing. "Every schoolchild hereabouts knows that much of the tale. I'm afraid his majesty made himself rather unpopular, however. For one thing, he ordered that all game within a radius of sixteen miles should be preserved for his own pleasure, and he apointed keepers to deal with poaching."

"See here," exclaimed his lordship, looking at Abberley, "don't your estate date from before the Stuart reign?"

"It does," acknowledged the earl, "and in answer to the question hovering upon your lips, it also falls within the designated radius. My ancestor of the time was not a particular fan of James the First's either. There was dissension, not to say dismay, when he was informed that the game on his estate was to be preserved for the king's pleasure. There was also, I imagine, more than a little disobedience to the royal order."

"He said the hunting was for the benefit of his health, did he not?" asked Margaret, racking her brain to remember the little she knew about the matter and raising her voice so that the two riding ahead would hear her.

"That's right," Pamela said. "He enjoyed such felicity in the hunting life at Royston that he desired his council to take charge of the burdens of state and see that he not be interrupted nor troubled with too much business."

"Which was all very well and good," said Abberley, grinning, "but in 1605, while his majesty was shooting quantities of little birds on Royston Heath, his secretary of state, Sir Robert Cecil, received his first intimation of the Gunpowder Plot in the form of an anonymous letter addressed to Lord Mounteagle of Furneux Pelham, warning him not to attend the opening of Parliament, and such was the royal devotion to sport—or was it to health?—that two full days were allowed to pass before James was informed."

"Only just in time to assure the safety of Parliament," inserted Pamela, "not to mention that of the king himself, for naturally he would have deserted the heath to attend the opening."

"I say, Miss Maitland," said Kingsted, looking at her respectfully, "that's fascinating. Of course, I ain't such a dunce that I never heard tell of the Gunpowder Plot, but I'd no notion such a little town as Royston figured in the tale."

"Oh, we were involved in more of James's history than that, sir. Why it was right here on the heath that he signed the death warrant of Sir Walter Raleigh in 1618."

"And," added Abberley, looking back at Margaret, who in her enjoyment of the conversation had fallen silent beside Kingsted, "he was still shooting little birdies on Royston Heath a month before his own death in 1625. Look here, John," he added suddenly, "if you're so set on learning the entire history of the place this morning, why don't you ride up here alongside Miss Maitland? I am persuaded she will get a crick in her neck if she is forced to talk over her shoulder. She can tell you how it was that the townspeople finally managed to express their hostility toward the mighty hunter."

"I know that tale," Margaret said, chuckling. "You mean the Jowler story, don't you, sir?"

"Right," said Abberley, reining in beside her and allowing Kingsted to take his place beside Miss Maitland. "You tell it, then."

"Well, Jowler was the king's favorite hunting dog," Margaret said, "and supposedly one day he was found with a note round his neck that said, 'Good Mr. Jowler, we pray you to speak to the king (for he hears you every day and so he doth not us) that it will please his majesty to go back to London, for else the country will be undone. All our provision is spent already and we are not able to entertain him longer.'"

Kingsted roared with laughter and demanded to know if King James had taken the hint.

"No, of course not," retorted Abberley. "Royalty never takes hints, as you should know from your own experience with them. Uh, oh," he added, reining in, "I think Apollo has picked up a stone. If Miss Caldecourt doesn't mind, you two can ride ahead while she bears me company. We'll catch up before you reach the hill road."

The other two, already engaged in a discussion of Charles the First, who used Royston Palace on his way to and from Newmarket, went on with barely a nod to acknowledge having heard the earl's suggestion. Margaret, to whom the facts were quickly returning of stories heard throughout her childhood, wondered if Pamela would have reached the part about Charles being held a prisoner in the palace before they caught up. It was just as well, she decided, watching Abberley examine first one of his horse's shoes and then another, that Kingsted had not seen Royston Palace before hearing the tales of its early history. Much of the original building had been replaced less than forty years before with an ordinary eighteenth-century house whose greatest claim to distinction was a shell-hooded door set beneath a Venetian window. Though the palace was still crown property, it didn't look as though it ought to be. In fact, one could easily pass along the street in front of it without noting its existence.

"Have you found the stone, sir?" she asked politely.

Abberley looked up at her, grinned, and dropped the hoof he was holding. His horse pawed the ground as though to scratch an itch. The earl chuckled. "Couldn't find a thing. If he picked one up, he must have got rid of it himself." He swung up into his saddle.

"There was no stone," Margaret said, watching to see if he would insist that there was.

He didn't. "True. I wanted to talk to you. Are you annoyed with me?"

Surprised by the direct attack, she stared at him.

"Well, out with it. Are you? You've scarcely spoken a word today, and you haven't said much the last few days either."

"I haven't seen you to speak to," she pointed out.

They were moving forward again, but the others were well ahead of them now, and Abberley didn't seem in any hurry to catch them up. Other travelers were fewer now that they were farther from Royston, although there were still passersby and occasional family groups, some enjoying picnics on the grass alongside the road.

"I have visited the manor every day since my other guests departed," he said. "I have spoken to Timothy, but I seem to meet you only in passing."

"You have made little point of looking for me," she said calmly.

"Well, I have been busy," he said. "There is more work at the hall than I had imagined. After being lazy for so long, I find it is taking more energy than I'd anticipated to get my affairs in order again.''

''I cannot think why you should believe me to be angry with you, sir,'' Margaret said, returning to the point at hand. ''I have no right to be. You are carrying out your duties with regard to Timothy as well as anyone would.''

''Thank you,'' he said dryly, ''but I did give him that damned pony.''

''You weren't responsible for the thorn,'' she retorted. ''Moreover, we have discussed the matter already.''

''Very true, but somehow it is difficult to forget that if I had left well enough alone, the opportunity for mischief would never have arisen.''

''Don't be daft,'' she scolded, her brows forking above her eyes. ''If it hadn't been a thorn under the saddle, it might have been something else. Something more certain,'' she added with a sigh.

''All right,'' he said, suddenly smiling, ''if it wasn't giving Timmy the pony, what have I done?''

''I told you, nothing.'' She was startled by her reaction to the smile. It was almost as though he had caressed her. She looked away, trying to calm her feelings.

''Then, why are you so quiet today. You do like John, do you not?''

''Yes, of course I do,'' she snapped, ''but I shan't marry him, so you needn't think I shall.''

Abberley stared at her, pursing his lips in a silent whistle. ''So that's the rub.'' He was silent for a moment, but he didn't take his eyes off her, and though she refused to look at him, she knew she was blushing furiously. What a discussion to be having with a gentleman on the high road. ''It was all that talk of mine about how he'd come to Hertfordshire in search of an heiress, wasn't it?'' he said gently.

She nodded, still blushing.

''You are not precisely an heiress, are you?''

She shook her head.

''I thought I must have heard if you had come into a great fortune.''

Margaret raised her head, glaring at him now. "I am very well to pass, however, sir. You know that."

"True." He appeared to think the matter over. "There is also the fact, as John himself pointed out, that he is not in need of a true heiress."

"Although he would not turn one down," Margaret said, unable to stop herself.

Abberley chuckled. "Do you know one who would offer to oblige him?"

"No." She looked at him more directly now. "You did make me think you meant to look out for my best interests, you know, just as you did in the old days when you and Michael were always telling me what to do."

"For your own good. Yes, I see how you might have thought I would be capable of such manipulation. However, I can assure you that I do not look to see you married to John. He would not do for you."

"Now you sound like Aunt Celeste, who said the very same thing about Frederick Culross."

"Sensible lady."

"You did not think so when she had you shut up in the north tower," she reminded him, not caring to discuss Culross.

"Of course not. That was different."

"Well, I think it was entirely sensible. You had no business to be going off to London when you were needed here."

"Did you need me, Marget?"

The tone was a new one, and she glanced at him sharply. He was looking straight ahead. Oddly, she didn't wish to answer the question. Even the thought of admitting that she had needed him was frightening. The muscles in her stomach tightened and she couldn't speak. She turned away, staring hard at the road in front of her.

The Pen Hills were on their left now, rising to chalky crests. There was no hedge on that side, only turf and scrub, marked for many yards here and there with tracks made over the years by wagons and coaches pulling off the main road when it was too rutted for easy passage. The land, a canvas of assorted shades of green, brown, and yellow, dotted everywhere with brilliant wildflowers, rose up to considerable swells of chalk, cloven sometimes gently and sometimes abruptly into deep narrow valleys, some smooth as lawns, some beautifully filled with thick stands of oak, beech, or hornbeam trees. Tumuli—those artificial hillocks or mounds believed by many and actually proved in more than one case to be ancient graves or barrows—were scattered over even the smoothest parts of the greensward, and down from the ridge of the high land came more and more deep, curving trackways. There were people walking for pleasure on the grass above the road, and Margaret could hear the sound of children laughing, although she could see no children at the moment.

"Are you going to answer me?" the earl asked quietly.

"You were meaning to shirk your duty," she muttered. "Timothy had been injured."

"There was nothing I could do about that. He was in good hands, and I thought you would be happier without my face about for a time. I thought then that you would blame me for giving him the pony."

"Don't be foolish, Adam." How could she explain to him that the pony had nothing to do with anything, that it was merely the instrument of Timothy's fate, that something would have happened to the boy no matter what Abberley had or had not done, merely because she was coming to love the boy as though he were her own child. Abberley would scoff if she tried to explain that, would he not? So, instead, she said, "I didn't blame you then, nor am I angry with you now. Should we not be catching up with the others? I am persuaded that the track we want is just ahead, before we come to Odsey village."

He favored her with a long look but made no attempt to continue their private conversation. Within moments they had ridden up behind Kingsted and Pamela, and the turnoff they wanted came some ten minutes later.

The narrow dirt road wound steadily upward into the hills, but it was not so steep as to prove difficult for the horses, and the ride was an enjoyable one. No longer did they pass groups of people. The only sounds they heard, aside from their own voices, were the chirps of sparrows and the songs of meadowlarks and bobolinks. They rode past the white wall of a chalk pit, with roses and privets overhanging, and black bryony and elder growing below.

"How pretty!" Pamela exclaimed.

"How dangerous," Abberley said soberly. "These hills abound in disused pits like this one, but they are not all so easily discernible. It's as much as a man's life is worth in some areas to leave the road. What looks like a patch of low-growing scrub can in fact be a deep pit. At the very least, one's horse will founder; at worst, one can fall through a bunch of thick growing alder or other scrub and be seriously injured. Getting out again can prove to be impossible without assistance."

Pamela drew in her breath and Margaret bit her lip, knowing he was right, but Kingsted said reprovingly, "Look here, by gad, no sense in alarming the ladies. We don't mean to leave the road, do we?"

"No, John," said the earl, "and I'd no intention of alarming anyone. I just think something ought to be done about marking the chalk pits—those that are naturally formed as well as those that are manmade—to make them safer. Some of them, of course, have been as they are since ancient times, so I daresay it will be some time longer before anything is done about them."

"Imagine some Neolithic man hunting across the chalk," said Margaret, smiling.

"And making weapons out of the branches of one of those elm trees," said Pamela, entering into the spirit at once. "Flint for their arrows can be found in many places hereabouts. Did Neolithic man use a bow and arrows?"

"If he did," Abberley told her with a chuckle, "he didn't carve them from any of these elms. I doubt that any one of them is more than two or three hundred years old."

"Just infants, in fact," said Kingsted.

The earlier, serious mood was broken completely, and they whiled away the rest of their uphill journey by making up outrageous stories about the way ancient man must have entertained himself along the Chiltern crest. At last, however, they reached the crest itself at the point known as Periwinkle Hill and were rewarded for their exercise by a fine view of some ancient castle ruins. Not much remained of the castle other than a few piles of weathered stones, but there were more elm trees for shade and lush green grass upon which to spread their saddle blankets. Abberley had provided a picnic, and both gentlemen carried saddlebags filled with delicacies. Mrs. Puddephatt had outdone herself, and there were cold chicken legs and sliced ham—not so cold now after some hours in the warm saddlebag, but delicious nonetheless—and bread and cheese and fairy cakes. There were also apples from the hall's fruit cellar, still crisp and juicy even after the long winter, and jugs of lemonade and wine.

It was cooler on the hill than it had been down on the Icknield Way, for a breeze was blowing, but it was not so cool as to be uncomfortable, and Margaret found herself relaxing as she had not done for some time. Even when she thought of Michael and how much he might have enjoyed such an excursion as this one, her feelings were soft and warm and loving. It was the first time she was able to think about him without sadness welling up within her. She glanced at Abberley and saw that he was watching her. His look was one of those she had come to know as a child when she had fallen into some scrape or other, at once protective and understanding. Big brother, she thought, smiling back at him, but feeling somehow even warmer inside, and softer too. He stood up and began to help Pamela put the remains of their feast into the saddlebags, but when Kingsted moved to assist with the task, Abberley left them and came to stand beside Margaret.

"You were thinking about Michael," he said quietly.

She nodded. "Remember how we used to ride into the hills together when we were children?"

"I remember when Michael and I used to ride into the hills to go fishing or hunting," he corrected her, "and how you would always catch up with us after the first hour when it was too late to take you home again.''

"You both scolded me dreadfully the first time I did it,'' she reminded him, "and Michael told me to turn around and ride straight home again by myself, but I said I couldn't because I would get lost, and you convinced him to let me stay with you." She twinkled up at him from under her lashes. "I wouldn't really have got lost, you know."

"I know. I seem to recall wondering about that as I stood on the carpet in the bookroom and listened to my father explain to me exactly why it was that I was being punished. His point was that we ought all to have turned around and ridden home, so that your people wouldn't have had to spend the entire day in a fret about your safety."

"Surely you weren't punished every time," Margaret ex-claimed, wondering if it were possible for such a thing to have come to pass without either her brother or Abberley ever telling her.

"Of course not." He chuckled. "They soon learned to expect you to be with us when you couldn't be found, and it rapidly became apparent to everyone that Michael and I were not to blame for your disappearances."

Kingsted interrupted their tête-à-tête just then to invite them to accompany himself and Miss Maitland in a stroll through the ruins, so Margaret accepted Abberley's hand and let him assist her to her feet. When he tucked her hand into the crook of his elbow afterward, she made no demur, think-ing it felt very comfortable there. Besides, the terrain was a little uneven here and there, and it would not do to trip and fall.

By the time they returned to the horses and saddled up for the return journey, she was completely in charity with the earl again, and if she occasionally intercepted a look from him that was not particularly brotherly, she did not give the matter a second thought. The weather, although cooling somewhat as the afternoon advanced, remained comfortable, and there was nothing at all to mar the return ride. Even the market-day crowds had thinned to the point where their passage through

Royston was scarcely impeded at all. The men and Margaret
accompanied Miss Maitland directly to the vicarage, politely
refusing the vicar's invitation to stop long enough for a cup of
something wet, then rode on to the manor. There, Abberley
jumped down from the saddle quickly enough to forestall
Archer, the footman, who was moving to assist Margaret.

"I should step in to bid my charge good day, don't you
think?" he said. She agreed and invited Kingsted to accompany them, which he did with alacrity, professing himself all
agog to continue an earlier conversation with Lady Celeste.
Her ladyship, as well as Lady Annis and Jordan, was found
easily enough in the drawing room, but Timothy was not in
the house.

"I'm afraid he's done a bolt again," said Lady Celeste
when they asked her if she had seen the boy. "Went to the
vicarage as good as gold this morning, but when Melanie left
him in the old schoolroom to finish up some lessons the vicar
had given him, he must have decided there were better things
to be done."

She did not seem at all put out by Timothy's behavior, but
Margaret could see at once that the earl was displeased. "I'll
send someone to find him," she said quickly.

"No, let him be," Abberley told her firmly. "Let us see
just how far he will carry it this time. When I come by
tomorrow, I shall insist upon knowing how long he was gone,
Marget. This behavior must be stopped. You'll never have a
comfortable moment if you don't know where he is from one
moment to the next. He's got to learn that I won't tolerate his
running off like this."

"Perhaps you would care to stay to dinner, Abberley,"
suggested Lady Celeste, watching Margaret. "If you intend
to read that rascal a scold—and mind, I fully approve of such
an intention—it would be as well if we were not all left in
suspense over the matter until tomorrow. 'Tis best to have it
over and done tonight."

But the earl refused politely, saying that it would do the
boy no harm to wait and that as it was already past four
o'clock, Mrs. Puddephatt would be wondering what had kept

them. "I know you keep country hours, too, ma'am, so I daresay your cook is wishing we would leave so that your dinner might be served."

"Goodness, Mrs. Moffatt won't be distressed over two more," said Lady Celeste. "Nor is it too much trouble for anyone else. I've merely to pull the bellrope and inform Moffatt that he must lay two extra covers for dinner. That will scarcely prostrate me or him."

The others laughed, but the earl insisted that while the Moffatts might be accommodating, he had no wish to give his head to Mrs. Puddephatt for washing. Kingsted, who had been listening with a polite ear to Lady Annis's latest symptoms, agreed promptly that it was time they were on their way.

Since Jordan had not returned by the time Moffatt announced that dinner had been served, the three ladies dined alone, and Margaret thought the meal a particularly dull one. She excused herself as soon as she could do so politely, saying she wanted to see if Timothy had returned from his ramble.

He had not, and Melanie was clearly worried.

"He hasn't done this for quite a time now, ma'am. I'm afeard summat must of 'appened to the lad."

10

Melanie's words were enough to rekindle Margaret's fears for Timothy's safety, and she decided she had to find the boy at once. Though it immediately occurred to her to send for Abberley, she dismissed the notion, deciding to go for the earl herself. After questioning Melanie more closely and learning that Timothy had appeared to be interested only in finishing the lesson set for him by Mr. Maitland, Margaret was more certain than ever that there had been foul play; however, she couldn't be sure Abberley would agree, that he wouldn't continue to believe that Timothy was merely up to his old tricks again. Her first act, therefore, was to scrabble back into her riding habit, and her second, before setting out for the hall, was to go in search of Jordan.

When he was nowhere to be found—his own man insisting he had not cast eyes upon him since midday—she fought the tension building within her and hurried to find Lady Celeste. Wanting only to inform that lady of her fears and consequent intentions, she ignored Lady Annis' disapproving exclamations of surprise at seeing her attired once more in her habit, and described matters briefly, never taking her eyes off her distressed grandaunt.

"Are you certain it is wise for you to ride to the hall, Margaret?" asked that lady when she had finished and was turning on her heel to leave the drawing room. "I am persuaded it must be nearly dark outside."

The heavy dark-blue velvet curtains in the room were

already drawn, of course; so, short of going to the window to look outside, there was no way to dispute that fact, but Margaret didn't consider it worth discussing, except to point out that it was then all the more important for her to make haste. On those words she took her departure, hurrying down the stairs and along the back passage to the garden door, then across the garden to the stable path, meeting no one on her way but Archer, the footman.

"Have you seen Sir Timothy this afternoon, Archer?" she asked hastily.

"No, miss, can't say as I have, but then I rarely do, you know," the man said, frowning.

Accepting his response as no more than she had expected to hear, Margaret thanked him and hurried on. At the stables she gave rapid orders for the formation of a search party.

"Call upon our tenants for assistance," she directed one of the stableboys as Trimby brought a fresh horse around for her, "and tell Mr. Farley what has happened. He will have more orders for you. I am riding to the hall to fetch his lordship."

The stable was abustle by the time she left the yard, and Margaret was certain the men would do all they could to help find the boy. She knew he was a favorite with them despite his odd and often unchildlike ways.

Darkness was indeed rapidly descending upon the landscape, and as she spurred her horse forward into the thick woods, it seemed to enclose her altogether. She heard Trimby shout at her to slow down. At first she chose, out of fear for Timothy's safety, to ignore the groom and trust to her mount. But when the horse stumbled only a moment later, although she managed to hold him together, she knew she was being foolish. She could do Timothy no good by killing herself.

Of course, she told herself bitterly, pulling the horse in to a bare trot, she hadn't done the boy much good anyway. It simply didn't do to care so much for someone. One practically guaranteed that something dreadful would happen.

"My, my, I had no notion you exerted such a powerful influence over Fate."

It was almost as though the words had been spoken aloud there in the darkening woods. But she knew she was merely hearing an echo in her head of the words she had once spoken to Abberley. But then, his attitude was absurd, since he seemed to believe some action or inaction on his part had been responsible for things that had happened—blaming his absence for Michael's death, for example, despite the fact that others (and perfectly capable others, at that) had been at Michael's very bedside and had been unable to do anything to help him. Or blaming himself when Timothy had been injured even after Farley had discovered that someone else had been actively responsible.

Her own feelings with regard to Fate were quite different. She didn't influence, she tempted. She had been warned time and time again, had she not, that she had only to care deeply for someone to lose him. Or her. The fact had been proven over and over again, all her life. And now, it was Timothy who would suffer. What if he were already dead? What if whoever had been threatening him—the thorn, the medication— what if that person had bashed him over the head and left his body under a rock somewhere? She shuddered deeply at the thought, and tears leapt to her eyes. Without thought, she dug her heel into her horse's flank, and the steed lengthened his pace. Only when she felt the first tear, chilly in the wind created by the horse's increased speed, spilling down her cheek, did her astonishment at the fact that she was crying— she, who rarely did such a pointless thing—cause her to realize what she was doing. She pulled up again in time to hear Trimby's indignant shout behind her.

"Sorry," she called back over her shoulder. "I'm afraid I was wool-gathering." There was no response, and she slowed even more to allow the groom to catch up with her. "I said I was sorry, Trimby. Did you hear me?"

"Aye."

"I suppose you don't approve of my rushing to the hall like this," she said with a sigh. After all, he had been at the manor long enough to expect some sort of explanation from her, servant or not. "I'm dreadfully worried about Sir Timothy, Trimby."

"Aye." It was little more than a grunt.

"He could be lying injured somewhere. He might even be dead." Her voice faltered on the last words, and she cleared her throat hastily, determined not to let her fears overcome the strong hold she kept over her emotions. "It is very worrisome," she added in a firmer tone.

"He b'ain't dead, miss."

"How do you know?"

"A cause that lad most allus lands on 'is feet, 'e does. Summat 'appened, certain sure, if 'e's gorn and missed 'is supper, but I gie ye odds, 'e ain't stuck 'is spoon in the wall."

She sighed. "I won't take the wager, because I wouldn't want to win, but I certainly hope you've got the right of it."

He grunted. A moment later the darkness ahead thinned. They were nearly out of the woods. As soon as she could see the road clearly, Margaret increased her speed again, and this time the groom made no protest, urging his own mount to keep pace with hers. Fifteen minutes later they reached the hall, and Margaret slid to the ground without awaiting assistance.

"Wait here, Trimby. I'm just fetching his lordship. I won't be long," she said quickly as she tossed him her reins. Without waiting for a response she turned and hurried up to the entryway, lifting the knocker and banging it as hard as she could. The door was practically thrown open, and Puddephatt stood looking at her in amazement.

"What's wrong, Miss Margaret?"

"Where's his lordship, Pudd? I need him."

"Here," Abberley said, coming out of the bookroom with Kingsted right behind him. The earl strode forward, his expression anxious. "What is it, Marget?"

Suppressing a strong urge to fling herself into those strong arms and weep out her worries on that broad shoulder, she clenched her fists, driving sharp fingernails into her palms, then pressing her sore palms against her skirt. "It's Timothy, sir. He's still gone. I think something has happened."

"Why didn't you just send one of the grooms for me?"

"Because I didn't know if you would take a message like that seriously," she said, knowing even as she admitted it that she had been wrong. His expression told her more than words would have done. "I guess I needed to do something," she said more calmly. "Just sending someone wouldn't have answered the purpose, and I knew Aunt Celeste would stop me—forcibly, if necessary—from setting out in search of him myself."

"Good gad, Miss Caldecourt," exclaimed Kingsted. "I certainly hope she would have stopped you from doing anything so foolish. Not the thing for a gently nurtured female, not the thing at all. Men's work, searching is. Just you leave it to us."

"No, my lord, I cannot do that," she said firmly, not daring to let her gaze clash with Abberley's but meaning her words for him as well. "I must help look for him."

"No." The word came from the earl. Just the one word, quietly spoken, but she reacted to it as though he had shot a quiverful of arguments at her.

"You cannot stop me, Adam," she said, her temper rising quickly. "If you will not take me with you, I shall simply look for him on my own. There is no way I shall meekly turn about and ride home to wait. I'm worried sick. I need to do something constructive."

"Talk some sense into her, Adam," Kingsted said, shaking his head. "I'll just change into my boots and get my gloves and whip."

"Get a duffel coat, too, John. If it hasn't already turned nippy, it will. And ask my man to give you one for me, too, if you will. I don't need to change, and I think my gloves and whip are still in the bookroom, where I left them earlier." Like Kingsted, he had not changed from his buckskins for dinner, but unlike his lordship, he had kept his boots on. The other man was wearing comfortable slippers instead. Clearly, they had stood on no ceremony at dinner, Margaret thought, as the earl, a firm hand to her elbow, guided her into the bookroom.

"Fetch your things, by all means," she told him, "but do not think to talk me out of taking part in the search. You know it will be useless, sir," she added, smiling crookedly at him. "I haven't changed all that much."

He had turned to face her, his eyes narrowed, his expression grim, but at these words a ghost of a smile tugged at his lips. "Someone ought to have beaten you the first time you followed us after having been ordered to remain at home," he said, only half-teasingly.

"As I recall, Papa did," she retorted. "I cannot recall, however, that the treatment proved efficacious."

"Stubborn little brat," he said.

She glared at him, daring him to continue to dispute her right to accompany them, and he met the look head-on, holding her gaze for a long moment. At first it was merely a challenge. She would not look away. For a brief second, she remembered childhood again and was determined now as then to outstare him. But suddenly she felt something else, something quite unexpected, something she could not understand. In that moment she wanted to look away and could not. His gaze held her, pinned her in place, and she felt vulnerable as she had never felt vulnerable before. She could *feel* his look, feel it as though he actually touched her. And he touched her all over, although his eyes were stationary, unmoving. She could feel caressing fingers everywhere, and they were like firebrands, for they set her aflame. The heat coursed through her, and she drew a quick breath, her lips parting involuntarily. Without thought, feeling drawn but not knowing whether it was by her own will or his, she took a step toward him.

The look in his eyes softened. He opened his arms to her, and she took another step toward him.

Kingsted's voice came to them from the stairs as from another world. "I say, Adam, should we send word to some of your tenants to help with the search? Perhaps you ought to rout out your bailiff."

Margaret had stiffened the moment she realized they were no longer to be alone. Abberley let his arms fall to his sides and stepped to a nearby table where his whip rested next to a pair of wash-leather gloves. "Time to go," he said gently.

"You'll take me?" She felt curiously weak.

His smile was one-sided. "Can't see that you've left me much choice in the matter. You were very quick," he added, looking beyond her shoulder at Kingsted, who came into the room just then.

"Must have set a record," his lordship replied, tossing him a heavy duffel coat. He was wearing a similar one. "These will scarcely set a fashion, old boy," he said.

"You'll survive. Did you think to send someone to saddle our horses?"

"I did that, m'lord," Puddephatt said, coming into the bookroom behind Kingsted. "I also took the liberty of sending one of the lads round to the farms. The tenants'll be wanting to help, and the more we get out, the quicker the lad'll be found, I'm thinking."

"Thank you, Pudd. Did you think to tell them all to meet in one place? It won't do to have them scattered all over the downs all night, not knowing whether the boy's been found."

"Aye, sir. Told them to come here to meet wi' Mr. Clayton first. That way, those that don't have suitable mounts can get them, and they can all ride to the manor together to find out what's what."

"You did well, man," said the earl, causing Puddephatt to color up to his ears in gratification. Abberley grinned at him, then turned back to the others. "Shall we go?"

They rode out a few moments later, and Margaret, who had expected Abberley to head toward the chalk hills, saw the thick beech wood ahead and was dismayed and angry to discover that he meant to ride to the manor instead.

"We're just wasting time," she cried as they slowed their horses.

"Not at all," he retorted. "I'm not so daft that I intend to ride into the hills without knowing how many men are looking for the boy and where they're looking. There must be order to a search, Marget, or the boy could be ten feet from the house and never be found. If your Farley's half the man I think he is, he'll have everything under control. Timothy may even have been found already.''

"You mean to leave me at home, after all,'' she muttered.

"Of course he does,'' said Kingsted in surprise. "Told you before, a search is no place for a lady.''

Margaret ignored him, watching the earl, wishing she could see more than the shape of him, but having the distinct feeling, nevertheless, that he was annoyed with her. When he spoke seconds later, his tone confirmed that fact.

"I gave you my word, Margaret. There is one thing, however.''

"What?'' She held her breath, wondering what conditions he would make.

"You won't go haring off by yourself. You'll stay with me.''

She released the breath. "Yes, sir,'' she said quietly. Then a moment later she said, "Adam?''

"What?''

"I apologize for doubting you. I know your word is good.''

"He's daft,'' opined Kingsted before Abberley could speak. "You ain't seriously meaning to take Miss Caldecourt along, are you, Adam?''

"I am.'' Was she mistaken, or was there a smile in his voice?

"But she'll only get in the way! Beggin' your pardon, ma'am, but you will. And we could search much more efficiently if we don't have to be looking over our shoulders every moment to be sure you haven't fallen behind.''

"More likely we'll be hard-pressed to keep up with her,'' Abberley told him, and this time there could be no mistaking the laughter in his voice.

Margaret chuckled.

"Don't enjoy yourself too much, my girl,'' the earl promptly warned her, and there was not a trace of laughter now. "I meant what I said before, and you'd be well advised to remember it, for if you flout my orders this time, you'll answer to me, and you'll find that *my* methods of dealing with disobedience are most efficacious.''

A chill raced up her spine. She knew he meant precisely what he said, and she had no urge to demand to know what he would do to her if she disobeyed him.

"That's the dandy," approved Kingsted.

"Put a sock in it," recommended Abberley.

They finished the ride in silence, arriving at the manor stableyard to find a number of men carrying lighted torches, just about to ride out. Farley stood in the midst of them, feet spread, hands on hips, bellowing orders. The men on horseback surrounding him made a path for Margaret and the two gentlemen.

Abberley spoke to Farley. "There are others coming. I take it you've had no word of the boy."

"Nay, m'lord. An we find him, we'll light a signal fire in the west barley field. Some of the lads are preparing it now. That field's new-plowed and visible from the downs and the hills. Not everyone'll be able to see the blaze, o' course, but we'll fire three rounds of shot as well. One way or t'other, we'll get word out when he's found."

"Good man. His lordship and I will ride with Miss Margaret toward the hills. Have you sent others that way yet?"

"One group, five men. They've torches. You'll see 'em."

Abberley wasted no more time. Taking an unlit torch from one of the men, he led the way out of the yard and followed the back road, skirting the woods and riding across open fields. They made good time. Stars blazed overhead in a clear sky, but the light was even better some fifteen minutes later when the moon began to rise above the eastern horizon. Before long Margaret realized that unless they rode into woods again, they would have little need for the torch the earl carried, for the moon was past the third quarter and bright enough to light their way. In fact, she decided, it was as well it lay behind them, for to have ridden into its light might have caused difficulties, it was so bright.

In the brighter light, the earl increased their speed, but Margaret had no difficulty keeping pace with him. Nor did Kingsted. She could see that he was grinning, enjoying the wild ride, and she realized that if she were honest, she was enjoying it, too. If only Timothy were safe. The thought sobered her.

"How long will it take us?" she shouted to Abberley.

"Another twenty minutes, this pace," he shouted back. "There are several chalk pits below the spring line. We'll check them before we ride any farther into the hills."

The thought of the chalk pits sent cold rivers of fear washing through her, and her stomach lurched as her imagination presented her with a picture of Timothy lying crushed by his fall at the bottom of one, hidden from view by overhanging shrubbery. She swallowed carefully, fearing to disgrace herself. Abberley would scarcely thank her for getting sick, and Lord John would no doubt then believe his disinclination to bring her along fully justified. The nausea passed, but not the fear. Before the twenty minutes had passed, her shoulders began to ache and she realized that her fear had caused tension in them, stiffening them. At the same time, she became conscious of pain in her lower lip and released it, licking the indentations made by her teeth. The way they were riding, she realized, she was lucky she hadn't bitten it clear through. Forcing herself to relax, she concentrated on the landscape ahead, trying to remember where even one of the chalk pits Abberley had mentioned was located.

Just then the earl's horse swerved slightly to the right, and she knew he was adjusting his direction purposely. He, at least, knew exactly where he was going. Less than ten minutes later he drew rein and slipped to the ground, dropping his reins with a low command to his horse to stand.

"This way," he said, using a match and tinderbox from a pocket of his saddle to light the torch.

Hoping her mount would not try to take French leave so long as Abberley's horse remained standing, Margaret looped her reins around a branch of a nearby shrub and followed

him, hearing Kingsted right behind her. It was a matter of but
a few moments to find the pit, a fairly shallow one and not
completely overgrown, by any means, but even with the torch
it was difficult to see the bottom well enough to be certain
Timothy was not down there. Abberley circled nearly the
entire pit, shouting the boy's name, but there was no answer.
Silently, he led the way back to the horses. An hour later,
they had examined four more pits in the same general area
without success. They had also caught sight finally of the
other searchers, but that group seemed to be riding farther
into the hills. Margaret wondered if she and her companions
ought not to be following their example. She was becoming
more and more certain that Timothy must have wandered into
unfamiliar territory and become lost. In order for him to have
done that, considering his propensity for wandering, she knew
he would have to have traveled quite a distance from the
manor.

"There are three more over that ridge yonder," Abberley
said. She thought he sounded tired.

"Maybe someone else has found him," Kingsted said,
"and we are out of sight of the signal fire and the sound of
the shotgun."

"No such luck," the earl said wearily. "Margaret would
have heard the shotgun blasts even if we did not, and we
should have a clear view from here of any fire they build in
the west field. Once we're over the ridge, of course, it's a
different tale, but from here, we'd know."

Kingsted fell silent, and Margaret moved up to walk beside
the earl. When they reached the horses, he put his hands at
her waist and lifted her to the saddle as he had been doing all
night; and despite the fact that at the first pit there had been a
perfectly good log she might have used as a mounting block,
she had not once protested. Independence could be carried
too far, she told herself, still aware of warmth where his
hands had been.

It took another fifteen minutes to reach the far side of the
oak-dotted ridge and five more after that to locate the first pit,
this one more overgrown with shrubbery than any of those

they had previously searched. Abberley had to use extreme care with the torch to avoid setting the shrubbery afire. All three of them took turns shouting as they carefully circled the rim. A false step and the chalk could crumble beneath their feet, sending one if not all crashing to the bottom. In a moment of silence between shouts, Margaret thought she heard something. Hastily, she shushed the others, and with heads cocked toward the pit, they listened.

There was only silence, then after some seconds, the low cry of a night bird behind them.

"That's what you heard," said Kingsted, straightening and cupping his hands to his mouth to bellow Timothy's name again.

"No!" she said quickly, reaching to pull his hands down again.

"What is it, Marget?" the earl demanded in a low voice. "Isn't that what you heard?"

"The note is wrong," she told him.

"Good gad," said Kingsted, "he's probably got more than one note in his throat."

"Hush," Margaret said, a note of desperation in her voice.

"Stifle it," ordered the earl, moving closer to her. "If she says the note was wrong, she means it was wrong to be a bird."

"There!" Margaret had heard the sound again.

"In the pit?" Abberley asked her. He hadn't heard anything over his own voice.

"Behind us," she told him. "Almost the same place as that bird, but a different sound altogether. Listen."

In the ensuing silence they all heard it, a human voice, faint and faraway, but definitely a human voice.

"Good girl," Abberley said. "We'll go on foot." He began shouting Timothy's name again, but at longer intervals now, and they all listened carefully afterward until they heard the voice and could follow it. After that it was but the work of a few minutes to find the boy. He was indeed in a chalk pit, one that looked to have been hollowed out by nature rather than by the human hand. It was narrower than the others they had seen, though not so deep as some. It was too deep, however, for Timothy, with his injured arm, to climb out.

"Aunt Margaret! Sir! Is that you?" the boy cried when Abberley held the torch over the pit.

"It is, indeed," the earl said, keeping his voice calm. "How did you manage to fall into this hole, young man?"

"Oh, Timmy, are you hurt?" Margaret called in the same breath.

"Just bruised a bit," he said. "My arm aches and I'm cold, but I didn't fall in, sir," he added. "I was dumped in here rolled up in a bunch of burlap." He picked up a corner of a large piece of material and waved it at them.

"Well, never mind how you got there," Abberley said. "We'll soon have you out."

It was necessary to get a coil of rope from his saddle, so Margaret waited with Timothy while the men went for the horses. Abberley also had a thick blanket rolled up behind his saddle and this was wrapped around the shivering boy once he was at ground level again.

"Thank you," he said gratefully. "That bit of burlap kept my head from being bashed in, I think, but it wasn't too much good against the cold."

"We'll soon have you warm again," Abberley assured him as he lifted Margaret to her saddle, then mounted his horse. "Hand him up, John."

Kingsted complied willingly, then asked if the earl thought he ought to ride after the men who had ridden farther into the hills.

"No need. By the time you'd catch up with them, we can be back at the manor, and they'll see the fire from where they'll be by then easily enough. Tell us what happened, Timothy," he added then, turning his horse toward the nearest track leading back toward the manor.

They didn't reach the track until they had crossed over the ridge again, and by then they had heard all Timothy could tell them. He admitted he had become bored with the lesson the vicar had given him to do at home and had decided to take a break and walk in the back garden.

"Only the back garden, young man?" Abberley's tone was skeptical.

"Well, that's as far as I got," Timothy said. Moonlight lit his narrow face, and Margaret could see from his expression that he hoped the earl would not pursue the matter.

All Abberley said was, "Go on."

"That's pretty much all there is," Timothy said with a shrug followed immediately by a low cry of pain and a grimace. "Forgot. I must have hit my arm a couple of times on the way down. It hasn't hurt like this for days."

"We'll go slowly," Abberley said. "What happened in the garden?"

"I was near the hedge, and there must have been a break in it, for somebody threw the burlap thing over my head," the boy said indignantly. "Can you believe that? Right there in the garden. Anyone might have seen."

"If they had, we'd have been denied our midnight adventure," said Kingsted cheerfully. "What a shame that would have been."

Timothy glanced at him as though wondering if the man were mad, but when Abberley recommended that Kingsted put a sock in it, the boy grinned. "I'm glad you enjoyed yourself, sir," he said. "I didn't like it much. First, I didn't like having the thing over my head, but then whoever it was that did it threw me over his shoulder and muttered something about throttling me and making the whole job easier if I didn't shut up, so I did."

"Did you recognize his voice?" demanded Margaret.

"No. He had a horse nearby and he tied me all around with rope. I could hardly breathe, and I hope I never have a ride like that again, for he tossed me over his saddle like a sack of barley and we rode for hours and hours, I think. A couple of times he stopped and clapped a hand over my mouth. Once I thought I heard horses when he did that."

"Took cover when he saw someone approaching, no doubt," Kingsted said.

Timothy leaned back against the earl and yawned. "Maybe. Anyways, then he dumped me where you found me."

"You weren't tied up, though," Margaret said.

"No, he took the ropes off except the one tying the burlap round my head and shoulders. By the time I got all that off me, he was long gone. I think I must have been unconscious for a time, because I didn't hear him leave. I was scared when I found I couldn't climb out, Aunt Margaret."

"I'm sure you were," she said with a shiver. "It's a good thing his lordship knows where all the chalk pits are around here."

"I didn't know about that one," the earl said grimly.

11

Timothy was sound asleep by the time they reached the manor, and even the clamorous excitement in the stableyard that heralded his return failed to rouse him. He did stir slightly and mutter incoherently when Abberley dismounted, still holding him, but by the time they reached the nursery, where Melanie was anxiously awaiting them despite the advanced hour, he was deeply asleep once more.

Kingsted had not accompanied them upstairs but had joined a sleepy Lady Celeste in the drawing room in order to comply with her demand to be told exactly what had happened. Thus it was that Abberley and Margaret had a few moments alone after Melanie had taken charge of the boy. At the top of the stairs, Margaret turned to face the earl.

"Did you truly mean it when you said you hadn't known before about that chalk pit?" she asked quietly.

His lips tightened briefly. "I would scarcely jest about such a thing. I was aware of only one other pit in that immediate vicinity, and we would have moved well away from Timothy in order to search it. Had he not mistaken the bird's cries for those of searchers and begun shouting, and had your sharp ears not picked up the sound of his voice . . ." His voice trailed away suggestively.

"He would be there yet," she said, finishing his sentence. "That's what you mean to say, is it not?"

Abberley nodded. "It is a good thing you insisted upon

accompanying us. Is that what you wanted to hear me say?''
he asked with a weary smile.

She dismissed his question with a gesture. "We now have
the proof we were seeking."

"What proof?"

"Why, that someone means to do away with Timothy, of
course,'' she said, surprised that he had not followed her
reasoning. "Surely that is perfectly clear now."

"Well, as to doing away with him, I cannot say that this
incident is proof of anything of the sort.'' When she opened
her mouth to protest, he silenced her by placing a gentle
finger to her lips. "Not so quickly, *my love*. In so isolated a
spot as the one in which we found Timothy, has it not
occurred to you that it would have been quite a simple matter
to have strangled him or bashed his head in?''

Margaret scarcely noted the endearment, so anxious was
she to prove her point. "But that's just it!" she cried. "Don't
you see, the murderer didn't think he would have to do
anything so violent. What with the cold, poor Timothy would
most likely have perished from exposure long before he
starved to death. And didn't he say the villain just dumped
him into that pit? That if he hadn't been wrapped in the
burlap, his head might well have been bashed in? What about
that, my lord?''

"I haven't said your villain wouldn't have been pleased if
the boy had died. I am saying that he did little to ensure that
such a fate would overtake him. He left a good deal to
chance, my dear.''

"He wanted it to appear that Timothy had met with an
accident, that's all,'' she said flatly. "If anyone *had* found
him dead, that is.''

Though Abberley remained frustratingly unconvinced that
more than mischief was meant, Margaret found support for
her view of the matter in the drawing room.

"Look here, Adam,'' Kingsted said the moment they had
entered that room and shut the door behind them, "I dashed
well didn't wish to say anything earlier—before the boy, that

is—but her ladyship here and I both think there is something dashed smoky about this business tonight.''

"That dratted boy never walked so far as the place Lord John tells me you found him," her ladyship said flatly, "and his pony has been in the stables all day.''

"No one has suggested that he walked," pointed out the earl calmly.

"Well, I thought he might have done so," Lady Celeste told him, "for a prank, you know. Even at such a distance, he might have taken a horse and then turned it loose later. But we know he never did either. And he never walked so far as that," she repeated.

"Someone carried him off," Margaret said. "We know that much. I think someone meant Timothy to die.''

Kingsted shook his head, but whether at the horror of such a thought or in denial of the suggestion Margaret wasn't sure, until he said, "Dashed awful thing to do, killing a child.''

"We don't know that murder was intended," said Abberley, sticking to his guns. He proceeded to explain that there was no actual proof that anyone meant anything more than to play the sort of practical joke it had already been suggested Timothy might have played.

But Lady Celeste had no patience with the niceties of legal points. "Fustian," she said crossly. "No adult would waste his time with such a game. The boy was meant to die. Lord John says Timothy quoted his abductor as saying that to throttle him would make his job easier. Therefore, we know he had some reason for not throttling him. And the only reason I can think of is that murder wasn't to be thought of by whoever found him—if anyone ever did find him.''

"That is precisely what I said earlier," declared Margaret with satisfaction, "but why would anyone be so roundabout?''

"Cowardice," suggested Kingsted.

"More feeling for the boy than he thought he had when he set out to do the dastardly deed," suggested Lady Celeste. "Decided to give Timothy a sporting chance. Wouldn't happen on the Continent, of course, but that's a very English thing to do, is it not?''

Abberley awarded her a wry smile. "I doubt that attempted murder and sportsmanship go hand in hand, ma'am," he said, "but there is one reason I can think of straightaway." The others gave him their full attention. "By law, one cannot inherit if it can be proved that one committed murder in order to do so."

Margaret's lips folded together grimly as the others exchanged looks. It was she who gave voice to the name the others were thinking. "Jordan Caldecourt."

Abberley nodded. "We still have little evidence, but perhaps the time has come to have a chat with that young fellow."

"I don't even know if he has returned yet," Lady Celeste said. "We have not set eyes upon him since early afternoon, you know."

"He said he had important business to attend to this morning," Margaret said, remembering with difficulty that it had been only that morning when they had all set out for Periwinkle Hill.

"Well, I don't know what his business was," Lady Celeste said, "but I do know that he didn't set foot outside his dressing room till almost noon. He was dressed as fine as fivepence—" She broke off with a thoughtful frown. "He wasn't dressed merely to go riding into Royston on a matter of business but more as if he meant to impress someone with his sartorial splendor. Come to think of it," she added, frowning more deeply, "he didn't look like a man about to commit an abduction either."

"It is possible that he wasn't expecting the opportunity to arise," Margaret pointed out. "When it did, he didn't care how he was dressed. He simply took advantage of catching Timothy in the garden unawares. He is the only one who can benefit from Timothy's death, after all."

"I think we should get to the bottom of this," said Lady Celeste, "and there is no time like the present."

Although still obviously reluctant to confront Jordan without something solid in the way of evidence, Abberley agreed to let her send for Archer to arouse the young man from his sleep. The footman was found in the front hall, waiting for the gentlemen to depart and the ladies to retire so that he might snuff the candles and get to bed himself. His demeanor upon being informed of what was wanted of him was not conciliating. He had clearly hoped to be told he might begin to lock up. Some moments later, when he returned to inform them that Mr. Caldecourt was not in his room at all, let alone sleeping, he looked a good deal more cheerful.

" 'Tis just as well," the earl said. "This business will be better dealt with after we've all had some sleep."

Lady Celeste didn't agree with him, but she did exclaim over the late hour when she looked at the little gold watch pinned to her bodice. "Merciful heavens, I'd no notion it was this late. Do you realize it is nearly two o'clock in the morning? I haven't been awake at this hour since we left Vienna.

Abberley smiled at her, then reached for Margaret's hand and gave it a little squeeze. "We'll return tomorrow. I'd like to say we'll come over first thing in the morning"—they heard Kingsted utter a long-suffering groan—"but I won't promise anything so foolish. Besides, if Caldecourt isn't back yet, he won't be stirring before noon. I do have some people coming to see me on matters of business early in the afternoon," he added, "but I'll get rid of them as soon as I can."

"You'd best plan to dine here, then," Lady Celeste told him. "Since Annis insists upon sitting down to table by half past four, you'll no doubt be here when she does, one way or another."

He didn't argue with her, but once the gentlemen had gone and Margaret had made her way to her own bedchamber, it occurred to her that there might be something a trifle awkward in Abberley's accusing Jordan Caldecourt of attempting to commit murder one moment and then sitting down politely to dine with Jordan's mother the next. She was too tired to consider the matter at length, however, and once she had wakened Sadie, sound asleep on a bench in the window embrasure, and sent her off to bed, Margaret slipped out of her clothes and into bed, intending to go straight to sleep.

However, a distressing thought occurred to her and refused to be dismissed, so she got up again, wrapped herself in a woolen robe, and hurried up to the nursery floor. Discovering that Melanie had set up a truckle bed beside Timothy's cot, she smiled in relief and went back to bed, secure in the knowledge that the boy was safe enough for the night.

Though it was not yet noon, it was still late the following morning by the time Sadie came to wake her. At first Margaret was annoyed, but once she discovered that Jordan had still not returned to the manor, she relaxed, and when she discovered how stiff she was from the previous day's riding, she experienced a feeling of fond gratitude for her woman's thoughtfulness. Dressing as quickly as her stiffness would allow but with an eye to the fact that Abberley and Kingsted might arrive at any time during the afternoon—it would not do to appear dowdy, after all, no matter what the occasion— Margaret emerged from her bedchamber at last, attired in a becoming light-wool morning dress of silver gray, its sleeves and hem edged with dark Naples lace. Her hair had been piled into an intricate twist of curls at the top that gave the appearance of a crown. She had pinched her cheeks to put color into them, not wishing to hear Lady Annis's animadversions on the sins of paint and knowing full well that that lady would not approve of even the slightest touch of rouge. Even so, she had touched her lips lightly with a finger dipped into the rouge pot. Her thick black lashes needed no assistance, and she knew she looked very well indeed for a lady who had gone to her bed in the small hours.

She found Lady Celeste discussing a hearty breakfast in the small parlor set aside for that purpose. "Good morning, ma'am," she said cheerfully. "Is there any more of that ham?"

"There is, indeed," replied her ladyship, setting down her fork in order to straighten the fluffy lace cap perched atop her stiff gray curls. "It is very tasty, moreover, but you must ring for Archer if you want him. I sent him away. Puts me off my food with that muffin face of his."

"He cannot help his looks, Aunt Celeste," Margaret told

her, giving a healthy tug to the cord, then helping herself from the pot of chocolate resting on the table before her ladyship. Sitting, she pulled her cup closer, then took a careful sip. It was tepid.

"No more, he can," agreed Lady Celeste once she had finished chewing a bit of marmalade-covered toast. "But I don't have to look at him. When are we going to find another footman or two? I am persuaded you ought to do so."

"Yes, I think we should. Of course, Quinlan will be back the end of the month—"

"I ought never to have given him leave," mourned her ladyship.

"Nonsense, ma'am. He had not seen his people in eight years. What else could you do?"

"True. Annis will not approve of hiring another man, however."

"That is not her decision to make, is it?" It occurred to her that it wasn't entirely hers either. "I shall have to ask Abberley, I expect."

"He said you had the run of the house," Lady Celeste reminded her.

"Yes, but another footman would be expensive. I ought at least to go through the formality of asking him."

She decided to ask the earl about hiring more servants just as soon as he arrived, so as to get the matter out of the way before they got onto more serious business. However, it was after three before the gentlemen arrived, and they did not come alone.

Hearing a commotion in the drive, Margaret looked out the drawing-room window to see Abberley's barouche drawn up at the door with Lady Annis's landaulette just rolling to a halt behind it. Hurrying downstairs in the hope of speaking privately with the earl, she discovered that Pamela Maitland had arrived with Lady Annis.

"I found Miss Maitland walking alone while I was out driving," her ladyship explained to them all. She had taken Pamela up with her, and upon discovering that the vicar was to dine with a friend some miles distant, she had remembered

Lady Celeste's having told her that the gentlemen were to share their dinner that evening, and she had invited Miss Maitland to join them. The only person who looked to be particularly gratified by the news was Kingsted.

He stepped forward enthusiastically. "Good show. Glad to see you again, Miss Maitland. Hope you weathered yesterday's expedition well."

"Yes, indeed," she told him, coloring slightly as he clasped her hands between his own but making no effort to withdraw them. "I was not even sore, despite the fact that it has been some time since I last was on a horse for nearly an entire day."

"You heard about the excitement last night, I expect."

"Oh, yes." She turned to Margaret, including the older ladies in a gesture. "You all must have been quite distracted. Naturally Papa was not expecting Timothy to come to lessons today. Is he quite recovered from his dreadful ordeal?"

"Yes," replied Margaret, who had seen the boy earlier and given orders to Melanie not to let him out of her sight for a minute. "Today he thinks it was merely an adventure."

"We've not heard the details, of course," said Pamela with becoming hesitation, "and I am persuaded you will not wish to dwell upon the episode—"

"That is kind of you," interjected Lady Annis before anyone else could speak. "The child was very naughty to have wandered off as he did, and even naughtier to be making up tales to protect himself from well-deserved punishment. It is not the first time, as I'm sure you are aware, that he has served such a trick to those whose duty it is to care for him. If Abberley were to do his duty properly, that lad would smart for it."

Margaret, opening her mouth to defend Timothy, encountered a direct and clearly silencing look from the earl, and shut it again.

"Now, dash it, ma'am—" began Kingsted.

"Not now," said the earl firmly, silencing him as well. "I am persuaded Lady Annis does not wish to hear any more on the subject. Shall we adjourn to the drawing room? Surely you will appreciate a nice cup of tea, my lady.''

Lady Annis shot him an enigmatic look, but she agreed that tea would be very nice, and no more was said about Timothy's adventure. Since they could scarcely allude to their suspicion of Jordan's guilt with regard to that same adventure in front of Lady Annis while she drank her tea, or in front of Pamela, for that matter, the conversation in the drawing room and later, over dinner, remained desultory. There was still no sign of Jordan by the time they had finished their leisurely meal, and when the ladies retired to the drawing room again, leaving the gentlemen to enjoy their port, Lady Annis said caustically, ''You'd think someone might spare a thought to what has become of my son.''

''I am certain Jordan is quite well, ma'am,'' Margaret told her gently. ''If we do not seem to worry about him in the same way that we worried over Timothy, it is because we are convinced that Jordan can take care of himself. Timothy is just a child, after all.''

An odd, undecipherable look crossed Lady Annis's face, and Margaret assumed it was a look of resentment, though it more nearly resembled one of guilt. No doubt the woman must have some idea of what had happened to Timothy, despite her staunch insistence upon the notion that the boy had invented the tale he'd told out of whole cloth. If she was truly worried about Jordan, Margaret told herself, it was probably because, no matter how staunchly she might deny it, she knew he had done something dreadful and was afraid he had taken himself off rather than face the consequences.

The notion grew stronger that Jordan had fled, so that by the time the gentlemen joined them, she was bursting to lay her ideas before them, but she could not do so with Lady Annis right there; so, remembering her earlier intention, she asked Abberley what he thought about hiring another footman.

''Good gracious, Margaret,'' said Lady Annis immediately, ''have you no sense of economy? What, pray, is there for a footman to do in this establishment that Archer cannot do? And that Quinlan fellow who arrived with you and went off again the next day, is he not returning soon?''

"The end of the month," Margaret admitted, "but Quinlan is a lady's footman, Annis. He is not accustomed to cleaning silver or boots other than Aunt Celeste's (and mine when we travel), nor would he appreciate being sent into town to purchase produce. For that matter, Archer is your footman, is he not? He does not take direction from Moffatt very well, only from you."

"I brought him with me, yes," Lady Annis told her. "He is accustomed to my ways and did not wish to remain with the people who hired our house. And having him, I saw no reason to retain the others. There were far too many menservants in this house."

"Well, now there are not enough," Margaret retorted flatly. "We ought to have done something to rectify the matter sooner, but we need at least one more footman if for no other reason than when you are out with Archer, Aunt Celeste has no one to go out with her. And even when Quinlan returns, if both of you are out in separate carriages, Moffatt will have only the maids to assist him with all the housework. It takes a man to do the brass curtain rods properly and to polish the tables and the rest of the woodwork. Women simply are not strong enough to give wood the glow it requires. The house looks dingy."

"Well, I like that—" Lady Annis began indignantly, but when Margaret tried to apologize, Abberley cut in to say that from what he knew of the matter no one had anything but praise for Lady Annis's attempts to keep order during a time of confusion. Her look at him was anything but grateful. "It was hardly my responsibility, sir, but I am certain that dearest Jordan did only what he thought best," she said stiffly.

"To be sure, ma'am, but Sir Timothy is scarcely purse-pinched, you know, and I'm persuaded that things here will run a deal more smoothly with two or three more menservants." He turned then to Margaret, winking at her. "You may do as you like."

"Thank you, sir." His wink stirred odd tremors in her

midsection, and she was grateful for Kingsted's immediate description of his mother's favorite footman. His anecdote was a funny one, and everyone laughed but Lady Annis, who gathered together the fancywork upon which she had been engaged and announced that she believed she felt a headache coming on.

"Oh, dear, ma'am," said Pamela, immediately rising from her place and stepping toward Lady Annis. "Is there anything I can do to make you more comfortable?"

"No, thank you," replied her ladyship. "I am often a victim of pain, and my woman knows precisely what will serve me best." Without another word to any of them, she left the room, shutting the door quite softly behind her.

For a moment there was silence. Then Lady Celeste said, "Gone to sulk, most like. Though she denies taking the responsibility upon herself, you shouldn't have criticized her housekeeping, Margaret."

"No, I suppose not," Margaret agreed. "My tongue ran away with me. Must I apologize, do you think?"

"Certainly not," replied her ladyship without elucidating.

Abberley had taken the opportunity to speak quietly to Kingsted, and that gentleman rose now to inquire whether Miss Maitland might care to take a hand at piquet.

Pamela, clearly as a second thought, glanced at Margaret. "Should we not play something that the others can play as well?" she asked politely.

"Nonsense," said Abberley before Margaret could think of anything to say. "You teach Kingsted how to count his cards properly. I've a wish for some conversation with Margaret, if Lady Celeste doesn't mind."

"Not a bit," replied her ladyship. "You will give me a chance to read a chapter of my book. And don't you worry about me, Miss Maitland. I detest playing cards unless I am made to do so. Too many years of making a third or a fourth when I didn't really wish to. I shall be perfectly content with my book. You needn't spare me a second thought."

So saying, she picked up the volume in question, moved a branch of candles a trifle nearer, adjusted a pair of wire-rimmed spectacles upon her nose, and turned her attention to the story.

Pamela and Kingsted were soon seated comfortably at a card table near the crackling fire, discussing the play of their cards, and Abberley drew Margaret to a sofa some distance away from them near the front window.

"We need to talk," he said.

"I think Jordan has run away," she said at the same time.

He looked at her, considering her words. "There would be no point to that," he said at last, keeping his voice low.

"If he thought he had been found out?"

"Why would he think such a thing? He might have heard somehow that Timothy had been found unhurt, but there has been no overt suggestion of foul play, certainly none that involves him."

"What if he thinks Timothy recognized him?"

"He took good care to avoid that."

"But—"

"No, Margaret, we have no reason to suspect that he's flown. He has too much to lose, after all, and if he did what we think he did, he did it to acquire the manor. For him to run now would be absurd. He'll turn up with some tale or other. Most likely he's found a woman to entertain him, for he certainly needed some excuse for being away yesterday afternoon. What better than one of his barques of frailty. Lord knows, he seems to have any number of them hereabouts."

She hadn't thought of that, but she had to agree that Abberley's words made sense. He was looking at her now in such a way as to stir that odd tremor again, so she said quickly, "I wish Jordan would come back so we can tell him we know what he's up to."

"We cannot do that," he said quietly.

Her eyes opened wide. "Of course we can."

"No, we cannot. I've thought about it a good deal, but the fact remains that we still have no proof. All the man has to do is say he had nothing to do with the matter. It would be our word against his, and we don't have anything to put behind the accusation beyond our suspicions."

"And good cold logic," she said, anger rising at his stubborn attitude. "How can he deny what he's done if the question is put to him directly?"

Abberley chuckled, shaking his head at her. "There are no rules of conduct covering attempted murder, sweetheart," he said. "Caldecourt will scarcely confess merely because we've figured out the puzzle. He'll tell us to go soak our heads. We must find a way to catch him out."

"A trap?" She looked at him hopefully. His use of the endearment had not escaped her notice, and she remembered that he had called her something else the night before. Then it had been his "love," now "sweetheart." Rakes, she told herself firmly, no doubt grew into the habit of using a good number of such terms without thinking much about them. Still, there was a small feeling of disappointment that he could use the words so casually to her. She gave herself a small shake, realizing that after nodding in response to her question, he had fallen into a brown study. "What sort of trap?" she asked.

"I'm thinking."

"Perhaps we could get Timothy to say he recognized his voice," she suggested. "If we set it up properly, we'd be able to judge from Jordan's reaction whether he's guilty or not."

"I thought you were certain of his guilt."

"I am, but you said we need proof."

"Well, that would scarcely be proof. The only proof that would come out of such a daft notion would be that he would make a stronger push to kill Timothy to keep him quiet. That's not the sort of proof I desire."

"Well, do you have a better idea?" she demanded, not appreciating his opinion of hers.

"Keep your voice down," he said in a sharp undertone when Lady Celeste looked up from her book with a slight frown. "I've no wish for this discussion to become general. I've been thinking this might be a case for the Runners."

"Bow Street! You are all about in your head, Abberley. Can you imagine the scandal that would result from an action like that? Why, everyone here and in London would then know precisely what had happened here.''

"I would insist that everything be kept confidential.''

"And how would you guarantee that?'' she demanded. "Doubtless you would have to do as your illustrious ancestor did to guarantee the secret of his hidey-hole, for the only way to be sure no scandal arises would be to shoot the Runner once he discovers the evidence we need.'' Her tone was sarcastic and she glared at him. He said nothing. Neither did he look away, however, and a moment later she was certain there was a glint of amusement in his eyes. "Are you laughing at me, Adam? Because if you are, so help me——''

"So help you, what?'' he asked conversationally. "I hadn't thought of shooting the Runner, that's all. It would wrap things up rather neatly, don't you agree?''

"I don't think any of this business is funny,'' she said, although she was finding it difficult not to laugh. "Oh, Adam, you didn't really mean to call in Bow Street, did you?''

"No, but I confess I don't know of anything better to do. There has to be a simple way to get to the bottom of things without blowing up a scandal, but I want to protect Timothy, too. I'd as lief the boy never know that someone meant him real harm.''

They continued to discuss the possibilities, bickering amiably and sometimes not so amiably, while Kingsted and Pamela finished another several hands of piquet. Time passed quickly, and when finally there came a pause in the conversation between Abberley and Margaret at the same time that Pamela threw down her cards in mock disgust, Lady Celeste closed her book with a sigh and suggested that someone might be so kind as to ring for the tea tray.

"I don't know how it comes about that I am so weary,'' she said, "for unless my watch has stopped, it is not yet even half past nine.''

"Perhaps the fact that we were all up rather late last night accounts for it,'' Margaret said, twinkling.

"Very true,'' agreed her ladyship without a blink. "Lord

John, you are nearest. Will you just give that red cord two good tugs?''

Kingsted complied, but the door to the drawing room was pulled open well before they might have expected the tea tray to arrive, and a rather flushed Moffatt approached Abberley, wringing his plump hands.

''If you please, my lord, there's a bit of a turn up in the stableyard and Mr. Farley desires you to come at once.''

''What is it, Moffatt?'' asked Lady Celeste.

The butler looked anxiously at Abberley, but the earl crooked a grin at him. ''I'll come, of course, but unless you wish for her ladyship's company as well, I'd advise you to answer her question.''

'' 'Tis Mr. Caldecourt, m'lady, and some person from Royston, I believe. The man leapt upon Mr. Caldecourt as he was giving his horse into a groom's keeping.'' Moffatt hesitated, clearly uncomfortable, then added in a rush, ''Mr. Farley said to tell his lordship the person bellowed something about his daughter's honor.''

12

"Merciful heavens!" exclaimed Lady Celeste, but there was little by way of consternation in her tone. Indeed, Margaret thought the old lady was more amused than anything else.

Abberley did not know their grandaunt so well. "I'll send the fellow packing, ma'am, never you worry," he said.

"Nonsense," she said tartly, stopping him halfway to the door. "If Caldecourt has wronged the gel, the matter must be set right. I wish to hear what this person of Moffatt's has to say, if you please. Bring him up here straightaway."

"But, ma'am," protested the earl gently, "I am persuaded that whatever the man's tale might be, 'tis certainly not one for delicate ears to hear."

"Pish tush," retorted the old lady, "what delicate ears? Mine are no such thing, I assure you, and Margaret is no mealymouthed miss to be distressed by what will no doubt be a common enough tale. As for Miss Maitland, she is a vicar's daughter, is she not? The tale will be nothing new to her ears, will it, my dear?" Her glance dared that young lady to contradict her.

Miss Maitland's soft eyes gleamed with suppressed merriment. "No, ma'am," she replied obediently, "I daresay it won't be."

"Well, then?" Lady Celeste turned a basilisk glare upon the earl.

His eyes had also begun to dance and his lips twitched as well, but he controlled himself with an effort and turned to

Lord John with a long-suffering sigh. "I suppose I shall have to fetch the fellow. Do you wish to lend your assistance to the task?"

"Not in the least," replied that gentleman, affecting a fastidious air. "If I may make so bold as to say so, old chap, this appears to be a family matter and not one in which I should involve myself." He made no effort to absent himself from the scene, however, nor did he suggest that Miss Maitland should do so. Instead, he grinned at the earl.

"Damn your impudence, John," Abberley said without rancor before turning his hand up in a polite gesture to the butler, who stood impatiently in the open doorway. "Lead on, Moffatt."

The butler turned with great dignity upon his heel, but at that very moment, from below, came such noises as to indicate that the stableyard altercation had moved into the front hall, and Moffatt's astonishment overcame his dignity at once. He fairly ran to see what was happening, and Abberley, his eyebrows raised but with no other change of expression, strode after him.

Without thought for propriety Margaret leapt to her feet and followed them. By the time she reached the landing at the top of the stairs, the others were in the hall, and since she had no wish to become involved in the altercation and could see and hear everything perfectly well from where she was, she stopped there, her hands resting upon the gallery rail. A moment later, she realized that Kingsted was standing beside her, his erstwhile, albeit spurious air of fastidiousness entirely overcome by his curiosity. Evidently, Pamela had been able to restrain so unbecoming a trait and had remained with Lady Celeste. And while that lady had sufficient curiosity to put the rest of them in the shade, Margaret knew she would stay put at least until she began to doubt whether Abberley meant to bring the participants to the drawing room.

At first it seemed that he had no intention of doing anything of the kind. For that matter, it appeared that it would be beyond his power to do so. The front hall was alive with the sort of persons who would never be found in a lady's drawing room. At first glance there seemed to be an entire invasion force, but once Margaret had forcibly calmed herself, she realized that there were only five or six men below. Three of these, mere stablehands who had evidently followed the others, were speedily routed by the earl and Moffatt. That left Mr. Farley, Jordan, and a beefy man wearing a soiled apron under his tattered coat and over his dusty pantaloons in much the way that an innkeeper might. However, he carried a shotgun under his arm, which Margaret thought to be a trifle out of character for an innkeeper. His complexion was choleric. He bellowed indiscriminately, not seeming to çare who it was that he addressed.

Farley attempted to silence him, as indeed he had been trying to do before Margaret arrived on the scene. "Mr. Tuckman, an ye please, man!" he shouted.

"I'll see justice done, b'God," bellowed the beefy man, ignoring him. "Me own daughter, b'God, ruint by—"

"That will do," said Abberley. He had not shouted, but somehow Margaret had heard him very clearly, and his tone sent shivers up and down her spine, making her thankful that he had not been speaking to her, and causing her to remember that there had been moments before this one when she had thought him other than a harmless, gentle friend.

Evidently the others also heard him, for a silence fell immediately that was a good deal more unnerving than the uproar that had gone before it. Jordan opened his mouth twice to speak but shut it both times as if he had thought better of the notion, and Margaret realized she had not heard his voice at all among the bellowing. He was nursing a bruised jaw, which might account for his silence, and for once no one would mistake him for a dandy, so filthy and disarranged were his clothes.

Abberley turned his attention to the young man. "Explain this row, if you please," he said gently.

The gentle tone did not encourage Mr. Caldecourt overmuch. Indeed, he colored up to his ears and appeared to have more difficulty speaking than ever. His mouth, opening and shutting as it was, put Margaret forcibly in mind of a landed fish. Abberley waited patiently for some seconds, but when Jordan still said nothing, he turned to the beefy man.

"Perhaps you would care to explain your presence, Mr—"

"Tuckman, I be, m'lord," the big man growled, but he bent at the middle as he said it, clearly remembering at last that he was in a gentleman's house. "Landlord down t' the Fox 'n Grapes in Royston town, I be."

"I see. Well, perhaps you will not object to stepping upstairs with me so that we may discuss this matter," said his lordship calmly, remembering his orders.

"Upstairs?" the man repeated doubtfully, glancing upward and flushing even more when he caught sight of Margaret and Kingsted at the gallery rail. "Well, I dunno, m'lord. Ain't there—"

"It is quite all right," said Abberley with a wry smile. "We were just about to have tea, and you will no doubt be grateful for a mug of ale. Moffatt, in the drawing room at once, if you please."

"See here, Abberley," said Jordan, stirred at last by the indignation of seeing his assailant treated as a guest in the house, "you've no business to be inviting the man up to the drawing room. When you hear how he's treated me—"

"You'd best come up, too, I suppose," the earl drawled as if the notion had just occurred to him. "You may go, Farley, and take Mr. Tuckman's shotgun with you to the stables, if you please."

Jordan sputtered, but when Abberley, a solicitous hand under Mr. Tuckman's huge elbow, merely turned his back, there was nothing for the young man to do but follow. Margaret and Kingsted, turning quickly, preceded the others into the drawing room, Kingsted muttering irrepressibly that all the best seats would be taken if they didn't make haste. Margaret found herself chuckling as she entered the room.

"What is so funny?" demanded Lady Celeste. "Where's Abberley?"

"Just coming, ma'am," said Kingsted, frowning with mock fierceness at Margaret before turning with a grin to reclaim his seat at the card table opposite Miss Maitland. "High entertainment approaches, or I miss my guess," he told that young lady *sotto voce*.

Abberley entered with Mr. Tuckman just then and began to make introductions, treating the man with calm civility. The innkeeper was clearly taken aback by all the courtesies, but when Jordan entered the room behind them, a sulky scowl on his face, Mr. Tuckman recovered himself quickly.

"It be pleased I am ter make yer acquaintance, yer ladyship," he said to Lady Celeste, "but I didn't aim ter be speakin' ter no ladies, ye know. An it please yer lordship," he added, turning back to Abberley, "this business be best attended in private, an ye take m' drift, sir." He grimaced and made an awkward gesture that encompassed the three ladies in the room.

"Send him away, Abberley," Jordan muttered. "It is my affair, not yours. I'll attend to it in my own good time."

"Ah, ye will, will ye?" said the innkeeper, arms akimbo. "Like ye attended t' me daughter, I expect. Aye, man, affairs be the word fer it, belike. But I'll attend t' ye, me broad laddie, not turnabout. Ye'll do right by the lass, ye will."

"Mr. Tuckman—" Jordan began testily, but Lady Celeste's indignant voice cut him off.

"Good grief, Jordan, what have you done to the gel?"

"Ah, Moffatt," said Abberley at the same time, as the butler entered, carrying a heavily laden tea tray, "come in, come in. Here is your ale, Mr. Tuckman. Won't you have a seat?"

Jordan turned away in disgust, and Mr. Tuckman seemed dismayed rather than gratified by Abberley's invitation.

"As to that, m'lord, please believe I be flattered by yer condescension, but I knows me place—"

"Fustian, Mr. Tuckman," interrupted her ladyship as Moffatt set the tray down before her and turned toward Tuckman with a mug of ale. Lady Celeste went on sharply, "Sit yourself down, man, and give us a round tale. What has that rapscallion Caldecourt done to your daughter that hadn't been done to her before?"

Accepting the mug of ale with both hands, Tuckman sat

hastily before Lady Celeste had finished speaking, but her
last words brought him upright in his chair with righteous
indignation. "Me daughter's a good lass, 'n there be none t'
gainsay that, m'lady. She never strayed afore this . . . this
jackanapes done 'er wrong."

"Did you, Jordan?" inquired her ladyship curiously. "Do
her wrong, that is?"

"Is this absolutely necessary?" demanded Jordan angrily.
He glared at the earl. "I fail to see what business this is of
yours, my lord, or of Lady Celeste's or any of these other
people."

"But we are fascinated, Jordan," Margaret said sweetly.
"My favorite part of any play is the farce. Surely, you
wouldn't deny us a part in all this. Everything has been so
dull hereabouts until now. Have you not said so yourself any
number of times?"

"That's enough," said Abberley, but he was clearly struggling and not nearly in such command of himself as he had
been when he had said the same words below in the hall.
Still, everyone turned to look at him now, just as they had
before, and when he turned his attention upon Jordan
Caldecourt, the look in his eyes was stern. "Having brought
the matter to our attention the way you did, sir, you made it
the business of everyone here. If you wish such matters kept
private, then you must make it your business to see that they
remain so and refrain from engaging in brawls that wander
from the stableyard (where such activities belong if they
belong anywhere) into a proper house."

"Well, it wasn't my idea to do such a thing," retorted
Jordan, incensed. "I thought the matter *was* private until
Tuckman here leapt on me the moment I'd dismounted and
tried to hold me up at gunpoint. No man has to stand for such
a thing. But when I tried to wrench the weapon out of his
hands, he jumped me and well nigh bashed my head into the
ground."

"I come t' see justice done, is all," said the innkeeper
stubbornly. He swilled ale as though to punctuate his words,
but when Jordan had not said anything further by the time

he'd swallowed half the contents of the mug, he looked at the others and explained, "Follered 'im all the way from Royston town, I did. Wanted ter be certain sure I knowed who 'e was."

"And the shotgun?" Abberley asked gently, shaking his head at Lady Celeste, who was pouring out tea and had raised a questioning eyebrow in his direction. Though she nodded dismissal to Moffatt, that worthy moved only so far as the doorway, clearly reluctant to leave so interesting a scene.

Tuckman took a swallow of ale and cleared his throat noisily before answering Abberley's question. "Wanted ter see 'e did right by me daughter, is all. But all them others got into the scuffle, ye see, 'n the lad here run up ter the 'ouse. I tried ter fight off t'others afore I come after 'im, but they wouldna leave me be."

Lady Celeste, no longer looking the least bit sleepy, cocked her head a little to one side and asked curiously how it was that Mr. Tuckman was so certain Jordan alone was to blame for his daughter's ruin. "For, although I do not mean to offend you, Mr. Tuckman, it has been my experience that a gel who will . . . that is, one who—"

"It was no doing of Mandy's," said Jordan suddenly. "I still cannot see that any of this is the business of anyone but myself and her father, once he manages to calm himself, but I won't have you saying things like that about Mandy. What happened was my fault, not hers. She is a good girl, just as Mr. Tuckman says she is, and I seduced her. He's right about that, too, and right to say I was a heel to do it, and right to come after me with a shotgun, and—"

"Jordan, no!" shrieked Lady Annis, who had approached the open doorway unseen by the others because of Moffatt's bulk upon the threshold. At her cry, the butler moved hastily aside, and she plunged into the room, coming up short before her angry son. "What can you be saying? Why are all these people here, making all this row? What on earth have you done?"

Jordan glowered at her. "I've seduced an innocent girl, that's what I've done. And her father says I must marry her, though I cannot see what concern it is of yours any more than of anyone else's.''

"No concern of mine? After all I've done for you? After all the risk and botheration? You merely go out and seduce some common trollop without so much as a thought to your future or to your mother's precarious health? Oh, my God, seduced!'' She seemed to be approaching full hysterics, for her voice had risen from that first shriek into near banshee wailing. Margaret had stepped forward to attempt to calm her, when Lady Annis gave one last shriek and began flailing her arms and fists at her son. He had no sooner lifted a forearm in self-defense, however, than she clutched at her breast, gave a much weaker cry, and slumped at his feet.

Pamela jumped up from her chair and rushed to kneel at Lady Annis's side, feeling expertly for the pulse in her wrist.

Kingsted, at a more leisurely pace, followed to inquire in an interested tone if her heart had stopped. "Couldn't go the pace, I expect," he said.

Pamela shot him a furious look. "If you would be so good, my lord," she said in measured tones, "as to procure a cold cloth and some smelling salts or burnt feathers, your presence here will be all the more greatly appreciated.''

"Didn't think she was dead," he said, satisfied.

"Of course she isn't. How can you be so unfeeling, sir? She has suffered a great shock. Abberley, since his lordship prefers to stand like a stock, will you help me put her on the sofa there, please?''

The earl moved quickly to help her, although he, like Margaret and Lady Celeste, had been staring oddly at Lady Annis since nearly the beginning of her outburst. When Pamela glared at Kingsted again, he moved at last to assist Abberley, turning first to Moffatt with a curt demand that he do as the lady said. "Get a cloth and them feathers or whatnot, man!''

Lady Celeste spoke for the first time. "If Annis hasn't got a vinaigrette by her, it must be for the first time," she said calmly. "Look in the pocket of her gown, Pamela. 'Tis a cut-crystal bottle.''

"I know," said Pamela, searching. "Here it is. Come, my lady," she murmured, putting a solicitous arm around Lady Annis's shoulders, "breathe deeply. Ah, I think she's coming around already. Steady, Lady Annis, you merely fainted."

Her ladyship stirred uncomfortably and reached for her breast. "M-my heart," she moaned weakly. "My palpitations, oh, what is to become of me?"

"Shhh," said Pamela, taking the cloth that Moffatt was now offering her and laying it upon her ladyship's brow. "You must breathe deeply and evenly now, my lady. Your heart is fine. Your pulse is very strong, you know."

Lady Annis glared at her from beneath the damp cloth.

"I'll wager she don't thank you for telling the world she's got a strong pulse," Lady Celeste put in acidly. "What was all that chat about risk and botheration, Annis?"

Margaret exchanged a glance with Abberley. Neither had missed Lady Annis's words, and they, too, wanted to hear how she would answer that question.

Lady Annis moaned again, then began to complain in distracted tones. "Where is my woman? Send for Wilson at once. Oh, I must rest. I should be in my bed, truly I should. Someone must assist me to my bedchamber."

"In a moment, my lady," Abberley told her. "First I should like very much to hear an answer to Aunt Celeste's question."

Jordan had not moved from the place where he stood while his mother railed at him. Now he said fiercely, "What can you be talking about, Abberley? Cannot you see that she is distraught, that she needs rest? For God's sake, man, get her out of here."

"In a moment," Abberley said. "I believe you ought to hear what she says, too, young fellow. If I'm not much mistaken, I was wrong about you." He turned back to the woman on the sofa. "Was I not, my lady? You see, we thought Jordan was responsible for the odd things that have been happening lately."

"What things?" The voice was still weak, but Lady Annis's eyes had focused sharply and steadily upon the earl.

"Abberley," warned Margaret, looking pointedly from Tuckman to Moffatt, "not here, not now."

"Don't worry," he told her. "Lady Annis, I believe you know what I mean, and I'm persuaded that you would be as loath to hear the details repeated to you here and now as Margaret and the others would be to hear them. If you admit your responsibility, however, and promise me that nothing further will occur, I will do my possible to see that your son gets out of this bumble broth with a whole skin and with at least the shreds of his reputation intact."

Lady Annis sighed and looked away. "Help him, Abberley. Whatever I may have done, I did for him, and he doesn't even care. I shan't apologize."

"You admit your guilt, however?"

"As you wish." She would not look at him, nor would she respond to anything Pamela Maitland said to her.

Abberley nodded. "Leave her be, Miss Maitland. She will recover more quickly if she is left in peace. Mr. Tuckman, I am prepared to discuss the ins and outs of this affair with you at your convenience, but I can see no further reason to do so with such an audience. Perhaps you will come downstairs with me now to a private room."

"See here, Abberley—" Jordan protested.

"You may come, too, if you like," the earl told him kindly. "I shall do nothing that does not meet with your approval, but since I regret my misjudgment of you most sincerely and since I realize you do not possess the financial wherewithal to conduct this sort of affair properly, I am prepared to disburse whatever sum is necessary to see you safely out of it."

"I cannot let you do that," Jordan said stiffly.

Abberley's eyebrows rose to high peaks. "Dear me," he said, "I hadn't thought the impropriety of accepting money from me would affect you so strongly. It is your affair, sir, but I promised—"

"Impropriety be damned, my lord! I collect that you mean to buy off Mr. Tuckman."

"Buy me off?" demanded that worthy in high dudgeon.

"I'd just like t' see the day. Ain't no man'll put a price on me daughter's honor me lord, beggin' yer pardon fer the offensive nature of me speech, but no man kin spout such claptrap ter me."

"Gently, Mr. Tuckman," said Abberley.

"Puts a rub in, don't it?" observed Kingsted, who had returned to his seat. His eyes were twinkling again.

Abberley silenced him with a glare and turned his attention to the indignant innkeeper. "Mr. Tuckman, please believe I meant no offense to you or to your daughter, but surely you must see that she cannot marry Mr. Caldecourt."

Jordan muttered something, but no one paid him any heed, for Mr. Tuckman had leapt up from his chair and was advancing ominously upon the earl. Margaret gasped in dismay at the murderous expression on the huge man's face. Surely he could squash Abberley flat with one of those hamlike fists.

Tuckman growled, "I see nothin' o' the sort, me lord. Young Caldecourt b'ain't no nobleman, after all, 'n me daughter's good enow fer better nor the likes o' 'im. But 'e's the one she wants, odd as it may seem ter any man o' sense. If'n ye dispute the matter, per'aps ye'd care t' dispute it wi' me outside. The man ruint me daughter, ruint 'er chances fer a decent match, 'n 'e's b'God gonna do right by 'er."

The earl stood his ground, meeting the angry man's gaze directly and without a jot of fear. "Mr. Tuckman, there is no cause for your distress. I can promise you that a decent match will be made for your daughter. Mr. Caldecourt admits his fault, so the very least we can do is to help you set things right. You know who I am. You know my reputation. Do you for one moment think I would make a promise I did not mean to keep?"

The innkeeper halted, glaring. "Ye've not been much about these past years, m'lord, if ye'll pardon the liberty o' me sayin' so. Yer reputation b'ain't so fine as ye seem t' think, b'God. How 'm I ter know whether yer still a man o' yer word or no?"

Abberley flushed. "You've an undebatable point there, Mr. Tuckman, but my word is good and I've given it before witnesses. Suppose we go downstairs, and let these ladies get to bed as they must be yearning to do. We'll discuss the matter calmly, and I will do my possible to convince you that nothing will be done that you do not approve." He turned purposefully toward the door, clearly expecting the other to follow. Over his shoulder he said, "Caldecourt, you coming?"

"I won't let you buy him off, Abberley," Jordan said again.

"Jordan!" Lady Annis pulled herself upright. "You just do as Lord Abberley thinks best. You'll only make a mull of it if you don't."

"Dash it, man," Kingsted told him, "she's right about that. You listen to Abberley. Handled any number of irate fathers, he has."

"No one doubts that," said Lady Celeste dryly.

The earl looked back over his shoulder, his lips pressed together firmly, and Margaret expected him to issue a blistering order to Kingsted to hold his prating tongue. Instead Abberley's gaze shifted to her, and his look was a speculative one. When she grinned saucily at him, he seemed to relax, responding with a rueful smile.

Jordan had remained silent during this interplay, but he had made no move to follow Abberley. Now, as the earl turned once more toward the door, he said abruptly, "I won't let you buy him off, and I won't let you find someone else for Mandy. I want her for myself!"

His mother gave a weak cry of dismay and clutched at her vinaigrette. The others simply stared at Jordan. Abberley was the first to find his voice.

"What did you say?"

"I said I want Mandy."

"Ye've got 'er," said the innkeeper promptly, holding out his hand. "I knew ye'd see the right of it, sir. Me girl wouldna throw 'er 'eart after scum."

"Jordan, you mustn't," Lady Annis wailed. "You can't."

Kingsted scratched his head. "Dash it all, I thought this whole business came about because he already had."

Pamela shook her head at him, but there was laughter in

her eyes when she looked down again at the hands folded
neatly in her lap.

"Mr. Tuckman," said the earl with a sigh, "I don't think
you understand Caldecourt. He merely said he doesn't want
someone else to have your daughter. He never said he wanted
to marry her, and while I admit the attitude is a detestably
selfish one—"

"It's not, I do want to marry her!" shouted Jordan.

Staring at her son in disbelief, Lady Annis slumped against
the sofa cushions again, sniffing desperately at her vinaigrette. Even Lady Celeste was taken aback. Only Mr. Tuckman
seemed at all pleased by Jordan's burst of temper.

Abberley threw out his hands. "Caldecourt, for the love of
heaven, show some sense. I can appreciate the fact that you
feel some responsibility for this girl, but you cannot have
thought at all sensibly about the matter. You cannot wed the
girl."

"I can do as I like," muttered Jordan stubbornly.

"Nonsense, boy," Lady Celeste told him, "such a match
is entirely unsuitable. The girl will tell you so herself, and so
would her father if he weren't so taken by the notion of
marrying his daughter into the gentry. And so you are, my
man, and you needn't deny it," she snapped, turning her
guns on Tuckman. "For all that folderol about Mr. Caldecourt
not figuring among the nobility, you still cannot deny that he
is several cuts above your precious daughter. Have you stopped
to consider how miserable she will be among his friends, or
are you too enamored of the idea of having such as him for a
son-in-law? If you truly think that is a goal for which one
ought to strive, may heaven help you. He's more like to hang
upon your sleeve than to enhance your family tree."

Dismayed silence followed this piece of plain speaking,
even Mr. Tuckman not daring to cross swords with her
ladyship. He shifted his feet and twisted his apron between
his hands and looked everywhere in the room but at Lady
Celeste.

Lady Annis continued to moan upon the sofa, and Pamela
Maitland had not dared to look up from her lap. Only Kingsted

frankly enjoyed himself, surveying the others as though he were sitting first row, center, at Drury Lane Theater. Margaret's eyes met Abberley's briefly, but the glint of amusement she encountered there was nearly her undoing. Quickly, she imitated Miss Maitland, looking for perhaps the first time in her life the picture of demure young womanhood.

At last Jordan drew in a long breath and straightened his shoulders. Margaret thought for a moment that he meant to tell Abberley he would submit to whatever course the earl thought best. Instead, the young man turned to face Lady Celeste.

"Ma'am, everything you've said is true. I have done little in my lifetime to make anyone think well of me. I have been a hanger-on, content to let my mother or anyone else call the tune. Following the crowd has always been easier than doing anything off my own bat, for until I met Mandy, I had no reason to consider anyone but myself or to strive for anything beyond the mediocre. Even after I met her, and knowing how I felt about her, I thought of some of the things you have just said, but I lumped them all together into one large excuse for seducing her. Her father is perfectly right in saying that I wronged her. I did. But there is one thing he cannot know, for I've never even told Mandy. I love her."

"Unnatural boy!" cried Lady Annis, collapsing again.

As though nothing out of the ordinary had occurred, Jordan turned from Lady Celeste to face the earl. "Please believe me, sir. If a way can be found to effect a marriage between us that will not make Mandy miserable for the rest of her life, I mean to marry her at once."

13

Everyone, even Kingsted, stared speechlessly at Jordan, for no one in that room had ever before seen the young man so thoroughly in command of himself. Margaret thought she had never liked him as well as at that moment.

Lady Celeste broke the spell. "It cannot be done," she said grimly. "Whatever one may think about the rights and wrongs of classing people according to their standing in life, that's how the world goes about its business. Like unto like and Nan unto Nicholas—anything else brings unhappiness to both. You may put the right gowns on your Mandy, young man, but you'll not make a silk purse out of a sow's ear, and that's a fact. Her speech alone would make her unacceptable to polite company and therefore render you both acutely uncomfortable. She would shame you among your friends and you'd feel out of place among hers."

"Then we must live where no one knows us."

"You would each still be recognized for what you are," said Abberley gently.

"Not necessarily," Margaret said. She had been watching Jordan carefully. "Are you sure of your Mandy?" she asked. "Have you even known her very long?"

"Since we arrived in Hertfordshire," he replied gruffly. "I'm sure."

"But you've flirted constantly, and with anything in skirts," she protested.

He shrugged, glancing obliquely at Lady Annis. "Only so

that Mother wouldn't realize I'd got serious about one girl. I knew she'd kick up no end of a riot and rumpus, because she was after me to make a dead set at you, but I knew that wouldn't answer.''

"Then you truly mean to marry Mandy?"

Several voices raised in protest, but Jordan, recognizing a possible ally, ignored them. "I do." he said firmly, "if it can be arranged so that she won't regret it later."

"Well, I believe there is at least one place you could go where she might not do so," Margaret said slowly.

"Where? We'll go at once."

"The colonies . . . that is, America," she said. "Now that things are peaceful there again, I should think it might provide the answer for you. We have been told—have we not, Aunt Celeste?—that people there care much less than we do here for the rigidities of the social structure.''

Lady Celeste nodded, albeit doubtfully.

Jordan's eyes had lit the moment Margaret mentioned America, but now his face fell again. "I'd go in a minute," he said, "if Mandy agreed, but the devil's in it that I don't have enough money for passage. Heaven knows Mother won't help me.''

The only response from Lady Annis was a low moan, which was ignored by everyone. Abberley had been listening thoughtfully, however, and now he said, "I would be willing to make you a loan, Caldecourt. I know you would not care for me to pay your fare outright, but perhaps we can come to terms that will not bankrupt you. I would certainly be willing to discuss it further, once you have had a chance to talk with Miss Tuckman.''

"B'ain't no need fer talkin'," the innkeeper said with a chuckle. "That lass'd foller 'im anywheres. Not but what I'm so certain I takes kindly ter the notion, meself. Goin' all the way ter Americky, where she don't be knowin' a soul and don't know what ter be expectin'. There be savages in Americky, b'ain't there?''

"There are also any number of civilized towns, Tuckman," Abberley said with a smile. "Your daughter needn't end up in the backwoods. We can discuss the whole tomorrow, if you are willing. Caldecourt and I will ride in to Royston during the afternoon if that will be convenient. He can discuss the matter first with your daughter, and then among us we can make a suitable plan.''

"Abberley, how can you?" wailed Lady Annis. "My only son—encouraging him to travel thousands of miles from his nearest and dearest, across a dangerous sea, to live like a heathen. It is too much, my lord, and so I tell you."

"We will discuss your position in all this after Mr. Tuckman has gone, ma'am,'' Abberley said ominously, silencing her. "Are you satisfied, Mr. Tuckman?"

The innkeeper declared that he was quite satisfied, thank you, and soon took his departure, rubbing his hands together and murmuring to himself joyfully.

Kingsted watched him go, then shook his head. "A happy man. Who'd have thought we'd see such a sight tonight? I daresay it all goes to show that miracles are not so uncommon as one has consistently thought them to be."

"The miracle," Abberley told him, narrowing his eyes menacingly, "will be if you get to see the light of day, dear fellow."

"Indeed, yes," agreed Miss Maitland. "You have passed the line of being pleasing more than once tonight, my lord, and so I do not scruple to tell you."

"Do you not, ma'am?" inquired Kingsted with interest. "Then, perhaps you have more to say to me?"

"Indeed, sir . . ." She blushed. "Oh, you are abominable and deserve that someone should read you a severe scold, but of course it is not my place to do any such thing, so I shall say no more, sir. You must hold me excused if I have already said more than I ought."

"Nonsense," returned his lordship bracingly. "I am intensely interested in anything you have to say, ma'am. Indeed, I make so bold as to suggest that since the hour grows late and since your reverend father has no doubt returned from his dinner and has already begun to fret about your whereabouts, 'tis my duty to see you safely restored to his care. You may say whatever you like to me on the way. I shall need your carriage, Abberley.''

''Oh, will you?'' demanded the earl, diverted. ''And how am I expected to get home, if you please?''

''Oh, 'tis a simple matter. I shall be pleased to swing past the manor on my way back to the hall—unless I forget,'' he added innocently.

''Never mind.'' The earl chuckled. ''I daresay I can borrow a horse from the stable here. Heaven knows how long I'd have to wait for you.''

''That's the dandy,'' approved Kingsted. He rose to his feet and held out his hand to Pamela. ''Come along, Miss Maitland.''

She had been staring at him as though she thought he was out of his senses, but at this high-handed gesture, she gathered her forces and, with a martial light in her eye and a tightening of her soft lips, took his hand and allowed him to lead her from the room. The earl and Jordan escorted Mr. Tuckman to the stableyard some few moments later, Moffatt moving quickly in their wake, and Margaret was left alone with Lady Celeste and a weeping Lady Annis.

Margaret exchanged a look with her grandaunt. ''What now, ma'am?''

Lady Celeste shrugged, picking up her knitting but showing no indication that she meant to retire for the night in the immediate future. ''I daresay Abberley will have more to say when he returns. He didn't say good night, you know, and he would not be so unmannerly as to take his departure without doing so.''

These words caused Lady Annis to moan again, but she forced herself to an upright position on the sofa and, clapping a hand to her breast, announced that she must, simply must be got to bed. ''Where is Wilson?'' she demanded. ''Surely, someone has rung for her. Does no one care what I have suffered tonight?''

''Piffle,'' retorted Lady Celeste. ''No more than your just deserts, if you ask me.''

''Oh, you don't understand,'' the younger woman said, her

voice rising into a whine that set Margaret's teeth on edge. "Nothing has gone the way it should. Nothing. My poor boy, throwing himself away on a common innkeeper's daughter, when he should by rights be Sir Jordan Caldecourt."

"By what rights, ma'am?" Margaret asked in a dangerous tone. "Jordan has no right to the title unless Timothy dies. Is that why you tried to murder him or to have him murdered?"

"Oh!" The hand clasped to Lady Annis's breast jerked, then tightened into a fist. "I never . . . that is, it wasn't meant to be—"

"Providence didn't mean it to be, certainly," Margaret said tartly, "but that was through no fault of yours, was it?"

"Oh, my dear, you cannot think I would do anything so, so dreadful. Truly, if Archer was motivated by something I said . . . if, indeed, he did that terrible thing, wishing to please me, well, I can scarcely be held responsible for that, can I?" Her eyes shifted from Margaret to Lady Celeste. "Well, can I?"

"Not for me to say," the old lady responded with a disgusted twist of her lips. "I collect you refer to the business of the chalk pit."

Lady Annis nodded.

"Are you trying to tell us that Archer carried Timothy into the hills and dumped him into that pit in an effort to please you?" Margaret demanded. "That you knew nothing of the business?"

Lady Annis shrugged helplessly.

"I don't believe that for a minute," Margaret told her flatly. "You would have us believe that you are some modern-day Henry the Second and Archer no more than a follower who would heed your slightest wish and rid you of your Becket. 'Tis utter nonsense, ma'am. I daresay Archer was responsible for the thorn under Timothy's saddle, but he had little opportunity to meddle with Timothy's medication. His presence in the nursery wing would be remarked, while yours would not."

Unable to meet the accusing look in Margaret's eye, Lady Annis turned her head away, then snapped it around again when Abberley spoke from the doorway. "There was not enough of anything in Timothy's medication to kill him," he said. "After you told me about what had happened, Marget, I spoke to the doctor, who had already determined that somehow a stronger medication, one similar to that which he'd prescribed for Lady Annis, had been substituted for Timothy's stuff. I stupidly assumed that Jordan had done the substituting. Nonetheless, Fennaday assures me the strength of the substituted draft was not great enough to be fatal. What did you hope to accomplish, Lady Annis?"

Tears spilled down the woman's cheeks. "I didn't know whether my medication would kill him or not. I just thought if he died after taking it, it would be a sign that the Fates had meant it to be. Archer would have killed him, I expect, but I couldn't let him do anything truly violent."

"You were afraid Jordan would not inherit if it could be proved that Timothy was the victim of foul play. Is that it?"

"Oh, no. Is that truly the case?" Lady Annis's dismay seemed perfectly genuine. "I didn't know. Oh, goodness."

"Then, why?" Abberley demanded.

"Because I'm not a murderess, of course," she said indignantly. "If Timothy died of drinking the wrong medication, it would be an accident, an act of Fate. Or if he died from exposure to the elements or of the fall into the pit, well, that would be an accident, too. But if I had put real poison in the medicine or had let Archer strangle him—as I promise you, he wanted to do—well, that would be murder, wouldn't it?"

The other three stared at her, and Margaret felt a strange stirring of compassion. She said gently, "You hid Michael's will, did you not, ma'am?"

"Yes, of course. It was the only thing to do once we discovered he didn't leave poor dear Jordan so much as a brass farthing. Why, Jordan was his only heir up until seven years ago. Michael ought to have left him something." She was sitting properly now and seemed to be talking as much to herself as to anyone else. She went on musingly, "Of course, there was no particular reason to suspect that Timothy would survive childhood. So few children do, you know, so it seemed practical for Jordan to take control of the estate at once. Only then Abberley found a copy of the will, and the boy seemed to be so very healthy." She sighed, picking at the nails of one hand with the fingers of the other and seeming to concentrate heavily upon the task. "What will happen now?" These last words came as little more than a whisper.

Margaret looked at Abberley. His lips formed a tight, straight line. "My lord," she said softly, "I do not think . . ."

"Her ladyship must not be left alone, Margaret," he said when her words trailed into silence. "Have you a servant who will sit with her tonight?"

"Yes. She has her own woman, of course, though if you feel we ought not to trust Wilson, I daresay Mrs. Moffatt would sit with her."

"An excellent choice," Abberley said, ringing the bell at once. When Moffatt appeared with suspicious haste, he explained the matter, and the butler agreed to fetch his wife.

"What of that dreadful Archer?" Lady Celeste demanded. "The man ought to be hung, drawn, and quartered for his part in this business."

"Unfortunately, I believe Archer has taken to his heels," the earl said quietly. "I asked Moffatt about him after I discovered—when I escorted the worthy Mr. Tuckman to the stableyard, you know—that Archer had attempted to take a horse from the stables a short time earlier. Trimby saw him trying to saddle Dancer and put a stop to his intentions in short order, but now Moffatt tells me he is nowhere to be found. Just as well, I imagine, since we still have no hard evidence against the man, unless you believe Lady Annis here could be got to testify against him."

"How would he know—"

Abberley chuckled as Margaret began to form the question. "He's a footman, m' dear. Can't beat a footman for the ability to listen at doors. Plain as a pikestaff that something untoward was occurring here tonight. No doubt he saw the writing on the wall and decided the climate was becoming too unhealthy for his future well-being. Not a slowtop, Archer isn't. Must have known we'd cotton to him, soon or late.''

Mrs. Moffatt came in a moment later, accompanied by the bracket-faced woman who attended Lady Annis. Her ladyship seemed grateful to see them both and went away with them contentedly.

Margaret turned to Abberley as soon as they had gone. "Has this business turned her mind, do you think, sir?"

"Possibly, I suppose."

Lady Celeste clicked her tongue in annoyance. "She is overwrought, that's all. Annoyed to have her plans come to naught. Annis's trouble is that she can never take full responsibility for anything, so she's made a mull of nearly everything she's ever attempted. Timothy can thank those precious Fates of hers for that, I expect, but I don't believe for a moment she's deranged. Merely that she don't wish to face up to what she don't like. Been that way from a child. Still and all, if we are wise, we won't be deceived by her innocent airs now we know her to be dangerous. She ought to be clapped up somewhere safe with a keeper."

Abberley, who had been looking sober until now, was betrayed into a chuckle. "You are very harsh, ma'am. Not that she doesn't deserve a taste of harshness for her mischief, but I think we can manage the thing without clapping her into Bedlam."

"If you insist." Lady Celeste clearly didn't think much of his merciful attitude, but encountering a speaking glance from him a moment later, she sniffed and looked over at Margaret, who was fiddling with the folds of her skirt. Then with a sudden, understanding glint in her eye, Lady Celeste cleared her throat and announced that since she had meant to go to bed a deal earlier than this, she might as well take herself off. "Now that all the entertainment seems to be over," she added acidly. "You may say what you like about Kingsted, but he does know farce when he meets with it."

Margaret looked up then, surprised by her grandaunt's tone. "Farce is not usually so frightening, ma'am. I feel cold shivers running up my spine whenever I think of what might have happened to Timothy if we had not chanced to hear him cry out as we did.''

Lady Celeste shook her head. "It was meant that he be found, my dear. You were right about that. Providence interceded. Even if you had not heard him cry out, I doubt Annis would have stood up long to any direct questioning about his whereabouts. It must have come to that, you know, for we already knew that mischief was afoot, and Jordan would have been accused. Rather than see him suffering Abberley's no doubt rough cross-questioning, I daresay she would have opened the budget and told us where to look for the boy. Don't stay up too late, my dear.''

"Aunt Celeste is right, you know," the earl said quietly when the old lady had gone, leaving the two of them alone. "Lady Annis isn't the stuff of which martyrs are made. I would swiftly have determined that Jordan knew nothing of what was toward, and she would have been the only possible suspect left.''

"But it was Archer—''

"Archer had nothing to gain unless he was acting under someone else's direction," Abberley pointed out. "She must have known his general plan. For one thing, he doesn't know these hills. As it is, he must have stumbled over that particular pit, though I daresay she pointed him in the right direction. It is not the natural way of footmen to spend their idle hours on horseback or traipsing about unknown terrain on foot.''

Margaret nodded, accepting his explanation as a logical one. "What will happen to her?''

Abberley moved toward her. "I think it best that she be removed from here. No doubt Aunt Celeste is in the right of it, and her mind is not truly affected by all this, but I see no reason to put that theory to a test when Timothy's safety, and yours, might be in jeopardy as a result." He sat down in the chair beside her, pulling it nearer to hers as he did. "If you do not dislike it too much, perhaps we could send her to my estate at Pytchham. The house is a small one, but I keep a skeleton staff there all the time, and her woman would go with her, of course. It would be easy enough to arrange for her to be looked after there, at least until we know her mind is whole. By then, her own house will be free again.''

''Oh, the very thing,'' Margaret agreed, regarding him warmly. But then she frowned. ''Only, will she not refuse to go, sir? You have no authority over her, you know. She is no connection of yours at all.''

''Well, I had thought of that,'' he confessed, ''but perhaps I have an answer to that problem as well. Do you not think she would be more willing to accept my hospitality if I were more closely linked to the Caldecourt family?''

Margaret's breath stopped in her throat, and she pushed her hands against her skirts in order to wipe away the dampness suddenly coating her palms. ''Wh-what do you mean, sir?'' she asked, wondering if the voice she heard was actually her own, it sounded so odd.

He leaned closer, reaching out to take her chin in his hand, to turn her face toward his. ''Look at me, Marget,'' he said quietly. ''I want to ask you something very important.''

''Oh, sir, please,'' she said, feeling a surge of panic, ''please, don't.''

''Don't?'' He watched her closely for some moments, then said, ''I realize the time is not the most romantic I might have chosen, but you have known me all your life and you must have felt the warmer feelings developing between us these past weeks.'' He smiled gently. ''No one will take it amiss for me to offer your aunt the hospitality of one of my manor houses when I am betrothed to her niece.''

''I am not . . . that is, she is *not* my aunt,'' Margaret muttered, refusing to look at him, ''and I take leave to tell you, sir, that that is the most absurd reason for offering one's hand to a lady that I think I have ever heard.''

''That is not my only reason, Marget,'' he said quickly. ''I've fallen in love with you. You must know that. Dammit all, I've moved heaven and earth these past weeks to restore my house and estates to order. Surely you must have guessed I did it all with an eye toward a more settled future.''

''Fustian,'' she said, straightening and giving him look for look. "I know nothing of the kind, sir, and you speak very glibly of love for one who less than a week past had a houseful of ladies who traveled all the way from town to seek you out, so intensely did they bewail your continued absence. Well, now that the danger is past, I assure you I have nothing on my mind other than to put this house back in order and, with Aunt Celeste's help, to raise Timothy to be a proper gentleman. You need not bother your head about us, either. You may go back to your raking with a clear conscience."

He did not bother to dispute her description of his house party. Instead he asked quietly, "Is there someone else, Marget? Someone you left behind in Vienna?"

"You must know there is not. I have no intention of forming a lasting passion for anyone, Abberley. It will not do, and can only lead to further heartache. If you are truly in love with me—which I don't believe for a minute—you will get over the affliction in time. I daresay you have fallen in and out of love any number of times in the past and have survived every time. You have merely looked upon me as a younger sister for so long that you have become accustomed to looking after me, and this business has made you think I need you more than ever. Well, I thank you, but I don't want to marry you."

He reached to grip one of the hands in her lap. "Can you deny your feelings for me so easily as that?"

She swallowed, then forced herself to look at him. "I deny nothing, sir. I do care for you, very much. You know I do. I always have. But my feelings are sisterly, just as your feelings for me are those of a brother." She gave a gasp of pain when his hand tightened on hers, but when he released it with a muttered apology, she said calmly, "I believe I am meant to remain a spinster, sir. I am not emotionally suited to the married state."

He made a sound low in his throat that sounded like a growl, and she felt cold thrills shoot up her spine that this time had nothing to do with fear. But then he got to his feet and stood for a moment, silently and a bit stiffly, before he said, "Very well, I shan't impose upon your sensibilities any further. You needn't fret about Lady Annis or Jordan," he added brusquely. "I'll see both matters attended to, one way or another. Good night, Margaret."

As he strode to the door, she leapt to her feet, calling his name sharply. He turned, his eyes alight with hope. When she said nothing further but merely stood with her mouth agape, staring at him helplessly, he said, "Well?"

"Adam, please don't leave this way," she begged. "Not when you are so angry with me that you call me Margaret. I cannot bear it," she added, her words spilling over each other in her haste to make herself clear. "I know I haven't said all that is proper. You have done me a great honor, and I was probably rude, but you must believe that I am fully conscious—"

"Stuff! You aren't conscious at all, my girl. You are blind and deaf to your own heart's desire. You've pushed your feelings down inside you so that you won't have to be surprised by them, so you won't have to be hurt again. But the feelings are there, Margaret, and they'll haunt you if you don't face up to them."

"That isn't so," she cried, clenching her fists against her ears so she wouldn't hear any more. "You shan't say such things to me just because I embarrassed you. No doubt you are accustomed to your advances being met with immediate acceptance. In fact, you've probably never even had to make advances. As I recall, you are said to be one of the best catches on the Marriage Mart, are you not? The matchmaking mamas fairly fling their eligible daughters at you. But you prefer to take your amusements where you find them, and you no doubt find them easily, sir, so you are not accustomed to rebuff, and now that you have taken it into your head to marry me, your conceit is suffering, nothing else. You insist that I have the tenderest feelings for you and you refuse to believe me when I say I do not, but you are wrong. You are—"

"Enough, damn you," Abberley said sharply, striding back across the room and taking her firmly by the shoulders. "You may babble such nonsense to yourself if you like, but you'll not fling it at me and get away with it. Look at me, Marget," he commanded, giving her a shake. "Look me straight in the eye and tell me you don't love me."

Gritting her teeth, she did as he commanded, glaring at him. "A simple matter indeed, sir, for at this moment, I think I hate you."

"Good," he said, controlling his voice carefully, "then hate this." And with that he bent toward her, raising a hand to the back of her head so that she could not stop him, and captured her soft lips in a searing kiss.

At first, feeling as though she had touched flame, she tried to draw away from him, but the heat from that flame warmed her all the way to her toes in a way she could not deny, stirring feelings she hadn't imagined could exist. She was scarcely aware of the moment that her arms went around his waist.

The minute he sensed the response in her, Abberley moved his hand from the back of her head to her shoulder and then, caressingly, down to the flare of her hips. His other hand was busy, too, but Margaret was scarcely aware of either of them, only of those sensations deep within her body that threatened to overcome her reason. Her lips parted as though directed to do so by some unseen power, and his tongue gained entrance to the velvety softness of her mouth, darting, caressing, teasing. By then, she wanted only for him to continue what he was doing. When he shifted his position slightly, her arms tightened their embrace as though she feared he would stop. His lips twitched against hers, tickling, but even as she wondered about that, his kisses became harder and more demanding than ever and she felt the heat within her body turn to a veritable inferno of desire.

One of his hands moved between them, searching, still caressing, lighting still more little fires along its course. When his fingers moved across the tip of her breast, she moaned softly but pressed harder against him, feeling the tight muscles of his thighs against hers, more aware of the shape and feel of his body and of her own than she had ever been before. A moment later, his hands gripped her shoulders again as bruisingly as before, and he set her away from him. The look in his eyes was grim.

"I am sorry you feel you cannot return my regard," he said softly. "I hope we can remain friends." With those words, he was gone.

14

Margaret stood where she was for some moments, staring at the doorway, one hand pressed to still-burning lips. Her breath came in sobbing gasps, and her heart was pounding so heavily in her breast that she believed she could hear it. Then she realized that what she heard was the earl's footsteps as he pounded down the grand stairway. Moments later she heard the front door slam shut behind him. Her first thought then was to wonder if he had remembered to collect his hat and cloak. Her second, that he was not dressed for riding.

Slowly, her breathing returned to normal. When she noticed that she had been gnawing unconsciously at the back of her hand, she pulled it away, forcing it to her side. The tip of her breast still tingled where Abberley's fingers had brushed against it, but the flame in her midsection had cooled to a glowing ember. With another long, ragged breath, she straightened her shoulders and moved to regard herself in the mirror over the side table, feeling a need to restore her disheveled appearance before Moffatt or one of the maidservants came in to extinguish the lights in the drawing room.

She felt mussed, but when she examined her image in the glass, she could scarcely understand why she should feel so. She looked perfectly normal except for the heightened glow in her cheeks and a certain unnatural brilliance in her eyes. A strand of hair had come loose from her coiffure, to be sure, but there was nothing particularly dramatic about that, nothing that any casual observer would notice, at any rate. Absently, she pushed the strand back into place while scrutinizing her face for more visible signs of the disarrangement she felt within. There was nothing.

"Will there be anything else, Miss Margaret?" Moffatt asked quietly from the doorway. The sound of his voice startled her, making her jump and turn quickly, almost guiltily, but she could see nothing in the large man's expression to indicate that he suspected anything beyond the ordinary.

"No, no, nothing at all," she replied hastily, covering her confusion with a rueful smile. "You caught me primping, I'm afraid, but I am just going up to bed now, and everyone else has retired, I believe—that is, I don't know about Mr. Caldecourt," she added, feeling more foolish than ever. Primping! What a ridiculous thing to have said to him. As though anyone would worry about her appearance just before going to bed.

"Mr. Caldecourt has retired," the butler said in a perfectly normal tone of voice, "and Lady Annis is comfortably settled as well, the missus tells me. Shall I put out the lights, then, miss?"

"Yes, of course. Good night, Moffatt."

Scarcely daring to look at him and still feeling disoriented, she hurried up to her own bedchamber, where she submitted meekly and silently to Sadie's ministrations. Then, once her maid had retired, she settled back against her pillows in the certain belief that, exhausted as she was from the day's activities, she would fall instantly asleep. Half an hour later, after turning over for what seemed to be the fortieth time and attempting unsuccessfully to find a cool place on her pillow upon which to lay her head, she knew that she had judged the matter incorrectly.

Though he was long gone, she could still feel the effects of Abberley's kisses. Her lips were bruised, though only enough to make them seem as though they had swollen slightly beyond their normal size. But all she had to do was to think about the man to experience the full force of those burning tremors in her midsection, as well as an unfamiliar tingling sensation that attacked her lower down even than that. Hitting below the belt, she thought, nearly laughing aloud at the ridiculous thought but stifling the impulse out of fear that such laughter might well lead to an uncontrollable fit of the vapors.

"I am not in love with him." she said aloud suddenly, fiercely. "I cannot be. 'Twould be too cruel."

She would not think about the man, she decided. She would simply force her mind to contemplate something else instead. Certainly, enough things had occurred in the past two days that she ought to be able to think about something harmless. Or, better yet, she would consider ordinary household affairs. A new footman would be required at once, now that Archer was gone. Or even if he were not gone, for that matter, though the earl had said he was quite certain the man had fled. Abberley had also said, of course, that he was quite certain that he loved her, and that was nothing more than fustian, wasn't it?

Gritting her teeth, she turned over again, then was forced to turn again when she got tangled in the bedclothes. They felt damp and uncomfortable. She focused her mind on them at once, forcing herself to think of nothing more disturbing than the necessity of getting them straight and smooth again. But when she had done so and had lain back against her pillows once more, shutting her eyes with a long sigh, Abberley's face appeared in her mind's eye as though he had simply been waiting for her to finish attending to other matters before raising the question of his love for her—and hers for him—once more. She wanted to shout at him that he was crazy, that he was merely deluding himself out of a wish to punish her for rejecting his advances. But she couldn't shout at him, for he wasn't there, no matter how real his image might seem in her mind. Moreover, others would hear her if she shouted. Once they realized she was shouting in an empty room, they would think, and rightly, that her mind was as deranged as Lady Annis's.

For a moment then she succeeded in diverting herself long enough to consider the state of her ladyship's mind. Was

Lady Celeste right, and was the woman merely incapable of accepting responsibility of any kind, particularly the responsibility for her misdeeds? Or was Lady Annis demented? Either way, surely it would be better to attend to her within the family, rather than to allow her actions to cause a scandal about them all. Abberley would see to it that she never harmed anyone else. And he would protect her. He was rather good at protecting people, was he not?

So much for diverting her thoughts, she mused ruefully. It was unfair that he should monopolize them when she was so tired, though. At the moment, she could nearly imagine how lovely it would be to allow him to take care of her forever, to continue to protect her as he had done for the greater part of her life. But he had never been able to protect her against Fate, had he? She bit her lip, enumerating and remembering all those persons she had lost over the years. As she did so, however, she realized she had not spared a thought for Mr. Culross in weeks. That was odd, considering that she had thought of him constantly in Vienna. The matter could not be explained away by the fact that she had been very busy, either, for she had scarcely had a moment to call her own amidst the social whirl that was the hub of life in that frivolous city. No doubt, the answer lay in the time that had passed since Frederick's death. Time healed all, as Lady Celeste would point out.

Still, the lesson had been clear enough. She was not meant to form a lasting passion for anyone, and it would be particularly foolish to form one for Abberley when she already cared enough for him that she would mourn his loss almost as greatly as she would one of her own family. Pure foolishness to tempt Fate any further than that. Besides, Abberley did not love her. He had simply come to the realization that she had never set her cap for him, that she had never for a single moment numbered among the veritable host of eligible damsels who had flung themselves at him. No doubt that had stung him a bit, had put him on his mettle. Or perhaps he was merely bored after having rusticated in Hertfordshire for so long a time when he was clearly more accustomed to being surrounded by friends and flirts alike. The man was a rake, after all. Everyone said so, and he certainly had not denied it. And whoever heard of a rake kicking his heels in a well-nigh-empty country house for weeks on end? And what prey was there for him hereabouts besides herself? Only Pamela Maitland, and if Abberley had not fallen for Pamela in all the years they had known each other, he certainly would not do so now.

The thought did not cross her mind that Abberley—an earl, after all—might think himself a cut above Miss Maitland. She knew that would not weigh with him if he were truly in love with her. Not much, as a matter of fact, would weigh with him under such circumstances. Which, the little voice in her mind continued more forcefully, just went to prove that he was not in love with Margaret herself. He would never have taken his congé so lightly in such a case.

She turned that thought over and over again in her mind. Slowly, the panic underscoring all the other emotions that tumbled through her began to ebb. He did not love her. He had simply allowed his brotherly feelings to carry him away once his vanity had been piqued. No doubt it had been a game with him. What a relief, she told herself, to realize it was no more than that. Unfortunately, the sense of relief she wanted to feel seemed to be overshadowed by disappointment.

"Zany," she whispered, "you are as bad as he is himself. 'Tis no more than your own woman's vanity speaking. Still, 'tis better as it is, since you cannot return his love."

Believing she had discovered the truth of the matter, she finally achieved a comfortable position and gave her mind up to recurring memories of Abberley's kisses and caresses, wondering why he had been able to stir her to such passion when Frederick's touch had never done so. Neither Frederick nor any other man had ever touched her so intimately, of course, which was rather annoying when one wished to compare the results of such incidents. She could not help wondering if there were numerous other men trotting about the world whose touch could enflame her as Abberley's had done. No doubt there were, she decided at last. Any man with as much experience as the earl undoubtedly had should succeed as well. Frederick, she recalled, had been nearly as young as she was herself and probably as inexperienced. No doubt that accounted for it.

Experimentally, she touched the tip of her breast where Abberley's fingers had brushed. There was no particular thrill at first, but suddenly she found herself thinking about the earl again, seeing his face and figure, feeling his touch there, and suddenly there was a sharp tingling that radiated from the tip of her breast through her stomach to her loins. Quickly, Margaret snatched her hand away. Even though she was entirely alone in the darkness, she knew color had flooded her cheeks. Indeed, by the warmth she felt, color had flooded her entire body. What would Aunt Celeste, or indeed anyone else, think of such wanton behavior? Surely no proper lady would ever touch herself in such a way.

In a last desperate attempt to turn her thoughts away from the earl, she began to recite a long and boring poem her governess had taught her when she was about twelve. The first verse she said determinedly aloud. The second she recited in her head, and halfway through the third she fell asleep.

If her dreams were not entirely innocent, they had mercifully faded from her memory by the time she awoke the next morning to discover Sadie at the window, drawing the curtains. Margaret stretched lazily, savoring the first moments of the day, noting idly that sunlight poured through the window much as it would in summer, laying paths of gold across the highly polished floor.

"Good morning, Sadie." She yawned delicately behind her hand.

Sadie turned, smiling. " 'Tis a good morning, indeed, miss. A true spring day, it be, and there be buds forming on the rose bushes in the garden, Moffatt says." She crossed the room briskly to a table near the door. "I've brung yer chocolate. I'll just be putting the tray ter the bed, an ye'r ready fer it."

Margaret sat up, plumping pillows behind her, and allowed the woman to set the tray across her lap. Besides the pot of chocolate there was also a covered dish, and Margaret lifted the lid to reveal several slices of buttered, toasted bread. Inhaling the enticing aroma, she smiled again. "This is lovely, Sadie. I think Mrs. Moffatt makes the best bread for toasting in the entire world."

"Indeed, and she's a fine cook," Sadie agreed. "Will that be all, miss? I promised to 'elp the chambermaid wi' the others, Lady Annis's woman not coming down this morning, and that Archer gone like 'e is. Lady Celeste's Millicent took 'er ladyship's tray up an hour ago, of course, but you'll not find her helping no one else."

Mention of Lady Annis's woman brought memories of the previous evening back with a vengeance, and the toast Margaret had been eating paused halfway between her mouth and the tray as she gaped at her tirewoman.

"Miss? Be somethin' wrong, Miss Margaret?"

Margaret collected herself quickly, setting the toast down with a hand that shook slightly. "I apologize, Sadie," she said at last. "My thoughts wandered for a moment. I expect you've heard a good deal about what happened here last night. No," she added quickly when the woman's eyes lit up and she opened her mouth, clearly with the intent of repeating to her mistress exactly what she had heard, "I don't wish to discuss it now. Moreover, I should take an extremely dim view of your repeating elsewhere anything you may have heard."

Sadie gasped indignantly. "As if I would, miss! A tattle-monger I ain't, 'n I'll thank you ter remember ye've trusted me afore this."

"All right." Margaret held up her hand and said apologetically, "I know I have no cause to believe you would say anything out of turn, Sadie. Just mark it up to the fact that such a bumble bath as this has not turned our lives upside down before. I know I can even trust you to depress any tendency in one of the maids to gossip about our affairs. Do forgive me." The hand was held out, and Sadie stepped forward to squeeze it.

"Ye've known me many a day, miss. Never yet fret about the goings-on hereabouts these past weeks. They be over and done, now 'is lordship 'as taken 'em in hand. He'll see all right and tight. 'E was fair muddled 'isself, I 'ear, afore we came home, not that I'd believe it if I 'adn't seen m'self 'ow those Mustons an' the others was livin'. But 'e's isself again, 'n no mistake." Sadie smiled knowingly, and Margaret winced but didn't say another word about the matter, merely dismissing Sadie to help with the morning routine, saying she could manage her own dressing well enough without assistance.

Finishing her chocolate at leisure, Margaret put the tray aside long enough to get out of her bed and then set it outside her door for one of the maids to retrieve. Deciding to take a morning ride in order to enjoy at least a portion of the beautiful day before she had to face the details of reality, she donned her green habit, the gray one seeming entirely too drab for such a day, and brushed her hair into shining splendor before confining it in a net at the back of her head. Putting on her green felt hat, she collected whip and gloves and hastened downstairs and out through the back garden to the stables with a cheerful greeting to each servant she met along the way.

She saw Lady Celeste in the breakfast parlor, seated near the window, and waved to her. Though Margaret knew the old lady was no doubt waiting for her so they could discuss what was best to be done in the interval before Abberley arrived, she knew, too, that Lady Celeste would contain her impatience, realizing that Margaret needed to gallop the fidgets out of her head before she would be able to think clearly about anything.

Trimby was waiting with the black mare already saddled, clear evidence that word of ructions in the big house had reached the stables, for Margaret had not sent word ahead that she wished to ride. She said nothing to him about his prescience, however, merely accepting a leg up into the saddle and telling him she meant to ride out across the downs. He swung up into his own saddle, prepared to follow, and she led the way out of the yard. For a full hour she rode, trying Dancer's assorted paces and her own capabilities in a series of maneuvers she had not attempted since her teens. Not since the days when she had practiced such things daily in order to appear to advantage whenever Michael and Abberley had been at hand to see her had she worked herself so hard on the back of a horse. She did not think about her brother or her brother's friend now, however, concentrating instead upon her horsemanship. By the end of the hour she was content to ride back to the manor at a walk, talking amiably with Trimby about unimportant matters.

As she had expected, though she took time to go up to her bedchamber to change into a dark-gray frock with silver buttons all down the front and silver braid at the cuffs and at the high waistline just beneath her breasts, Lady Celeste was still in the breakfast parlor. The old lady was reading the London *Times*, which was delivered to the manor twice a week with the morning post. A cup of tea sat by her elbow. At Margaret's entrance she lowered the paper and reached out to feel the teapot beneath its embroidered cozy.

"Tepid," she said. "Ring for another pot, dear."

Margaret obeyed. "I apologize for keeping you waiting, ma'am, but the morning was so magnificent I couldn't resist a long ride."

"Pish tush, don't apologize. 'Tis nothing to me. I've been amusing myself with the paper, as you see. There are the most entertaining items. Here, for example"—she raised the paper again—"listen to this. 'Tis a story about two convicts who have been hung at Newgate. First they received a visit from a reverend. It says here that 'Brandeth' (that's one of the convicts, not the reverend) 'got a long new pipe in his mouth, which he held by his right hand, while he kept his left hand in his pocket. He dashed his chains about as if he felt them not, and seemed quite composed and at his ease while he looked coolly around him and smoked his pipe.' Oh, I see," she went on in a different tone, "he was in his cell, for it says he looked out the window, 'through a small grated window,' it says here. One would almost think the writer to have been sitting beside him, wouldn't one?"

"Really, Aunt," Margaret protested with a weak smile, "I'd as lief not discuss a pair of convicts. Particularly if their crime was murder, as I suspect it probably was, considering the reverend. A reverend visiting a pickpocket would hardly be noted by the *Times*."

"No, I daresay he wouldn't," agreed her ladyship, scanning the rest of the article rapidly. "They are indeed murderers, though of course one of them at least denies it, and they are also convicted of high treason. Still, it appears that they cannot be monsters, for one of them, when on the scaffold, requested the Bible out of which the reverend was reading, kissed it, and then requested that it be given afterward to his younger sister. Oh, how melancholy this is. He said that he hoped a book given in such circumstances would be afterward read with greater attention and profit."

Margaret grimaced. "Trading upon the feelings of the spectators at his execution, no doubt. I should be surprised if such a man even had a sister."

"Now, dearest, anyone might have a sister," said her ladyship in a calming tone. "Not but what you are quite right," she added, folding the paper and laying it aside. "The subject is not one we would wish to discuss at the present. Not that Annis is on her way to the gallows, nor more unfortunately is that muffin-faced footman of hers, but still we ought to discuss more cheerful subjects. Have you seen Timothy this morning?"

"No, but I saw Melanie when I was leaving my bedchamber to go to the stables and he had already had his breakfast. I told her there was no reason he could not go to the vicarage as usual this morning, so I assume that is where he is now."

Lady Celeste nodded. "Then, what shall we do today, dear? Mrs. Moffatt was saying only a day or so ago that it is high time and more the linen closets were turned out and a new inventory made of the contents. She usually does such a turnout this time of year, you know, but being shorthanded, she wasn't certain she ought to begin yet. Still, it ought to be done.''

Margaret knew the linen closet ought to be done. Like all the other large closets, it needed doing at least twice a year. That was when anything that hadn't been mended before got mended, when old sheets were torn into dust rags and sheets of lesser age got their hems turned, and when lists of what was needed to bring the numbers to their proper levels were drawn up. It was not a chore left to one's housekeeper in a well-regulated house, no matter how trustworthy or expert the woman was. It was a chore that must be directed, at least, by the lady of the house. Still, Margaret knew perfectly well she wasn't up to dealing with sheets and towels and table linen. Not today. Not until certain outstanding matters had been attended to.

"Have you seen Jordan this morning?" she asked.

"Well, that is hardly an answer to the question I put to you, but I must confess I have not," replied Lady Celeste, regarding her closely. "What do you want with him?"

"Oh, nothing, I merely wondered if he and Abberley had set a time for going into town."

"I expect they did, you know," her ladyship said placidly. "No doubt Jordan will meet Abberley on the road. Pure foolishness for Adam to ride over here and then backtrack to reach Royston."

Margaret nodded, telling herself that she ought to be relieved the earl wouldn't show his face at the manor, but feeling disappointed in spite of herself.

As it happened, however, he did pay them a visit that afternoon. She was descending the stairs, having formed the intention of routing out her housekeeper and informing her that she would help her attend to the linen closet on the morrow, when the front door was pushed open and Jordan entered.

He was chuckling. "As easy as kiss your hand," he said. "Who would have thought the matter could be arranged without setting everyone at sixes and sevens?"

"What was so easy?" Margaret asked, drawing in a quick

breath when she realized he was not speaking to her but to Abberley, who followed close upon his heels.

Jordan looked up at her, grinning and looking more like a carefree young man than he had looked since she had first seen him at Caldecourt. "I am to be married by special license," he said cheerfully. "Mr. Maitland has agreed that it would be best for all concerned and is at present engaged in composing a letter guaranteed to wring the heart of the archbishop, to whom I must make my application."

"Then, you must go to London?"

"Immediately," he agreed, "and Mandy and Tuckman go with me. Everyone seems to agree that the sooner the thing is accomplished and we are off, the better. There will be any number of ships sailing now that the weather has improved, so we should have no difficulty booking passage. I cannot thank you enough," he added, turning back to the earl. "Without your assistance, I doubt things would be going so swimmingly now."

"Think nothing of it," Abberley said quietly, his eyes on Margaret. "I felt it was the least I could do after so badly misjudging you."

Jordan frowned. "You know, I cannot help fretting a bit about Mother, though you have told me time and again that I needn't do so. If it weren't for my feelings for Mandy and everyone's concern that we leave before even a whisper of our intentions begins blowing about, I know I should never allow you to take the burden of all this onto yourself, sir."

"Don't think about it," advised the earl. "Your chief concern is to get yourself leg-shackled without pain to your intended. Believe me, if she is as sweet as I believe her to be, now I've met her, she would be deeply hurt by the sort of comments that would come her way the minute your intentions become known. The quicker you're away, the better. Your mother will be in good hands, I'll see to that."

"I know you will, sir, though I still don't know why you'd allow yourself to be saddled with such a business. It won't be easy, you know. She will fight you tooth and nail. Perhaps I ought at least to speak to her, to tell her that I have agreed to your plan and that it is the best course for her to take."

Abberley shook his head, but his voice was gentle. "I have no right to order you to do nothing of the sort," he said, "and if you truly feel you must speak to her, then you must. But do not think anyone else expects you to do so. You have made your feelings with regard to her activities—supposedly on your behalf—well-known to the rest of us. What I fear is that you will try to make her understand them as well. You won't do it. She has clearly managed to hide herself behind a wall of misunderstanding. She has convinced herself that she did nothing wrong, that whatever she did, she did for you, and that Fate determined that her plans should go awry. She takes no responsibility whatever for her deeds. At best you would have dozens of recriminations flung at your head for your ingratitude. At the worst you will have to suffer through a series of spasms and palpitations."

Jordan snorted derisively. "I know that much, sir, but surely you must realize that I have scarcely ever held a conversation with the lady when I haven't suffered through exactly the sort of scene you now describe. No, I shall go to her and tell her what I intend to do. She will be no more pleased about Mandy now than she was last night, but she deserves to hear the whole from me."

Margaret, watching and listening from the stairway, was impressed by Jordan's attitude. No longer did he seem to be nothing more than a dandified fop with no more than solid bone above his eyebrows. He was confident. His shoulders were squared and his back was straight with resolution. It was a change, she decided, definitely for the better.

She had avoided looking at Abberley, but when Jordan passed her on the stair on the way to visit Lady Annis, she had no choice, for to ignore him when there was no one else in the room would be churlish. Feeling self-conscious, she said stiffly, "Would you care for refreshment, sir?"

"I wouldn't say no to a glass of Madeira in the drawing room after I've paid my respects to my ward," he said affably. "Is he in the schoolroom?"

"Yes," she replied, feeling slightly deflated. Abberley seemed not to be affected in the least by the happenings of the previous night. In fact, she thought, as he too passed her—with a cheerful grin, no less—that he had entirely forgotten all that had passed between them on that occasion. She turned on the step to stare after him in dismay.

15

The following morning dawned in much the same blaze of brilliant sunshine as its predecessor had displayed, but when Margaret awakened, she was not granted the same blissful few moments of forgetfulness. She had not slept well, for one thing, and when she had slept, her dreams had disturbed her more even than her waking thoughts had done. Worst of all, she remembered the dreams. It seemed as though they had followed, one upon the other, all night long, and that she had wakened after each with the memory of it lingering all too clearly. Each dream had been of Abberley, with each more disturbing than the last. Not that the dreams had been particularly frightening, merely disturbing. From more than one she had awakened moaning, but the moans had not been moans of pain. Not by a long chalk. Remembering certain portions of these dreams now, she blushed scarlet.

There was another reason she failed to welcome the sunlight with the same sense of well-being that she had welcomed it with the previous day. Today there would be no time in which to gallop the fidgets out of herself on horseback. Her services had been bespoken for another task, one not nearly so pleasing to her tastes. She was to escort Lady Annis into Royston and to help her hire a post chaise and four to carry her to Pytchham.

Surprisingly, her ladyship had not cut up stiff over the prospect of her banishment to Lincolnshire. On the contrary,

Margaret had thought her rather flattered by Abberley's decision to send her to his manor house there.

"Why, how kind of his lordship to invite me," she had said the previous afternoon when Margaret, finding her in the drawing room with Lady Celeste after parting with Abberley on the stairway, had thought to inform her of the earl's suggestion. "He must know it will be just the thing for me after all this upset. My nerves would never recover here, you know," she had added complacently. From all appearances, her ladyship was exactly as she had always been. Her reference to upset was made in a tone of slight distaste, much as though someone other than herself had been responsible for causing her distress.

When Margaret opened her mouth to point out to her that she had no one else to blame for her present circumstances, Lady Celeste intervened, saying mildly, "I am persuaded Abberley thought you would enjoy a space of peace and tranquility, Annis, and Lincolnshire, you know, is particularly lovely in the springtime—and quiet, too, now that the hunting season is done." When Margaret moved to pull the bell, Lady Celeste asked if Abberley had arrived, and upon being answered in the affirmative, went on, "Then, he will be able to tell us just what arrangements he has made for your comfort, Annis. I know you will want to depart as soon as may be."

"Indeed," agreed Lady Annis, "although I could not contemplate traveling into Lincolnshire unescorted, you know. I am persuaded there must be any number of highwaymen and footpads along the way. And, of course, now that Archer seems to have disappeared so oddly, there will be no one to make arrangements for me along the way—meals and so forth. The journey is too long to be made comfortably in one day. Oh, I am certain it would be entirely too difficult without a proper escort." Her hand went to her breast, and her agitation was visible. Margaret felt strangely sorry for her.

"Indeed, Annis, I doubt Abberley would consider for a moment the thought of sending you alone. He will have made all the proper arrangements. You will see."

And so it seemed he had done, for when he entered the drawing room after spending some ten minutes with his ward, he informed them that it was his intention to send Lady Annis to Pytchham by post chaise.

"Oh, no," she had protested, "you cannot have considered, sir. 'Tis monstrous expensive, you know. I couldn't think of such a thing for a moment."

"Nonsense, ma'am," he had replied earnestly. "*I* wouldn't think of sending you by any other mode of transportation. It will be my pleasure to do this for you, so you must not be fretting over the expense."

She seemed to be gratified by this indication of his regard for her and fairly preened herself as she began to make plans for a departure at some vague point in the future.

"You will depart tomorrow, ma'am," Abberley said in a tone of one bestowing a treat upon a child. "You will hire a post chaise at Royston."

"I will? But I quite thought you would be going with me." She regarded him wide-eyed, her hand once more clutching at her breast.

"No, unfortunately I have business that will require my being elsewhere tomorrow, but I shall send my own carriage for you and Margaret before noon." Without so much as looking at Margaret, he went on blandly, "I am persuaded she will want to accompany you as far as Royston if only to assure herself that I have left nothing to chance where your comfort is concerned."

Margaret had opened her mouth midway through his words to deny any such intention, but as usual, by the time he had finished he had left her with nothing to say that would not sound impolite. And when Lady Annis turned to thank her profusely for her concern, she had merely smiled weakly and said it would be her pleasure. Abberley had looked at her then and grinned in such a way as to give her a deep desire to smack him, but she had taken pains to conceal these feelings and he soon took his leave of them. Later she had tried to convince Lady Celeste to accompany them on the journey into Royston, but that lady had stoutly refused her invitation.

"One of us would have to sit with her back to the horses, alongside that bracket-faced woman of hers, for one thing, and neither of us enjoys riding that way. Moreover, I've promised to visit some of the tenants tomorrow, and I'd as lief not put it off when I've told them I'll come."

"But you will have no footman to attend you, ma'am," Margaret pointed out, snatching at the only straw she could bring to mind.

"Pooh, I am not such a weak sister that I must have a man up behind me when I drive out. I have naught to fear among the tenants here or at Abberley, and John Coachman will protect me from anything else well enough." She raised her eyebrows haughtily. "Or were you thinking my consequence can be sustained only by parading a liveried footman about?"

"No, of course not," Margaret had replied, chuckling. "I thought only of your comfort, ma'am. Come to think of it, we shall not have a footman to attend us either. And Annis *will* complain of the lack."

But Lady Annis had no cause for complaint. When Abberley's barouche rolled up the drive shortly before noon, there were two staggeringly tall footmen perched up behind. The earl had not accompanied the carriage, Margaret noted with displeasure from the drawing-room window, but he had sent an emissary in the form of Lord John Kingsted, who rode just ahead of the barouche astride a handsome bay mare. He entered the drawing room some moments later in Moffatt's wake.

"You behold in me your courier, Miss Caldecourt," he said cheerfully after the amenities had been seen to. "Abberley thought you would not disdain to accept my company as far as Royston. In point of fact," he added, glancing around at the company in general—which, since Jordan had ridden out early that morning with the promised letter from vicar, included only Ladies Annis and Celeste, besides herself—"I am to ride as far as Baldock with Lady Annis. Then, as she will travel north along the Great North Road and I will travel south, we shall part company there—if no one objects to the scheme, that is."

"Of course we do not object, sir," Margaret told him, "but I did not know you had formed the intention of leaving us today."

"Hadn't," he told her, still grinning. "Formed it two nights ago, if you must know, but first I had to discuss certain matters with the vicar, who was so dashed disobliging yesterday as first to spend the afternoon composing young Caldecourt's letter to the archbishop and then to be called away to some feller's deathbed. He didn't return to the vicarage until Miss Maitland had ordered the tea tray."

"The vicar! What on earth had you to discuss with him, I wonder?" demanded Lady Celeste, fixing the young man with a speculative stare.

"Just so," he told her. "Daresay you've found me out, ma'am, but I'd as lief you don't open the budget till I've had time to tell the parents."

"Tell your parents," Margaret repeated, tilting her head to one side. Then, when he continued to grin at her, the truth of the matter warmed her with a glow of astonished happiness. "You don't mean to say you've offered for Pamela, sir?"

"Do mean to say that very thing," he said, his eyes twinkling madly. "Just what I mean to tell the parents, in point of fact."

"Oh, how very glad I am for you both," Margaret said, "but I hadn't the slightest notion. Indeed, I thought she had—" She broke off, blushing when she realized that it was not at all the thing to say the words perched on the tip of her tongue.

But Lord John was not offended. "Thought she had taken a strong dislike to me," he said wisely. "Thought so myself until she began ripping up at me the other evening. Too much a lady, Pamela is, to behave like a shrew to one she don't care a fig for. Knew then I could pop the question without having my head handed to me in a basket. Never had such a peal rung over me as what I suffered on the way back to the vicarage. Word of a Kingsted," he asserted.

Margaret laughed heartily. "And that convinced you to ask for her hand?"

He shook his head. "Convinced I ought to do it long before that," he said soberly. "Never met a sweeter female, nor one less conscious of being a beauty." Margaret stared at him, for it was the first time she had ever heard anyone describe Pamela Maitland as a beauty, but Kingsted went blithely on, unaware of her astonishment. "Never met one who treated me like I wasn't someone entirely different from the rest of the world, for that matter. But Pamela don't. Hasn't from the outset. She's as natural with me as she is with her cook. I like it. And she can talk like a sensible person. Chits I've met before only want to tell me what an intelligent fellow I am. She don't even always agree with me," he added in tones of astonishment.

"She certainly didn't approve of you the other evening," Margaret said with another chuckle.

"No." He grinned. "She was wonderful. Knew then I had to marry her."

"I cannot approve," said Lady Annis, speaking for the first time since her greeting to him. " 'Tis worse than dearest Jordan insisting he means to wed that dreadful innkeeper's daughter, for Pamela is too far removed from your high station in life, Kingsted. You must not forget that you might be a marquess one day."

"Heaven forbid," he replied. "My father's good for many a day longer, and I trust that my brother won't stick his spoon in the wall before then, but we Kingsteds are a healthy lot, so I don't anticipate the eventuality. If it should come to pass, however," he added in sterner tones than Margaret had yet heard from him, "I am convinced that no one would make a finer marchioness than my Pamela."

"Very true, no one better," said Lady Celeste.

Kingsted rewarded her with a grin, and Lady Annis, defeated, retired from the lists.

Some moments later she declared herself ready to depart, and less than a half hour after that, her trunk was strapped to the baggage shelf under the coachman's high seat, the top had been raised at her ladyship's request so that the sun would not damage her complexion, and the ladies themselves had been handed into the carriage. Miss Wilson, my lady's bracket-faced attendant, occupied the forward seat, and since the folding top only covered the rear seat, she received little protection from the brilliant rays of the sun, now riding high overhead.

When Margaret commented on the fact, saying that she was afraid Miss Wilson would be uncomfortable, the woman informed her stiffly that she had a parasol by her and could put it up if she did indeed become too warm. She did not sound as though she contemplated the necessity with any great distress, but Margaret received the distinct impression that Lady Annis's maid was not looking forward to a prolonged sojourn in the wilds of Lincolnshire. She hoped for Lady Annis's sake that Miss Wilson would not desert her. Lady Annis would surely think herself ill-used if such a thing should come to pass.

The journey into Royston was uneventful, although Miss Wilson did have recourse to her parasol before the barouche had passed into the town, where she was shaded by the tall buildings lining the narrow streets. At last the carriage drew into the yard of the Stag's Leap, a posting house located at the crossing of Ermine Street and the Icknield Way, the latter here taking the name of Baldock Street from the town ahead on most waybills. Kingsted jumped down from his horse even as the footmen moved to assist the ladies from the barouche, so that they might refresh themselves.

"Abberley sent ahead to order the chaise," he said a few moments later in the taproom, where he had ordered tea for the ladies and a mug of half-and-half for himself, "so there ought to be one awaiting you." When Lady Annis murmured distractedly about highwaymen, he hastened to reassure her. "Doubt the postilions will be armed unless it's the policy of the inn to arm them," he told her, "but I know for a fact that your footmen are prepared for anything, m'lady. Can't ride up behind a chaise, of course, but they're to have horses and will ride escort. Abberley was persuaded that Pytchham would be understaffed without them, so they are to stay with you. One of them comes from that neck of the woods, any gate, and the other said he'd as lief be in Lincolnshire as anywhere, so they'll serve you well enough.''

"Both of them are going?" Margaret had just realized this fact from his conversation, and stared at him. She had assumed that there were two men because one would be riding back with her. Kingsted heard the note of dismay and smiled at her.

"Is this the intrepid Miss Caldecourt speaking? Surely, ma'am, you are not afraid to ride back to the manor with only Abberley's old coachman for protection. You need not fret, you know."

"I know," she replied. And truly, she did. She told herself she was merely suffering from foolish fancies, for nothing would happen to her between Royston and the manor. Nothing had ever happened before. Still, she had the oddest premonition fifteen minutes later as she watched the post chaise roll out of the innyard, preceded by Kingsted on his handsome mare and followed by two mounted footmen, that she was being basely deserted.

Abberley's horses had been watered and rested, so the barouche was ready to depart. As John Coachman climbed onto his seat, Margaret settled back against the squabs and relaxed. It occurred to her while the barouche rolled along Ermine Street in Royston that she ought to have made herself a list of errands to accomplish since she had to be in town. Since she had not done so, she amused herself by watching the people on the flagway until they were on the open road again.

As John Coachman stirred his charges to a neat, high-stepping trot, Margaret was conscious of a slight prickling sensation at the tips of her thumbs. She rubbed them together briefly, folded her hands in her lap, and concentrated on relaxing. Annoyed with her odd fancies, she leaned back and closed her eyes, forcing herself to breathe evenly and deeply. The trip back to the manor road was no longer than fifteen minutes, after all. Nothing could happen in so short a span of time. Certainly not in broad daylight.

But less than ten minutes later the coach lurched and one of the horses—or perhaps more than one—let out a frightened scream. Margaret opened her eyes to discover no less than four masked men thrusting their way through the hedges that lined the road. Two had already grabbed the leaders' harness and were forcing them to a halt.

"Footpads!" she exclaimed. "Oh, John Coachman, pray do nothing foolish. Once they see we have nothing for them to take, perhaps they will leave us be."

"Aye, mistress," muttered the old man under his breath. He had all he could do to keep his horses from leaping out of their traces, so it would have been unlikely in any event for him to have attempted anything heroic.

Frightened, Margaret watched the men approaching, wishing she had a pistol by her. There was a holster fitted into the offside door, but there was no weapon in it. An oversight? she wondered. Or did Abberley refuse to trust women with weapons? Whatever the reason, she was helpless against so many. Never had she even heard of footpads traveling in so large a gang. She drew a deep breath, determined to appear calm.

"I have no jewelry or money," she said to the first man, a large fellow with a brown woolen scarf wrapped around his neck and over his head in such a way as to hide all his features but his eyes.

He said nothing but pulled open the door and, without letting down the steps, leapt in beside her. Margaret stifled a scream, then wished she had not, since on the public road the chances were excellent that another vehicle might be just around the bend with someone who could come to her assistance. By the time she had thought better of her bravery, however, the footpad had revealed that he held a large, snowy-white handkerchief and a burlap sack of the sort that barley was carried in to Ware. Quickly, before she had a chance to do more than flail her arms about and aim a fruitless kick at the man's moleskin-clad shins, he had stuffed the handkerchief into her mouth and bundled the sack over her head. He then tied the sack around her waist and looped a rope around her wrists, tying them uncomfortably behind her back. She struggled more, managing to dislodge the handkerchief gag, but she was too frightened now to scream. Moreover, her struggles had released a cloud of dust within the sack, bringing on a fit of sneezing. Once she had control of herself again, her captor had only to rest a burly hand upon her shoulder to make her stop wriggling. He did not sit beside her but across from her, and although she had seen no weapons, the coach began to move, so she decided the men must have threatened the coachman to make him do what they wanted.

Not a word had been spoken by any of the men, and no one else attempted to climb into the barouche. Nonetheless, Margaret felt more vulnerable than she could remember ever having felt before. The men had her at their mercy.

"What do you want with me?" she asked, trying to ignore the brush of burlap against her cheek and trying to remain calm. When there was no reply, she tried another approach. "I truly have no money or valuables by me, and there is no one who thinks me worth much by way of a ransom, so I cannot think what you might hope to gain by this outrage. Won't you please tell me where you are taking me?" There was still no answer, and though she tried several more times to induce the man to speak, he did not, so she finally gave up the attempt.

Before long, the rough, lurching motion of the carriage told her they had left the main road for one of the tracks that led off it from time to time, and a change in lighting—which was all she could see through the burlap—told her they had entered some woods, which meant, no doubt, that no one would see her and think it odd to see a lady wrapped in burlap driving along the road beside—no, across from—a ruffian who clearly had no business to be riding in a carriage at all. She felt stifled in the burlap and nearly panicked, thinking she would suffocate, before she realized she could breathe quite easily if she remained calm. But it was more and more difficult as the time passed to remain calm. Her imagination began to suggest things the men might do to her, the very least of which was to slit her throat and leave her body in a ditch somewhere.

Maintaining her balance was oddly difficult on the rough track. She had not realized how much one depended upon one's vision and one's hands. The motion of the carriage swayed her from side to side, and it required effort to remain upright. After a time, however, as she grew more accustomed to the motion, maintaining an upright position became easier.

Where was Abberley when she needed him? So much for love and devotion, she thought bitterly. If he truly loved her, he'd be here, rescuing her. In books, the hero always rescued the heroine in the nick of time. So here was his chance to prove he loved her. And where was he? Some stupid matter of business occupied him elsewhere. And to think that she had been the one to tell him he ought to attend to his business and not leave others to attend to it for him. Why could she not have kept a still tongue in her head?

Try as she might, she could not keep the sardonic train of thought going for long. When tears of frustration and, if one had to admit it, fear welled into her eyes, she bit her lip angrily. She might never see Abberley again. There were four men nearby who would do as they pleased with her, and whether they left her alive or dead afterward didn't much matter, since they would most certainly leave her unfit for a decent marriage. Why had she been so stubborn? Why had she not admitted to herself before now that she loved him, too, that she had merely been afraid to commit herself to that love, for fear she would somehow lose him as she had lost everyone else? At least she would have had a few days of knowing she was loved and of loving openly in return.

Not that he really loved her, she reminded herself. She had suspected as much, even as he was declaring his love and proposing that she marry him. And now she could be sure of it, for he would never had given up so easily if he had really loved her. He had merely kissed her—well, she amended mentally, perhaps *merely* was not the word to describe that kiss. Still and all, after the kiss he had gone away, and since then he had given no sign of being a man suffering the pangs

of unrequited love. He had behaved perfectly normally, as
though nothing remarkable had occurred.

So it was perhaps as well that she had not confessed her
love for him. Once safely married to her, he might well have
waited until she had produced his heir for him before returning to his raking, but without love to bind him to her, he
would certainly have reverted to his old ways before long.
And she would still have loved him, for her nature was
tenacious rather than fickle, and his desertion would have
been exactly the sort of loss one might anticipate, exactly the
sort of blow one had come to expect from Fate.

So deeply sunk in thought was she that she did not realize
the carriage had left the rough terrain for smoother ground.
Nor did she immediately notice when it rolled to a stop. Only
when weight shifted as the man opposite her moved to get
out, did she stiffen in fear. Determined not to give them the
satisfaction of hearing her scream her terror, she caught her
lower lip firmly between her teeth and bit down upon it hard
enough so that she might concentrate upon the pain and not
give in to her fears. When she felt the man reach for her, she
leaned hard back into the squabs, but it was no use. He lifted
her as though she had weighed no more than a rag doll. As
she squeezed her eyes shut in an attempt to hold back the
tears, she thought she heard a murmur of voices, but so low
did they speak that she could not be certain she had even
heard them. Even as her captor's foot touched solid ground,
other hands reached for her, and though she struggled again,
she was as helpless against the second man's strength as she
had been against the first's and soon found herself slung
indignantly over his broad shoulder.

"Put me down!" she ordered him angrily.

No answer.

"Put me down. I can walk, damn you!"

Still no answer. He was walking quickly, in long strides,
and the movement made it extremely difficult for her to talk.
Also the burlap was pressing the linen handkerchief harder
against her face, over her mouth and nose, so breathing was
more difficult. After some moments, she began to fear that

she would lose consciousness, so she made herself breathe slowly and deeply once more, knowing she would stand no chance at all if she did not retain her faculties.

He seemed to be climbing steps now, she decided, and the temperature was cooler than it had been. It was also darker, so although she had not noticed the sound of a door opening, she decided they must be indoors. She had not the slightest notion of their location, having lost all track of time and distance as a result of the blindfold. After some moments he stopped. There was the sound of a dull thud before he took two or three more steps and set her on her feet. When she swayed dizzily, a hand came to her elbow to steady her, but still the man said nothing.

"Where am I?" Margaret demanded. "Who are you?"

There was still no answer, but when she heard the sound of a heavy door closing, she realized his hand was no longer at her elbow. There was the distinctly recognizable sound of a key turning in a lock, and she cried out, "Don't leave me like this!" before she realized he had not gone. The feeling she experienced then was scarcely one of relief, however.

She felt his hands again, this time at the knots of the cord around her wrists. A moment later, her hands were free, the rope was unwound from around her waist, and the burlap bag was pulled off over her head. The white handkerchief fell unheeded to the floor as she stared up, her mouth agape with angry astonishment, into Abberley's laughing eyes.

There was a brief silence. Then, thoroughly outraged, she launched herself at him, forgetting propriety altogether as she let her temper rule both tongue and fists. "Damn you!" she cried, beating her hands against his chest as hard as she could. "How could you do such a thing to me? Have you any notion how frightened I was? Who were those dreadful men? By heaven, sir, I don't know what you mean by this outrage, but I shall never speak to you again. Never!"

16

Though the laughter faded from his eyes, the earl made no effort to defend himself other than to fold his arms across his broad chest. He simply stood there, facing her, his legs braced against her furious onslaught. Undaunted, Margaret continued to berate him with angry words while pounding at him with her fists, but at last, frustrated by his silence and by the fact that she could not so much as budge him, she stopped and flung away from him, her breath coming in gasping sobs after the expenditure of so much energy.

"Have you quite finished?" he asked quietly.

Promptly deciding to give him a taste of his own medicine, she said nothing at all, focusing her attention on the need to restore her breathing to normal.

"I do hope you have finished," he said conversationally, "for I have learned a good deal these past weeks, you know, about how best to deal with recalcitrant persons—not just from Aunt Celeste, but also from you—so if you do not wish me to empty a basin of cold water over your head or to lock you up in this room until you have decided to behave yourself, you will do well to sit down in that chair and listen to what I have to say to you."

Margaret had not even noticed the chair, but she did now. Indeed, she noticed the entire room, and she did not require an echo of Abberley's words to assist her in recognizing the north tower room at Abberley Hall. The stone floor was bare, and the only items of furniture were the straight wooden chair, its padded seat covered in dark leather outlined by brass-headed nails, and a simple wooden deal table.

She felt reluctant now to turn and face him, but despite the conversational tone, there had been a note of implacability in his voice that put her forcibly in mind of several occasions in the past when she had been very glad he had been speaking to someone other than herself, and she did not dare to defy him. Slowly she turned, focusing her gaze upon the second button of his tan-colored waistcoat.

"Sit down, Marget," he said gently.

She glanced at the chair, even took a step toward it. But then she remembered there was only the one chair and looked back at him, more directly. If you please, sir, I would rather stand," she told him. "I find the very thought of sitting there whilst you tower over me, reading me whatever scold you mean to read, quite daunting."

"Scold? Why should I scold you, sweetheart? You are the one who has been abducted, after all. I shall not scold you for becoming angry."

"Well, I should think not," she retorted indignantly. "It was a dreadful thing to have done, sir."

"You have already rung that peal," he reminded her. "I let you say everything on that head that you could think of to say, and every word was as near the truth as can be expected under the circumstances. If you will recall, I have sufficient cause to know exactly how you felt."

Though she did not believe for a moment that anyone as big as Abberley—and male, besides—could possibly understand how helpless she had felt at the mercy of four masked men, she realized she would be as likely to gain satisfaction by railing at the moon as by trying to explain the matter to him, so instead she demanded to know how he had found it possible to subject her to such terror as he himself must have felt.

"Because Aunt Celeste's undeniably ruthless tactics served a useful purpose at the time," he replied, "and I hope mine will do likewise."

"What purpose do you have in mind, sir? Surely, you do not think to force me into marriage with you."

"I trust that you will agree to marry me before you leave this room," he said in that same conversational tone.

"You are as demented as Annis," she informed him roundly. "You cannot possibly force me to marry you by such a tactic. I collect that my abductors were Muston and the same crowd that waylaid you. Surely, you do not believe they will keep my whereabouts a secret from Aunt Celeste?"

Abberley shrugged. "I can deal with Aunt Celeste."

Margaret's lips twitched despite her annoyance. "I wish I may see the day," she said dryly.

There was an answering gleam of humor in his eyes as he said, "We may all live and learn, as she would say. Look here, Marget"—he took a step toward her, his hands firmly at his sides—"I shan't force you to do anything you don't wish to do. I resorted to drastic measures only because I knew I had to shake you as Aunt Celeste had shaken me. You do love me, I've seen it in your eyes and in the way you greet me when I have been away from you. But when you refused me, it was clear that you were not simply being coy in the manner of fashionable ladies who want to hear further declarations. I was certain that for me to have said more then, or even later, would have been disastrous and would have caused you to entrench yourself more deeply than ever in the foolish belief that you are not meant for marriage."

"It is not a foolish belief," she said doggedly, once more looking at the second button of his waistcoat. "How long do you think that you, who have always jumped from one woman to another like a child in a dormitory leaping from bed to bed, would be satisfied with me alone?" When he burst into laughter, she had to raise her voice for the last six words in an attempt to make him hear her, but since he was still laughing, she could not be at all sure he had. "Adam? Adam, stop that. What on earth did I say that was so funny?" she demanded, reaching for his arm in an attempt to make him heed her.

He bent to catch his breath, but he was still chuckling and

tears of laughter glinted in his eyes. "Ah, sweetheart," he said at last, "you have much to learn if you can ask me that with a straight face. Think about what you asked me and how you phrased the question."

She did, and she realized her choice of words had been unfortunate, but she did not blush and she did not look away from him this time. "The point is still relevant, sir," she said.

"Aye," he responded, reaching to grasp her gently by the shoulders, "but I was never in love before. The others bored me. I've known you all my life, and I know you won't do so. For that matter, I think I've probably loved you all my life. Lord knows my protective instincts have always gone wild when I've been around you."

"You were just missing having a little sister, sir, no more than that."

"Yes, it was more. When did I begin what everyone chooses to call my 'raking?' Do you remember?"

"How should I?" she asked reasonably. "You were off to London long before I was, you and Michael."

"Yes, we made our come-out together some eight years before you made yours," he agreed. "Was Michael a rake?"

"No, of course not."

"Was I?"

She thought about that for a moment before she realized that she would most likely have heard something about his behavior if it had been altogether different from Michael's. "All I ever heard," she said slowly, "was that the two of you and a number of others, when you were undergraduates at Oxford, made nuisances of yourselves at Melton Mowbray. I remember Papa was annoyed with you both over the cost of the damages, but I don't remember that there were ladies involved."

"There weren't. Take my word for it. That was just a bit of bobbery and nothing more than any undergraduate gets up to. That was before the time I'm speaking of, anyway, and since you cannot know anything much to my discredit, I'll tell you to your face that I didn't begin my so-called raking until you made *your* come-out.''

"Me! What did I have to do with that?"

"You treated me like another brother, that's what. Fobbed me off if you wanted to dance with someone else and expected me to dance attendance on you at your every whim, but it was perfectly clear that you didn't have a single romantical notion in your head where I was concerned. Besides, you soon enough fell tail over top in love with that idiot, Culross."

"Frederick was not an idiot," she said. "He was a very nice young man."

"I apologize, love," he said quickly. "I should not have said that."

She sighed. "No, but I think you and Aunt Celeste, too, are likely in the right of it. I have been thinking about him, and I think I fell for him more after he was so tragically killed than before. Is that possible?"

The look in his eyes was serious now. "Quite possible. You agreed to let him pay his addresses to you before he left in such a bang to make his attempt to rout Boney, and then when he was killed in the attempt—and at Waterloo, at that, making him a dashed hero—well, I think your reaction was perfectly normal."

"Perhaps." She looked at the earl, but her thoughts hovered for several moments upon Frederick Culross. Was it indeed possible that she had somehow formed the conviction that she had loved the young man out of some romantic bit of whole cloth? To be sure, he had been very handsome, far more handsome than Abberley, for example. Many young women had sighed over him and had flung their caps at him. Was she merely flattered that he had selected her? Surely not, for there had been others who had chosen her who were higher born, wealthier, and perhaps even as handsome. But none of them had proposed to her on the eve of departing to fight the dreaded enemy, Bonaparte. None of them had figured so dramatically in those fervently exciting, terrifying days after news of Bonaparte's escape from Elba had reached England. And she had promised none of the others that she would wait for his return so that he could resume his pursuit of her hand. Still, the fact remained that although she had agreed to allow him to court her, she had not fought Michael's decision to postpone any announcement of a betrothal.

Abberley had remained quiet for some moments, letting her think, but now he reached toward her, his hand just brushing her upper arm before he let it fall again. "Marget, he didn't have to go. He had already sold out."

"That didn't matter," she said quietly. "He was recalled and felt he had to go. He believed strongly that the Duke would need him." She tilted her head a little to one side and raised her right hand to touch the place on her left arm that still tingled from Abberley's touch. Strange that she could not remember tingling when Frederick had touched her. He had kissed her once, too, the night before he had gone away, but she could scarcely remember anything about the kiss except that it had happened. When she thought about Abberley's kisses . . . Warmth suffused her cheeks, and she moved to turn away from him.

His hands came to her arms again, gently. He would not let her look away. "Will you not tell me what you feel in your heart, sweet Marget?" he asked, his voice low.

She opened her mouth to tell him again that she was not suited to the married state, but before she could voice the words, a memory of her thoughts and feelings during the dreadful ride in the barouche stormed back into her mind and made it impossible for her to tell him she couldn't love him.

"Tell me," he said gently.

She raised her eyes to his. "I do love you," she said, "but I am still afraid of my own feelings. So many times—"

"No," he said, laying a finger to her lips, "don't say the words, for they are very foolish. You told me once that I was assuming that I had a great deal of power, to think that my actions affected the Fates in any way. And you understand that for Lady Annis to blame the Fates for her actions or for their lack of success is ridiculous and stems from nothing more than her own reluctance to take responsibility for what she has done. Yet you still persist in believing that one has only to be loved by you to be doomed, that your very happiness tempts the Fates beyond what they will resist.''

"Put that way, it sounds foolish, I know," she admitted, "and I don't think I have actually thought about it in so many words lately. Once I saw that what you were blaming yourself for was not your fault but more a wish that you might have been able to change what happened to Michael and to Timothy, I guess I began to realize that my own beliefs about myself were constructed on shaky ground. Still, it is hard to ignore the fear, Adam."

"Your fears stem as much from habit as from anything else," he said. "Indeed, many people suffer from a fundamental fear of happiness. But for either of us to think that we, personally, have any great influence over the tides of destiny is certainly foolish, even presumptuous. Besides, my dear, the damage has been done if all Fate requires is your love for someone. We might as well enjoy the time that precedes my doom.''

There was laughter in his voice, and she could not help feeling the lighter for it. She knew he was right. Over the past weeks, having come to understand him better, she had also found a deeper understanding of herself. And the same seemed to be true with him. Odd, she thought, how much easier it is to see others' faults than to see one's own. She believed him now when he said he loved her. How else could he have brought himself to use such rough and ready tactics with her? He had certainly never done such a thing before, even when she had displeased him. He had always been gentle with her. But looking at him now, she was not by any means certain that he would always be gentle in the future. Nor was she shocked by the notion that he might not. Indeed, the thought seemed to stir that tingling in her midsection again, to make her more aware than ever of his nearness, of the expression in his eyes when he looked down at her.

Margaret licked her lips carefully. "You are right, sir. I have allowed certain fears and worries to cloud my thinking. Perhaps, if you will give me time to consider the matter carefully—''

"Marget, cut line," he ordered crisply, his hands less gently now upon her shoulders. "Do you love me or not?"

She looked at the waistcoat button again. "I do love you, Adam, but—"

"No 'buts,' my girl. I wasted a deal of time by not making more of a push years ago to secure your affections."

"You always had my affection," she protested.

"Silence, brat, you know perfectly well what I mean."

"Yes, but you didn't know you wanted more than mere affection. You said as much before," she pointed out more reasonably.

"Well, I was a fool to believe I only thought of you as a sister," he retorted, "and not to realize before now that you mean a great deal more to me than that. But I do know the truth now, Marget, so will you please marry me?"

She hesitated, her eyes beginning to twinkle. "That depends, my lord, upon how far you intend to carry this abduction of yours. I am persuaded that my reputation must be sorely compromised already. After all, those men who waylaid the carriage must know that you have me at your mercy. If I stay up here much longer, alone with you like this, I shall no doubt be forced to accept your very flattering proposal."

"Stuff," he said with a chuckle. "Not that I wouldn't be willing to do whatever was necessary, mind you. Do you wish to be seduced, Miss Caldecourt?" He leered at her, his hands still firmly on her shoulders.

"You would force me?"

"If you like."

Her eyes narrowed speculatively. "I don't believe you, Abberley. You have spent the greater part of our acquaintance protecting me. I don't believe for a moment that you would . . ."

"Would what?" he asked, still smiling but more gently now, when her voice trailed away. His right hand had begun to wander down her arm, leaving little tingles of pleasure in its wake. When she didn't answer him and let her gaze lock with his without making any effort to look away, he bent his head nearer to hers. And when her soft lips parted slightly, he took advantage of their invitation, kissing her first gently, then more possessively, until her arms had gone around his waist and she was responding to his caresses with all the passion that had lurked so deceptively beneath the surface until now.

A moan escaped her when his hand cupped her breast, and his fingers moved gently across its tip, setting fire to the nerve endings. Her own hands were moving, too, exploring the contours of his body, enjoying the play of hard muscles beneath his soft shirt. His hand moved to the fastenings of her spencer, and seconds later to the bare skin above the lace edging of her gown. It was not a particularly low-cut bodice, but the touch of his fingers there was exciting, and Margaret yearned to feel his bare skin beneath her own fingertips. Without thought she began tugging at his shirt.

The banging on the door might have been going on for some time. She wasn't sure. There did seem to be an echo in her subconscious of the noise she was hearing clearly now.

Abberley bent his lips to the soft bare skin of her neck and right shoulder.

"Adam, someone is at the door," she said.

"Tell them to go away," he murmured, his breath, despite its warmth, blowing cold shivers in its path, making her neck arch in a tickle reflex.

"Abberley, you've been a very long time in there!"

"Aunt Marget, are you there? Aunt Celeste let me ride my pony all the way over here. I was her escort, so footpads would not attack her in the beech wood." Timothy's voice was high-pitched in his excitement. "Why are you in the tower room? Are you truly there, Aunt Marget?"

"I'm here, Timothy," Margaret replied, grinning at the earl. "I could have used your assistance against footpads myself."

"Were you set upon, Aunt Marget? Oh, open the door and tell us all about it. Do, please!"

Margaret chuckled, then said in an undertone, "I think if one of us is going to tell them to go away, it ought to be you, my lord."

"Damn." He straightened and stepped away from her. But despite the epithet, she knew he wasn't at all angry. His eyes glinted with suppressed laughter. "I wonder what they are doing here," he said innocently.

"Some seduction," Margaret retorted, unable to resist teasing him, "I expect they have been here all afternoon, just waiting to play gooseberry."

He did not deny it. Neither did he respond to the renewed battering at the door or to Lady Celeste's demands to be told whether he meant to stay in the tower room all day. Instead, he grinned at Margaret. "My intentions have always been honorable, sweetheart, though you might have at least have given me the satisfaction of doubting some of my methods."

"The abduction frightened me and made me angry," she told him, "but I couldn't fear you, sir, if that is what you intended. If my honor is in jeopardy, 'tis my own fault, not yours." There was warmth in his eyes now, a look that made her feel as though he still touched her, although he had released her when he had stepped away. "You must answer Aunt Celeste, Adam," she pointed out a moment later when neither of them had yet moved. "She is perfectly capable of sending for men to break the door down if you do not."

"So she is," he agreed.

"Did you truly think I would need the both of them?"

"No, merely that if I invited Aunt Celeste and you to dine with me, Timothy might feel neglected."

"Liar."

He grinned again. "You still have not agreed to marry me, sweetheart. If you do not do so by the time I count to five, I shall have to send Aunt Celeste and Timothy away again, shall I not?"

She grinned back, saying nothing.

"One . . . two . . ."

"Adam," she said softly, stepping toward him, "if you count more quickly, you can send them away all the sooner, you know."

"Abberley!" Lady Celeste's voice was sharp and clear. "Answer me, young man. I can hear the two of you muttering in there, and I demand to know how matters are progressing. Answer me at once. Has she agreed to marry you, or not?''

Abberley smiled at Margaret, now in his arms. "Yes, ma'am," he said, raising his voice enough so the words would be clear to the lady on the other side of the door, "I believe she has, so if you would very kindly take Timothy away and leave us to discuss the matter at some length, I shall tell you all about it later.''

Margaret stood on tiptoe to kiss him.

"If she has agreed to marry you," said Lady Celeste, "then come out of that room at once, the both of you. 'Tis monstrous improper, being locked in there together like that. I cannot think how I came to agree to be a party to all of this. Indeed, I cannot.''

"Aunt Celeste?"

"Yes, Margaret dear, what is it?"

"Go away, Aunt Celeste.''

There was a chuckle from the other side of the door. "One may play a good card too often," said the old lady. "I am glad to know that has not been the case today. I shall see you both at dinner.''

They could hear her footsteps and Timothy's going down the stairs. Then there was a small silence before Abberley said, ''Well?''

"Well, what?" She was looking at his waistcoat button again.

"You still have not said you will marry me.''

"Have I not, sir?"

"You know very well you have not.''

She regarded him from under her lashes. "Do you still intend to keep me here like this until I do agree, Adam?''

He chuckled. "I begin to believe you don't look upon those words as a threat, brat.''

"No, sir.''

He gave her a little shake. "Marget, dammit, will you say the words I want to hear?''

"But what of the Fates? Do we dare tempt them so sorely?''

"I'll show you 'sorely,'" he threatened, giving her another shake.

She snuggled against him. "You won't," she said confidently. "You are too much the protector, sir, and I have come to depend upon you too much in that role. You warned me once not to do so, but I do all the time and you have never really let me down."

"Yes, I did, once, but I won't let you down again, love. When I said those words to you, I was not myself. Indeed, I find I like myself a deal better now that I have taken command of things again. I don't mind at all that you or Timothy depend upon me."

"Well, I like it very much indeed. I should not like to think about a life without you, sir. Therefore," she added in more formal tones, "I believe I shall have to marry you."

"An excellent notion."

"Yes," she agreed. "Will you show me the secret panel in your bedchamber?"

"I'll show you anything you like," he promised, grinning at her.

SIGNET HISTORICAL GOTHIC

Her lips were still warm from the imprint of his kiss, but now Silvia knew there was nothing to protect her from the terror of Serpent Tree Hall. Not even love. Especially not love. . . .

DARK SPLENDOR

ANDREA PARNELL

Lovely young Silvia Bradstreet had come from London to Colonial America to be a bondservant on an isolated island estate off the Georgia coast. But a far different fate awaited her at the castle-like manor: a man whose lips moved like a hot flame over her flesh . . . whose relentless passion and incredible strength aroused feelings she could not control. And as a whirlpool of intrigue and violence sucked her into the depths of evil . . . flames of desire melted all her power to resist. . . .

Coming in September from Signet!